Beauty Has Her Way

NICOLA ITALIA

Copyright

Special thank you to Eddi Keller for reviewing the manuscript

Copyright © 2022 by Nicola Italia. All rights reserved.
No part of this book may be reproduced in any form or by any electronic or mechanical means, including information storage and retrieval systems, without written permission from the author, except for the use of brief quotations in a book review.
Cover Design by Agata Broncel, Bukovero
Edited by Sara Burgess, Telltail Editing

Also By

The Sheik and the Slave
The Tea Plantation
The Sheik's Son
The Reign of Love and Chaos
Love in the Valley of the Kings
The Three Graces
The Boston Girl
Seasons of Love
The Vaudeville Star
The Beauty of St. Kilda
The Savannah Stargazer
The Alchemy of Night
Sea of Revenge
Of Night and Dark Obscurity
Among the Darkness Stirs
The Imperial Orchid
In the Midst of Shadows

Author's Note

My eighteenth novel, "Beauty Has Her Way," takes place at the start of the early Georgian period in 1715.

This novel involves Alexander Mayson who was a secondary character in "Sea of Revenge" and his love interest Georgiana Gainsford.

As common with a woman of this time period, Georgiana is expected to marry, bear children and obey first her father and then her husband. Unfortunately for our heroine, her father is not at all choosey of who her husband should be though she is.

This causes friction between Georgiana and her father as she knows her own mind and will not settle.

Featured in this novel is colonial Boston. Though one of the characters has Puritanical beliefs and ways, the Puritans had almost entirely died out by this time period though some may have held on to their ways.

As always, I try to keep the historical accuracy intact while providing a story for readers to enjoy.

Chapter 1

WHITE'S CLUB

1715
London, England

Jonathan Gainsford sighed heavily as he settled onto the plush red cushioned seat and lit his pipe. He watched absently as the two gentlemen before him played a game of chess and was relieved that there were few men about White's that evening. He was in a foul mood and had no desire to bandy words with anyone or lose his purse to a card sharp.

He ordered a glass of port from the club servant and relished the thought of the drink even before it arrived. The two men before him were eyeing the other's moves with careful concentration, and already Jonathan knew that the man with the powdered wig and lavender breeches was going to lose. He had made several bad moves, losing a knight and a rook, and now his queen was in jeopardy. His drink arrived, and he sipped it appreciatively.

Just as he set his glass down, the man in lavender breeches lost, as Jonathan had predicted. He smiled inwardly to himself as the men placed their respective pieces back in the starting positions. As the two men began to play again, a young man took up the chair next to his. He ordered a brandy and nodded at Jonathan in greeting.

The man was dressed in a simple blue wool suit embroidered with a silver thread. He wore no wig, which was the fashion, and his dark brown hair was pulled back in a queue. Jonathan looked down at his own brown silk coat and waistcoat, which had been hand-embroidered and cost a small fortune. He smiled smugly at the knowledge that his beautiful clothes were handsome and had been worth the cost.

The young man in the blue wool suit extracted a newspaper from his coat pocket and stretched out his hose-encased legs in leisure as he began perusing it. Jonathan took another sip of his port and recognized *The Daily Courant* as the paper the man held in his hand. He glanced over at the two men before him and saw that the man in lavender breeches had made another bad move, putting his knight in peril.

He sighed inwardly, staring at the fireplace. It did him good to watch the two men battle over the chess board and the young man and his newspaper. It moved his thoughts away from his business, his government obligations, and his –

"How are you, Gainsford?" The older man in cream breeches, and the more skillful of the two players, suddenly looked up to see him. "We haven't seen you here in some weeks."

Jonathan sipped his drink and nodded at the man who was known to him. "Work keeps me quite busy, Duffin."

Duffin nodded. "How fortunate you are." He took the other man's knight as Jonathan had guessed he might.

"Fortune had nothing to do with it." Jonathan bristled. "Hard work and perseverance did, though."

"The British East India Company is nothing to sneer at," lavender breeches said. "Indeed no."

The young reader glanced over at him as the company name was mentioned but he said nothing.

"Well, if we have to bear a cross in this life, I do believe that is an excellent one to bear," Duffin said as he made a quick movement with his hand and captured his opponent's bishop.

"Damn!" lavender breeches cried.

Jonathan watched the younger man sip his brandy and return to his newspaper. He seemed a man capable of holding his tongue, which was an admirable trait to have. He was a handsome chap and probably somewhere about thirty years old or thereabouts. He had not seen him before in the club, but that meant nothing. His visits to his club were sporadic, as he was director of the famed East India Company and a member of Parliament, which kept him quite busy.

The chess players had brought him back to his troubles, and he pondered about his position at the powerful company and his government responsibilities. He enjoyed both, and they gave him the prestige and wealth he desired, but he wanted something for himself.

"I say, Gainsford," lavender breeches piped up again. "I meant to ask you. How is Georgie?"

Jonathan resisted the urge to close his eyes and sigh heavily. The two men had interrupted his quiet time, brought up his work, and now the one subject he truly did not want to discuss they had mentioned.

"Fine," he said curtly. "Just fine."

He could feel the young chap's eyes on him, and he turned his head to look at him. He stared back for a moment and then returned to his newspaper.

"Georgie," lavender breeches said with a warm tone in his voice. "She is the loveliest creature in London. Don't you think so, Duffin?" he asked his opponent. "The loveliest creature by far. I say, Gainsford . . . " He turned his attention to Jonathan, who stared back at him.

"Yes?" Jonathan said without a hint of invitation to continue the conversation.

"I remember her mother so long ago, and she was quite attractive, but Georgie surpasses even her." He smiled indulgently in his praise for Georgiana Gainsford, not realizing Jonathan was not in the least interested in his compliments about his daughter.

"Does she?" Jonathan asked coolly, raising an eyebrow.

"Indeed, yes!" Lavender breeches said warmly and nodded. "In fact, I recall seeing her as a young girl and thinking even then that she would grow to be such a beauty!" He smiled. "And so she has."

Jonathan eyed the man who was so effusive in his compliments, and an intense dislike swept through him. The dislike was not for the man before him but for the object of his compliments.

"Beauty, perhaps," he spoke slowly, twirling his drink in his hand. "And of course, beauty is in the eye of the beholder," he added. "But there are other traits much more important for a woman to have."

"Such as," lavender breeches asked.

"Obedience, humility, modesty." He checked off the traits as if they were items to be purchased at market.

"Absolutely," the man agreed vigorously. "But Georgie has all –"

"She has none of those qualities!" Jonathan hissed softly, startling the men.

The man in lavender breeches seemed confused, and his opponent looked on but did not appear shocked. The man reading the newspaper seemed intrigued.

"She's a frightful chit," Jonathan said passionately. "She has no sense of decorum, and she flits about from party to party with no thought of her own reputation!"

"I've never heard anything disparaging said of her," Duffin countered. "I've heard her called charming."

"Charming?" Jonathan repeated the word with a sneer on his face. "What is charming about staying out late, gambling with my money, and flirting with men? She's disgraceful!"

"She's young –" the man began to defend her.

"She should be married with a child in the nursery and another one on the way," Jonathan said firmly.

"Quite," the one man grumbled, though he didn't appear to agree.

The two men looked at each other. Duffin suddenly mentioned that the hour was late, and soon both men had bid their goodbyes and departed. Jonathan watched them both leave abruptly and was intensely irritated. They had brought up the one subject he loathed to speak about, and now that he had started, he wanted to continue to vent. She was a thorn in his side. An absolute thorn in his side!

"He was right about one thing," Jonathan said lowly to the young man sitting next to him.

The young man looked up and shook his head. "Excuse me?"

"What they said about Georgiana." He motioned to the empty chess table. "My daughter. She is lovely. That much is true but . . ." He shook his head.

"But?" the young man asked.

"What use is beauty when she has no understanding of her role?" Jonathan scoffed, brushing at a piece of nonexistent lint on his breeches.

"Her role . . . ?" The young man frowned.

"A woman's role is to marry and bear children. To serve first in her father's household and then her husband's. Georgiana seems incapable of that kind of life," Jonathan admitted.

"She has not had suitors?"

Jonathan smirked. "Several. And refused them all."

"On what grounds?"

Jonathan shook his head and finished his drink. He ordered another one before he answered. "On whatever ground suited her. One was too fat. One had odd smells. One was very short. One too old."

"Perhaps she's waiting for love," the young man offered. "Some women want to wait for that."

"No." Jonathan dismissed the thought quickly. "She's wild and unpredictable and delights in tormenting me. If I said the sky was blue, she would say it was green to spite me."

"She sounds quite a handful."

"I'm sorry to say but I find her very difficult," Jonathan confessed. "I have much to do with my work and in Parliament, and she – oftentimes – is an embarrassment."

The young man said nothing but appeared to be listening to the complaints.

"She's twenty-four." Jonathan shook his head. "She should be married."

"Surely there's time," the man pointed out.

Jonathan thought of the delectable widow Mariah Gower who traveled in the same circles as he and whom he wanted as his wife. He had long thought to make her the next Mrs. Gainsford, but the only cloud that hovered over their proposed union was Georgiana. Mariah was a virtuous, kind woman, and his daughter's fast and wild ways frightened his to-be wife.

He was sure that if his daughter was married and off his hands, he would be free to marry Mariah. Jonathan looked over at the man seated near him and realized they had not been introduced.

"I don't believe we've been introduced. I'm Jonathan Gainsford." He put out his hand out in greeting.

"Alexander Mayson." He took the hand offered him.

"Alexander May—" Jonathan stopped. "Are you Alexander Mayson of Mayson Shipping Line?"

"I am."

"How extraordinary!" Jonathan smiled wildly. "We were speaking about your shipping line the other day at the office. You've been in business what, four years?"

"Five."

Jonathan sipped his drink thoughtfully. "You ship to the colonies?"

"I do."

"What exactly do you ship?"

"Whatever the need is. Mostly manufactured goods, textiles, and furniture," Alexander explained.

"And from the colonies to here?"

Alexander shrugged. "Lumber, furs, whale oil, iron, gunpowder, tobacco, and indigo."

"Impressive." Jonathan nodded. "I have been thinking for some time to expand to the colonies. As a personal investment, you understand."

"Indeed?"

"Are you in need of an investor? I would be willing to be quite generous," Jonathan noted.

Alexander pondered his words. "I might be. A prominent investor such as yourself linked to the East India Company would be beneficial."

"Tomorrow evening we are having a supper party," he told the young man. "We can discuss in detail then."

Alexander nodded. "Very well."

"I'm fascinated with the colonies and all the opportunity it has to offer," Jonathan told him and gave him the address of his house.

"I look forward to our discussion tomorrow evening," Alexander said in what sounded like a sincere tone before they parted ways.

Alexander left the club and the contrary Jonathan Gainsford behind as he rushed to make his evening appointment at Haymarket Theater. It was past nine in the evening, and by the time he arrived, the theater was awash with several thousand people. The orchestra was playing loudly and a little off-key as he looked about for his friend he had planned to meet. He found his friend in the private box he rented. Peregrine Thornhill was seated with three ladies, laughing and drinking the cheap ale he had ordered from the theater.

Perry was the third son of a baron and had no chance at inheriting the title or money, which the two men had in common. Perry spent his days sleeping and his nights trying to bed the beauties of London. His tastes ran to music hall actresses and dancers, and he had a sense of humor most found appealing.

"Lex!" Perry spotted him coming into the box and sprang up. "I'd about given up on you."

Alexander nodded to his friend and was not immune to the three women whose eyes all turned to him. He was not unaware of his masculine beauty, and he found women intoxicating. He was known to be a ladies' man, but then most men he knew liked the ladies.

"Now look here, Lex," Perry said seriously. "The blonde is mine, but the other two are yours for the taking." He laughed, and the women laughed with him.

Alexander settled into the box seat, and immediately one of the women came to sit near him. She had small eyes and yellow crooked teeth. The women who frequented the theaters were prostitutes. He thought fleetingly of his mistress Philippine de Froissy. She was buxom and had a large appetite for sex, as she had been married to a man who liked his sex like horse racing, swift and over quickly.

Philippine had a small delicate face, and he enjoyed making love to her immensely. She had been in France the past month visiting her family so they had not been able to meet.

He peered out over the audience below and marveled at the throng of people inside. The theater seemed to have a heartbeat all its own, as the audience members could be loud, rude, or dangerous given the performance. Alcohol and food were consumed in large quantities, and people arrived and left during the performances. Audiences had been known to throw rotten fruit and vegetables at the actors, and things could become heated if the performance was not to their liking.

He glanced over at his friend and saw that the blonde was now seated on Perry's lap. His hand was under her skirts, and he knew the blonde was being penetrated by his friend's fingers. The woman's lips opened a little as she closed her eyes. He stood up abruptly.

"I'll return shortly, Perry," he told his friend. "I need some air."

Without waiting for a reply, he left the box and passed into the dark hallway, walking along the cavernous corridor, passing several boxes which were placed alongside the stage for persons of quality and money. Working men and women were squeezed together in the galleries, but at most theater performances, rich and poor people mixed together.

Several people were entering the box ahead of him, and he moved aside to allow someone to pass by him. The air was filled with smoke and laughter. The theater was an excursion for Londoners to enjoy themselves. He was able to purchase an ale, and the cheap liquor burned a trail down his throat. He preferred the finer things in life, but that would not be found at Haymarket tonight.

He turned to make his way back to the theater box. Several women were laughing ahead of him. He admired the cut of their gowns and the colors. They looked like vibrant flowers in the dark theater only lit by candlelight. One woman wearing a raspberry-colored gown broke away from the group.

He could not see her face, as her back was to him, but suddenly, he followed her inside the theater. There was no reason to do so except that he was bored and loathed to return to the box. As he watched the gentle sway of her hips, he played a game with himself. He tried to guess her identity. She was a governess who worked with three pampered children, and this evening was her only reprieve from them. She was enjoying the time spent at the theater before she had to return to them.

No! She was a lady's maid to a cruel, vicious countess, and tonight was the only night she was free of the torment and abuse heaped upon her by her lady. The woman moved to the right and down several steps, heading through the foyer of the theater.

He had it! She was a member of the royal family and incognito. No one knew who she was and she must stay hidden so it would never be known she had snuck out of the palace. He realized suddenly that she had come outside of the theater into a little garden. There was no one around, and she seemed to be breathing in the cool air.

He watched her secretly from his spot in the shadows and knew that whatever he had drunk should not have made him this stupefied. He felt a little giddy. But then there had been the brandy at the club, two rather. And listening to Jonathan Gainsford and those chess players. He suddenly recalled their conversation.

Did he really need Gainsford's money? No. He did not. But his connections with the British East India Company were invaluable. And though he had made his shipping line a success, there was always more money to be made in the world.

He thought of the woman with the crooked teeth upstairs in the box. Perry had probably given her a coin or two to sleep with him tonight. That would have been something Perry would think friendly, which did not appeal to Alexander at all. He had several mistresses, but a common prostitute was not something he cared to dabble in.

Perhaps the woman was not royal or a ladies' maid. Maybe she was plying her trade as well. The theater was known to bring together young men and women who would eat and mingle in the notorious pit. He had never done such a thing, but the alcohol seemed to sing in his blood. It made him high and foolish. He began to walk toward her.

He studied her back. Proud and erect, her body was slender and trim. He could easily span her waist with one hand splayed out and—

Suddenly, she turned around and walked towards him, passing him quickly. He had only a moment to gather himself and his thoughts before he followed her once more. He still had not seen her face. She was walking back through the foyer and into the theater again. His moment was lost. They were surrounded by so many people. She began to climb the stairs, and he realized she was headed back to the boxes. The boxes! So secluded. So dark.

He was suddenly mesmerized by the easy sway of her hips, her small waist, and the chestnut hair piled onto her head in soft curls. Why did his throat feel so dry? Why did he feel fuzzy and unfocused? The woman slowed her step as she entered the dark hallway that led to the theater boxes. The music could be heard playing on the stage, and boos and hisses were coming from the audience members. They were making their wishes known.

The soft candlelight flickered against the walls, and each step he took brought him closer to her. His heart beat faster, quicker. Without thinking about it for a second more, he grabbed her arm and pressed her up against the wall.

There, he dipped his head and kissed her once briefly. Then when he kissed her the second time, he deepened the kiss. His hand moved over the bodice of her dress, and he pressed his body into hers. She tasted so sweet, and he had the sense that – no. That was not possible. He could feel the warm flesh beneath the silk, and he felt the pull lower himself.

He pulled away from her and smiled down at her for a second before she slapped him across the face.

"Bastard!" she told him hotly.

He looked down into her face and wasn't prepared for that either. She had a perfect oval face, with delicately arched eyebrows over beautiful emerald eyes. Her nose was pert, her lips red and moist. Her hair was coiled up and held together by the ribbon he had seen as he walked behind her. How could she be so lovely?

Alexander shook his head. Jesus!

"Take your hands off me," she snapped, her cheeks flushed pink.

He didn't know what to say. What on earth had he been thinking? He had kissed a stranger. In the dark hall of the theater. What was in that ale he bought? He had been entranced. She was so enticing, and he had absolutely lost his head. He could blame it on the cheap alcohol as if he was some green lad barely out of school, unable to hold his liquor.

But even all that, he couldn't deny that the woman was stunning. Would a husband come bursting out of the box and demand a duel?

"I – " He didn't even know what to say to her.

"You low-class, uneducated beast!" she flung at him. "How dare you presume to touch me!"

She tried to wiggle out of his grasp, but he held her shoulders firmly. He had made a mistake, but a kiss was not the worst thing to have happened. Why was she so angry?

"It was only a kiss," he reasoned stupidly, and a grin appeared on his face.

She gave him a withering look. "And you're only a buffoon. Release me now!"

He was taken aback by the color of her eyes, which were a deep emerald green. He couldn't hold onto her forever, but he wanted to. He shook his head. He took his hands from her, and she stepped away from him.

"Swine!" she swore at him and then turned sharply away, wiping her mouth with the back of her hand before disappearing into one of the boxes.

Alexander shook his head and took a deep breath. It was best to call it a night.

Alexander woke up the next morning with a rather large headache. He remembered the conversation at the club with Jonathan Gainsford and the theater box with Perry, but he had an erotic encounter with the woman with the emerald eyes and wondered if it had all been a dream. He would never have taken a woman in the hallway? Kissed a total stranger? Impossible. Even if he could blame it on that cheap ale, it was not his style to accost a stranger in a darkened hall.

He had never been one to believe in love at first sight. If anything, perhaps lust. He had never lacked female companions either. A curvy milkmaid he had lost his virginity to when visiting his family's estate and several mistresses in quick succession after that. He tended to bore easily, and as he didn't need or wish to marry, he chose to remain a bachelor.

The dream last night had been odd. The emerald-eyed beauty had sighed in his ear and moaned, and he had taken her right there in the hallway. He had remembered pulling her hair down and the chestnut curls had bounced up and down as she wrapped her legs around his waist.

Damn! He shook his head. What a dream! He moved from the bed and poured water into the basin. He had no reason to dream about a stranger and a woman he would never see again. Philippine would be back soon, and there would always be a warm, willing woman after she was gone.

He had an appointment with his tailor and then the supper party that evening with Jonathan Gainsford. He was looking forward to discussing the plan in detail and seeing what the man had in mind. His valet helped him dress, then he made his way to the tailor.

Jonathan leaned back from his desk. He was pleased. Everything was coming together. The possible partnership with Mayson Shipping Line was something to look forward to. He wished to invest his own capital with the young Mr. Mayson and have something apart from the East India Company with which to use for his desires. Mariah Gower would soon be his wife, and he would lavish the wealth upon her. His daughter – well, he had thought about that as well.

He had decided that if the chit couldn't behave herself, there was one thing within his power to do. He would ship her off to his sister, Arabella, in Massachusetts. Georgiana adored her life in London. She loved to gamble, gossip, and flirt, and if she insisted on behaving as an uncontrollable slut, then he would send her to Massachusetts to curb her ways.

She would learn to control her behavior and act accordingly in London or off she went. He had already sent a letter to his sister, telling her that she might receive a visitor in the next few months. Arabella was the perfect choice, as she valued her place in society and would not allow her niece to misbehave.

He rubbed his hands together. The delightful little widow would be his at last. His daughter's wild behavior had frightened Mariah, and it was one of the few reasons she had not accepted his proposal before. But once Georgiana was gone, everything would fall into place.

A knock came upon his office door, and his clerk entered with Mariah Gower following behind. She was a slight woman with jet-black hair and piercing brown eyes. His heart warmed at the sight of her.

"Dearest Jonathan," she said as the clerk left them alone.

He came from behind the desk and kissed her intensely on the cheek, holding her tightly at the waist. "Mariah."

His eyes roamed over her slight figure, taking in the trim waist and slender bosom. She must have been in her thirties, but it didn't matter that he was ten years older. She was dressed in black silk, still in mourning for her husband, and he had the wildest urge to take her from behind right here on his desk – the mourning be damned! But he had waited this long and soon she would be his.

"I was on my way to pay a call to my cousin, and I thought to stop in to see you," she murmured, lowering her eyes demurely.

Jonathan wanted to take her in his lap and kiss her neck, but he restrained himself. "A delight to see you, my dear. As always." He motioned for her to take the seat before the desk, and he sat on the edge of it.

"I'm looking forward to the supper party this evening." Her face was flushed. "Will – Georgiana will be there?" she wondered.

Jonathan nodded. "I know she upsets you, Mariah, darling," he added, trying to comfort her.

"No, it's just . . . " Mariah clutched her fingers in her lap. "She's just so brash, and I don't understand her. But she's your daughter, Jonathan, so I try to love her."

Jonathan smiled at her thoughtful, kind nature. "You are too good. Your kindness is –"

"I do it for you, Jonathan," she said simply, her eyes wide.

"Perhaps when you have finally consented to be my wife, we may have children of our own one day," he suggested, smiling at her.

"Jonathan!" she said, shocked, and looked away from him. "What a thing to say!"

He was pleased by her modesty. "I look forward to seeing you tonight, dearest. Let me see you out."

"Until tonight," she said as he kissed the back of her hand.

Chapter 2

GEORGIANA LAY IN HER bed, staring up at the ceiling. She had wanted to rise for some time. The servants were moving about, getting the house ready for the supper party that evening. She had a slight headache from the ale she had drunk the night before, and the light streaming in from the windows hurt her eyes.

A knock sounded on the door, followed by the housekeeper telling her that her father wished to see her. She moved quickly, knowing her father did not like to be kept waiting. She pulled on a pale blue dressing gown over her chemise and tied it about her waist.

She brushed her hair out and then secured it back with a large mother-of-pearl comb. She made her way downstairs and knocked sharply on her father's study. There was no sound from within. She looked down the hallway and saw a maid dusting in the next room.

She knocked again. He was inside. She knew it. This was his way to curb her, and she willed herself not to fling open the door and enter his domain. She would wait. She would not knock again. Another minute passed before she heard the word "Enter" and she did.

She closed the door behind her and absently tightened the belt about her dressing gown. "Father," she greeted him.

"Hmph," he said and nodded to the seat facing his desk, which she took. "Why are you still in your dressing gown, daughter?" he asked, not looking at her. "It's midafternoon."

Georgiana looked down at her wrap and then back at her father. "I was out last night – "

He raised his hand, and she stopped speaking. "Say no more. I should have guessed. You were spending my money in town and wasting your time on nonsense."

"It was just the theater – " she began.

His eyes met hers then. "It was just the theater?"

Georgiana nodded. "You're right. It was a bit of nonsense."

"Of course, I am."

"And of course, you should know I spent much of the evening with Madeleine." She smiled brightly, knowing her father desisted her dear friend.

He narrowed his eyes. "You are well aware that I don't approve of Madeleine Mortier as a companion for my daughter."

"Why is that?" Georgiana asked, though she should not.

"You well know why. Ms. Mortier is a widow –"

"Her husband died," Georgiana interrupted and could have bitten her tongue.

"Don't interrupt me again," he told her firmly. Georgiana stared back at him. "Ms. Mortier may be a widow, but it has been said that she had gentlemen *friends* both before and after her husband died," he pointed out.

"Friends?" Georgiana repeated. "You mean friends like your Mariah Gower?"

Jonathan stood up and then caught himself and sat back down. "Do not speak that woman's name! I forbid it! She is a respected lady and may soon be your stepmother."

"Father, no!" Georgiana said in earnest. "The woman is a – " She stopped herself, but her father caught her gaze.

"The woman is what?" he asked in clipped tones.

Georgiana lowered her eyes and then met his gaze. "I've heard talk that she is a gold digger. She pays attention to you to be your wife because – because she wants your money and position."

Jonathan's eyes flicked briefly over his daughter and then he laughed. "Rather than try to denigrate an honorable woman, you should look to yourself, Georgiana."

"I've not said anything bad about her," Georgiana admitted.

"Yet you repeat gossip."

"I don't want you to marry the wrong woman," she said honestly.

"Well, here we finally have common ground." He shuffled the papers on his desk. "How many suitors have you turned down?" he wondered.

"I don't recall – "

"Four!" he barked.

"Four." She nodded.

"And do you think that the men in London will look favorably on a woman who has turned away four good men?"

"Four men, yes. Good . . ." She let the words hang in the air.

"There was nothing wrong with them."

"I disagree."

"Who do you want, Georgiana? Who? Because your dowry is enough to attract the highest circles. So, tell me, what will it take to get you married?" he said bluntly.

"You are so eager to be rid of me?" she asked softly.

"I want you married, as you should be, to start a family," he replied slowly. "It is the natural order of things. There's no reason with your dowry, connections, and looks that you should be an old maid."

She stared back at him but said nothing.

"What is not natural is my daughter galivanting about town at the theater, the gaming halls – "

"I don't gamble often – "

"Flirting with strangers – "

"I don't!" she argued and flushed warm.

Jonathan sighed. "I've no wish to play this card but you've forced my hand."

"What card?" Georgiana asked, her eyes widened with dread.

"If you cannot choose someone in two months' time to marry, I am sending you to your Aunt Arabella," he said with a glint of malice in his smile.

"Aunt Arabella!" Georgiana gasped with horror.

"Yes."

"Massachusetts!" A look of revulsion crossed her face. "I won't go," she said stubbornly.

"You will," he assured her.

"I won't!"

"I would not enjoy placing you in chains and putting you abroad a ship to the colonies myself, but you have an alternative."

"Marriage," she whispered.

"Marriage. I want a good man for you and someone who will provide you with the type of lifestyle you are accustomed to," he said amiably.

"And if I don't wish to marry anyone at this time?"

Jonathan smiled broadly. "That will be your choice. And you will spend the next year in the colonies with your Aunt Arabella and her husband, Richard, contemplating such a choice."

Georgiana felt her throat dry, as she knew her father would make good on his promise.

"Now, sweetheart," he said with no warmth in the endearment. "Why don't you put on one of those expensive dresses I've paid for and come down for your supper party?"

Georgiana stood and turned away from him.

"Georgiana," he said sharply and she turned. "I don't want to see one speck of rouge on your cheeks. Do you hear me? I won't have my daughter looking like a slut at the docks."

Upstairs in her bedroom, Georgiana slammed the drawers of her dresser with trembling hands. She hated him! He was a detestable man. She threw her shoes against the wall and willed herself not to cry. She had heard the stories but had never believed them. Her father had wanted a son to carry on his name, and her birth had been a disappointment. Her father had adored her mother, and when she gave birth to Georgiana, the occasion had been a happy one, but she was not the longed-for son.

When Georgiana was five years old, her mother had become pregnant again. Jonathan had been thrilled when his wife gave birth to a boy. But the child was weak, and within a week of the birth, the child and mother were dead. Jonathan had been distraught and had viewed Georgiana with distaste and anger after that.

Georgiana had grown up with a series of governesses and nannies while her father became more and more removed from her. As she grew into a lovely young woman, she was able to charm and flirt with those who fell into her path, and she surrounded herself with women who were not debutantes and men who allowed her to flirt but asked for nothing in return. In these men and women, she was able to receive the love and attention she never received from her father.

Her father despised her lifestyle and had always been openly judgmental of it. Most of the time, he dismissed her and went out of his way to avoid her. But now he had chosen Mariah Gower as his bride – Mariah Gower. Georgiana rolled her eyes. The woman was deceitful, but she would not warn her father off the woman again. She knew what she knew. Let her father be deceived in her character. What did she care?

And now Massachusetts. A backwater colony halfway across the world. Massachusetts! Where savages lived and she would probably not even survive the two-month-long ship ride there. She fumed at her father's suggestion. But marry? Never! She would never marry some man just so her father could be rid of her. She would never allow that to be her fate. Absolutely not. She stuffed several of her dresses back into her armoire, trying to stem the frustration and hate that flared through her when a knock fell upon the door.

Georgiana bid them enter and turned to see her maid, Flanna, step into the room. Flanna was ten years older than her and had been with the family for twelve years. She was from Ireland and had left her country for a better life in England. She had a soft brogue that always warmed Georgiana's heart. She acted as a maid and confidante, and Georgiana relied on her tremendously.

"Are you all right?" Flanna asked, watching her young charge's face carefully.

"I'm fine." She folded a garment and placed it back in its drawer.

"Did you and your father quarrel?" she asked, pronouncing the word quarrel in her unique Irish way.

"Yes."

"Do you want to talk about it?" Flanna asked.

Georgiana shook her head and then turned to her. "I must marry, Flanna. He wants me out of the house to marry that – that gold digger."

"Georgie!" Flanna said softly.

"No, it's true! She doesn't like me because I'm another woman to rival his affections. Only she doesn't know there's no affection to rival," Georgiana remarked.

"You always knew it would come to this," Flanna reminded her. "He's been talking of your marriage for some time."

"Well, I don't wish to marry," she said hotly, slashing her hand through the air. "I'm not going from my overbearing father's house to my husband's, so I can do what? Have children and be lucky enough to survive the childbirth bed? No thank you. I'll take my chances in Massachusetts."

Flanna frowned. "Massachusetts?"

"Oh!" Georgiana rolled her eyes. "According to darling Papa, if I don't find some poor sap to marry me, I'm shipped off to Aunt Arabella's."

"The colonies!" Flanna said, her eyes lit with excitement.

"Flanna!" Georgiana admonished. "It's not some grand adventure! It's a two-month ship ride to get there, and then once there, we'll be lucky enough to not be murdered in our beds by some red savage!"

Flanna bit back a smile. "You know very well it's not like that."

Georgiana looked over at her companion and then nodded. "I know what Aunt Arabella writes. That the conversation in Boston is as polite and refined as in most of the cities in England," she recalled from one letter she had received.

"There you have it!" Flanna said indulgently.

"She even said that a gentleman from London would almost think himself at home at Boston, as to the people and their houses, furniture, tables, dress, and conversation," she remembered. "She said that it was just as splendid and affluent as London."

"Exactly." Flanna smiled.

Georgiana narrowed her eyes. "Or she lives in a backwater savage land and wants us to think it's splendid when it absolutely isn't to save face."

"Ridiculous girl," Flanna remarked but smiled as she picked up a dress from the bed.

"So, this marriage mart business doesn't matter in the least," she assured her. "Because I won't marry, and if that means going to Massachusetts, then so be it."

"I could never change your mind, Georgie," Flanna told her. "So, if you've set yourself apart from marriage, then we best pack."

"He might change his mind," Georgiana added hopefully.

"Jonathan Gainsford?" Flanna raised an eyebrow. "I would not bet on that horse."

"Maybe not," Georgiana agreed.

"Come, Georgeen," she said with affection. "Let's pick out your dress and style your hair for the supper party."

ele

Madeleine Mortier was the first guest to arrive, and she was shown upstairs to Georgiana's room.

"You aren't ready yet, Georgie?" Madeleine asked, coming into the room in a swish of expensive gold and green silk. Her auburn hair was styled with heavy white powder, and she looked quite fetching.

"I got a late start thanks to you," Georgia told her widowed friend.

"Why me? What did I do?" She took up Georgiana's perfume and sniffed it.

"Last night. Haymarket Theater?" she pressed. "We were out so late."

"Oh, that!" Madeleine tried to hide the impish smile on her face. "Did you see that delightful Italian count? He was so handsome."

Georgiana tried to remember the Italian Madeleine spoke of but could only remember that ruffian in the hallway, the handsome devil pressing his body into hers and his mouth on hers. She felt a flush of heat rise to her face. How dare he? She angrily threw down her brush.

"Georgie?" She saw two pairs of eyes on her.

"I don't recall the Italian," Georgiana said, as much of the evening had been a blur except for the hallway kiss.

Madeleine made a humming sound. "Like a bull between my —"

"Ms. Mortier," Flanna interrupted her sharply, shaking her head.

"Oh my goodness," Madeleine grumbled. "If I can't talk about the most important thing in life—"

"Just be not quite so descriptive, please," Flanna countered, casting a glance at Georgiana.

"Well, yes. I don't want to get you in trouble with Papa Gainsford," Madeleine said, causing the two women to smile.

Georgiana stared down at the silver-blue gown thrown loosely over the settee and suddenly had no wish to attend the supper party. She didn't want to mingle with her friends and discuss frivolities when she should do as Flanna suggested and start packing. She would not bend to her father's will, and perhaps the colonies were the best place for her.

"Let me dress your hair and then we'll dress you," Flanna suggested and Georgiana nodded.

Georgiana watched her friend Madeleine as she moved to the window.

"I won't be too descriptive, my dears, but that Italian gentleman last night was quite handsome." Madeleine paused and sighed audibly, causing Flanna to look over at her. "What was his name?" she suddenly wondered aloud. "Giuseppe? Giovanni?" she asked herself while Flanna rolled her eyes.

"How did you meet?" Georgiana asked.

"I think it was after you went to get some air," she recalled. "He was in the next box and introduced himself to me. He had excellent manners!"

Flanna placed her mistress's hair up and pinned it as Georgiana remained glued to her friend's story.

"And?"

"Well," she looked over at Flanna, who narrowed her eyes, "I can't say much else to a young innocent woman's ears, but I will say the man was well-equipped." She licked her lips appreciatively.

"Ms. Mortier!" Flanna admonished Madeleine.

Georgiana frowned. "Equipped?"

"Never mind all that nonsense," Flanna said, glaring at Madeleine.

Madeleine smiled like the cat who had eaten the cream and nodded. "Yes. Best to leave the story there, my darling," she said, looking out the window and seeing a carriage pull up to the front door. The brass knocker was used on the door twice to alert the servants that someone had arrived.

"A guest already?" Georgiana wondered.

Flanna had a hairpin in her mouth but shook her head. "No." She placed the pin in her charge's hair. "I heard Master tell he was expecting a gentleman this evening to discuss business."

Georgiana looked radiant in her silver-blue silk gown, which was worn over the boned bodice and elaborate skirt. Her hair was laced with small diamond-encrusted pins that sparkled when she moved. Georgiana preferred not to use wigs and powder, as they made her head itch. She placed a hand at her waist and felt the whalebone stays that created the silhouette so admired by women.

"You look most becoming, Georgie," her friend complimented her.

Flanna nodded in agreement, and when the two women moved downstairs, the house was filled with flowers and the chamber music her father enjoyed.

Madeleine plucked a raspberry from the buffet table and placed it slowly in her mouth. The footman standing nearby seemed mesmerized by her, and Georgiana shook her head.

"Behave, wicked woman," Georgiana told her friend, nudging her. "He's only a mere mortal."

"Behave? I did that enough when I was married. Life is for the living, Georgia darling," Madeleine said, taking two glasses of champagne from the passing footman and handing one of them to her friend.

"Ah! Here's Nathaniel!" Georgiana remarked as a tall man came towards them.

"Georgiana, dear!" He leaned in to kiss her cheek and then spied Madeleine. "Madeleine, love."

Nathaniel Lindsay traveled in their circle and had for some time. He enjoyed the latest fashion and wore the finest silks and satins. He painted his face white and wore a beauty mark on his left cheek in the shape of a dot, as was the French fashion. He had spent time at the French court and it showed.

He had been quite taken with Georgiana when they first met, but those in their circle agreed it was because he liked pretty things and she was the loveliest of their group.

Madeleine believed the rumors that Nathaniel was a rich man's plaything and his way of life was bankrolled by the older baron. Either way, he had a razor wit and was filled with gossip and stories of London.

"Oh, my dears," he said, fanning himself with a silk fan attached to his wrist. "I cannot tell you; the gossip is true! Madame Laserie is pregnant!"

"So? That's not news," Madeleine retorted.

"Hmmm." Nathaniel made a sound. "The *bebe* is not her husband's. *D'accord?*" he said, his eyebrow raised.

Georgiana's lips lifted, and she grinned at him. "How do you hear everything?" she wondered. "It's uncanny."

Nathaniel took her hand in his and gave her a twirl. "If you would consent to be my wife, darling Georgiana, we could settle in the country and I would have no need for the tawdry *potins*."

"No need?" Georgiana's merry eyes met his. "But you live for gossip!"

"*Oui*, this is true. But a lovely woman on one's arm is a necessity as well," he answered her. "*Comprendre?*"

Georgiana ignored his false proposal but nodded. "Yes, I understand."

"Come. Let's say hello to everyone and eat. I'm famished," Madeleine told them both.

Jonathan nodded at Alexander as the young man took the chair facing his desk. "That's exactly what I want. I will completely fund the purchase of your next ship," he told him, "in return for eighty percent of everything you bring back from the colonies on your next run."

Alexander raised his eyebrows. "Eighty percent? Even with the generous backing of the ship, Gainsford, the percentage is steep."

"But in return is a ship that you will own outright for one shipment," Jonathan reminded him.

He had no desire to invest in another shipping line, as he already had that. What he wanted was the goods from the colonies to sell himself and earn a hefty profit.

"Do you have a date on when you would like to sail?" Alexander asked.

"A month after the ship has been commissioned."

"That would take some months," Alexander pointed out.

Jonathan shrugged. "I'm in no hurry."

"I'm intrigued, Gainsford. Let me think on it. It's a big decision," Alexander admitted to the middle-aged man in his long, neatly powdered wig and his expensive clothes.

"Of course," Jonathan responded. "Think it over. I never make rash decisions myself," he told the young man as he walked him out of his office.

Alexander glanced over his right shoulder. "The supper party?"

Jonathan nodded. "I have some letters that require my attention, but stay and have some food and drink. There's only a handful of people this evening and you're most welcome."

"Thank you. And let me assure you that I will give your proposal much thought."

The two men shook hands, and Alexander found himself alone in the hallway. He heard laughter and turned to see several couples gathered in the warm candlelight of the parlor. He recognized the music as the minuet. Two couples laughingly danced to the mincing steps, their movements perfectly aligned with the music.

He admired a woman with dark reddish-brown hair who was clothed in green and gold. She appeared to dance well and was enjoying herself. She giggled as she missed a step and her partner scolded her. A passing footman offered him a glass of champagne, which he took.

He thought over the conversation he had with Gainsford and was pleased, though he had not admitted it. An entire ship would be funded, and all he had to do was give his first shipment from the colonies to him. It was a fair exchange. The amount of money in goods he would return with in furs and tobacco and gunpowder alone would fund the ship twice over. He smiled broadly. He, in turn, would gain the backing of the East India Company through its director, which was impressive. The partnership might open more doors for his own shipping line, which must be construed as a good thing.

He heard others talking in another room and watched as the small group of five arranged their chairs in a circle.

"Come! We're playing Buffy Gruffy," one man called out to the others who were dancing.

The dancers joined the group, and soon ten people each had a chair with them, playing the game in the lowly lit parlor. Alexander knew the game well. He had played it as a child. The players would arrange their chairs in a circle and one person would be blindfolded.

The blindfolded person would approach a chair and push their knee forward to see if anyone was there. The blindfolded player would ask three questions to determine who was in the chair. The person in the chair would try to disguise their voice. But if the blindfolded person guessed correctly, they would exchange places. If not, the blindfolded person would continue until they guessed correctly.

He smiled at the simple game and watched as a woman in a silver-blue dress with her back to him was blindfolded. The woman in green and gold beckoned for him to take a seat, and he did so, placing his glass aside. The woman walked in a circle and then came to stand before him. She wore a white kerchief over much of her face.

She pressed her knee into the chair and her leg slid between his knees. "Nathaniel!" she guessed immediately.

"No," he said simply, and she frowned.

She guessed another name, and he said no again, not caring that she wasn't asking questions. He was not known to anyone here. She was unable to guess his identity and so she moved along in the circle behind him and immediately guessed the next person.

"Nathaniel!" she yelled. He immediately stood up and they switched places, laughing the whole time.

The game continued for a little while longer before they tired of it and suggested Blind Man's Bluff.

Alexander thought the games were childish parlor games, but the mood was light and silly, and everyone seemed to be enjoying themselves. Alexander knew this game as well. One person was blindfolded except now they were told to count to twenty and everyone else scattered about the room. The blindfolded person had to chase and catch someone and identify him or her correctly by touch only. Once identified, they would switch places and the game would begin again.

Again, he was at a disadvantage, as no one knew him and vice versa, but he picked up his champagne glass and watched the group blindfold the man named Nathaniel. Afterwards he chased after everyone. Alexander excused himself from the game and went in search of the buffet table.

He had not eaten much that day and suddenly found himself famished. He chose venison, asparagus, and an apple tart and was surprised at their rich flavors. He decided to leave the supper party since his business was concluded, and he walked back down the hallway past the parlor. Everyone was hiding behind furniture away from the woman wearing the silver-blue gown who was now blindfolded.

"Come out!" she commanded, but no one moved.

He crossed into the hallway, and his shoes echoed on the black-and-white tiled floor. Without warning, the woman in the silver-blue dress threw herself at him, pressing into him. He was taken aback at her actions and then realized she was playing the game.

Alexander stared down at the woman whose face was covered by a white kerchief. She was a stranger to him and he to her. She would never guess his identity. But swiftly all thought left him as her hands moved along his biceps through the fabric of his coat. He swallowed when her hands landed on his chest. He remained still with his arms at his sides, but it was difficult.

His heart thudded heavily as her hands moved upwards to his neck and then touched his hair at the nape of his neck. He felt aroused at the woman's touch, even though she was only doing so as part of a silly game. She moved her hands down again over his chest, and he realized he was holding in his breath. The woman frowned and shook her head. She reached up to remove the kerchief that covered most of her face.

"I don't know you –" Georgiana began, and in the low candlelight of the hallway, Alexander recognized her instantly even as she gasped.

It was the emerald-eyed beauty from the night before.

Chapter 3

"YOU!" GEORGIANA FLUNG AT him as an almost accusation.

Alexander gave her a lopsided grin. "And here I almost thought last night was a dream."

"Being pawed by some drunk animal is more like a nightmare," she sneered.

"You can continue to search me," he said, his grin larger now. "I wasn't complaining."

"My God!" Georgiana said, flushed and annoyed. "You think you are quite something!"

"Except for your injured pride," he said, leaning into her. "Did you really mind such a small little kiss?" His last words were a purr in her ear. "Don't tell me I was the first?"

Georgiana stared at the buffoon, willing herself not to slap him again when the door to her father's study opened and they both turned to see Jonathan standing there.

"Ah, Mayson. I see you've met my daughter, Georgiana." He nodded at the woman standing next to him.

Alexander swung his eyes to the emerald-eyed cat before him and recalled all the things that had been said about her.

"Georgiana," he whispered and then caught himself. "Ms. Gainsford," he said loudly for Jonathan to hear.

"This is Alexander Mayson, Georgiana," he introduced them. "We are working on a possible business deal."

Georgiana's dislike for the ill-mannered man turned to instant hate at her father's words. Anyone doing business with him was someone she wanted nothing to do with. All her father seemed to care about was making money and lavishing it on the many women he chose to spend time with in the evening.

A knock upon the door sounded, and the footman admitted Mariah Gower into the house. She handed her cloak to the footman and glided across the floor to where they stood watching her.

"Jonathan," she said in a soft voice.

"Mariah, my dear." Jonathan took her hand in his. "Don't you look fetching in your frock. Is it new? I've not seen it."

"It is, Jonathan." She looked down at the plum-colored gown. "You noticed." She glanced briefly at Alexander as Jonathan introduced them.

Stemming her aversion for the fortune-hunting widow, Georgiana excused herself from the trio. She was headed back to her friends, who sounded lively, as the music had begun again, when Alexander caught her arm and she turned to face him.

"Will you kindly keep your hands to yourself, Mr. Mayson?" She bristled at his hold, and he released her.

"Just a moment ago, you were caressing my arms and chest," he said lowly, a small smile on his handsome face.

"A parlor game, Mr. Mayson. And the only reason I would ever touch you."

"And here I thought you might have wanted to continue what we started last night." His words were a caress.

"Continue what *we* started last night?" Georgiana frowned. "Since when did anything start?"

He was about to respond when Nathaniel joined them in the hallway, pulling her playfully about the waist.

"Georgie, darling," he said, smiling at her. "Come back to the party. We can't decide on cards or dice." He pulled her with him just as Madeleine joined them.

"Who do we have here?" Her eyes moved appreciatively over Alexander.

"Alexander Mayson," he said, meeting her eyes.

"Alexander Mayson," Madeleine said, winding her arm through his and pulling him into the parlor. "Well, you must join our little party and tell me all about yourself."

Several people were playing cards and drinking champagne, while Nathaniel had cornered Georgiana by the fire.

"I'm Madeleine Mortier," she introduced herself, sitting back onto the sofa.

"Where is Monsieur Mortier?" he wondered.

"I'm widowed, as it happens." Her hungry eyes met his. "So, there's no husband to interrupt in the middle of the night. Some information you might find useful." She shrugged.

"I see," he said. But he thought, *Brazen hussy*.

"What do you do, Mr. Mayson? I've never seen you here before," she asked.

"Are you here so often to know the guests?" he asked.

"Often enough." She smiled. "Georgie and I are old friends."

"I'm here to discuss business with Gainsford," he explained.

"What business are you in?"

"I own a shipping line," he told her.

"A shipping line? Where do you ship to?"

"The colonies, mostly." His eyes followed Georgiana as she left Nathaniel sitting on the sofa and exited the room.

"I've never been," she said. "Though I'm not sure I'd want to."

"Afraid of the uncivilized heathens," he asked her.

"Something like that." She smiled.

Georgiana passed by them with a whisper of her skirts brushing her legs, and Alexander watched her figure as she retreated to the next room.

In the next room, Georgiana helped herself to a glass of punch that Cook had made specially for the evening. She poured the liquid into the glass goblet and tasted the orange and lemon mixed with rum, brandy, and champagne. She finished it quickly before she poured another glass and took it out onto the terrace. She was irritated with herself.

Haymarket Theater indeed! She had pushed the kiss from her mind and not told a soul about the evening, but it had aggravated her. At first, she had put it down to a drunk ruffian who had taken a chance and kissed a woman. But now seeing Alexander Mayson in her home, she knew he was everything she despised. He was arrogant, handsome, and a younger version of her father.

He was cold and money hungry, and in a few years' time, he would marry a woman, have children he would ignore, and his wife would be dissatisfied and die lonely and unfulfilled. He was just another one of her father's cronies. She pushed away the thought of her hands roaming freely over his biceps and chest as her cheeks warmed in the night air.

A sound came from behind her, and Mariah appeared. "Dear Georgiana." Mariah peered behind her out into the small garden. "You're all alone out here?"

Georgiana frowned. "Is there someone you were expecting to be out here with me?"

Mariah shrugged. "I'm sure we don't need to be coy with each other. I saw how taken you were with that young man. What's his name?"

Georgiana knew she was lying. Mariah was trying to get a rise out of her so that she could run to her father and complain about her once more. The sooner she was married or shipped off to the colonies, the happier Mariah would be.

"Alexander Mayson?" Georgiana asked her tartly. "My father's potential business partner."

Mariah smiled and moved to stand beside her. "Perhaps I misunderstood," she said with a simpering look on her face.

Georgiana said nothing as they stood together on the terrace.

"I have heard that the journey to the colonies is long and arduous at times," Mariah said, changing her tactic. "Almost two months aboard ship."

"Yes."

"I'm sure you'll understand that your father doesn't want to wait," she said slyly. "We'll most likely marry when you are away in Massachusetts."

"I'm fairly certain that you are kept up most nights thinking on how devastated you are at my not being in attendance at your wedding," Georgiana fired back.

Mariah's face became a smirk. "Most assuredly." She nodded and made a sound. "And your place in the home as its mistress? That will no longer be yours when I'm Mrs. Gainsford. How very sad for you."

"I wish you the joy of it," Georgiana said, trying to keep her composure.

"You must learn to call me Mama," she added sweetly. "After all, when your father and I marry, you'll be my dearest daughter."

Never! Georgiana swore inwardly, gritting her teeth.

Mariah sighed. "I've often thought that men who become fathers later in life are better suited to it. Don't you agree?"

"What?" Georgiana frowned.

"What I meant to say was that your father was so young when you were born," she elaborated. "Our child, on the other hand, will have the benefit of a successful businessman with wealth and love lavished upon them. A very happy home." She touched her belly.

Georgiana looked down at the woman's belly and then up into her devious face.

"Not yet, my dear," she said cunningly, "but it's only a matter of time."

Georgiana felt herself trembling. "Excuse me," she said, setting down her glass of punch and leaving the hateful woman behind.

She was light-headed as she made her way into the hallway. She walked quickly to the small sitting room at the back of the house that also served as a conservatory. She placed a hand at her waist and tried to stem her rapid breathing.

The woman was hateful! She was playing on her emotions. She knew full well that Georgiana's mother had died when she was young and she had grown up without her and only a cold, withdrawn father in her young life. She looked out the glass panes into the night and closed her eyes. She should pack now. She should go to her father and tell him to book her passage and leave this cursed house where there was little love and warmth in it.

But why should she give them the satisfaction of leaving early? If she had several months to catch a husband and drag them to the alter, so be it. She would use every minute of the time doing the exact opposite. When she finally failed, then and only then would she leave for the colonies with her head held high.

Her attention was diverted to the door of the room as a giggle came and two forms entered the conservatory. A man and a woman by the looks of the outline. One tall and broad-shouldered, the other petite.

"I thought you were showing me the house," the man asked quietly.

"I'm showing you the best part," the woman replied. Madeleine! Georgiana recognized her voice. Her friend leaned into the man as she wrapped her arms around his neck.

"Mrs. Mortier," the man said, stopping her movements.

"Yes, Mr. Mayson?" she asked coyly.

Mr. Mayson! Georgiana's eyes narrowed in the dark. Was the man no better than an alley cat? She knew her friend to be flirty, but this man? He was too brash and aware of his charms. He was handsome, and absolutely knew it. She hated him!

"I'm interested in doing business with the man of this house," he explained softly. "I don't wish to offend him."

"Offend him? What could we possibly do to offend him?" She giggled lightly.

"I don't think we should continue this," he whispered.

"Spoilsport." She pretended to be angry. "We could resume this later," she offered.

"Perhaps," came his comment.

"I'll return to the parlor. Wait a minute and then join us. Naughty boy," she said, grinning, and then departed.

Georgiana had been in society long enough to know that when men and women disappeared together at house parties, things happened between them. But Flanna explained that she was never to do such a thing until she was married. She wasn't even upset at Madeleine. Her friend was a harmless flirt. What aggravated her was this braggart, this unknown upstart coming into her house, engaging her friend as if she was a prostitute, and using her house as a brothel.

She was waiting for him to leave when she leaned against the pane of glass and disturbed a book that fell to the floor with a thud. Georgiana closed her eyes in frustration. She had no wish to come face to face with the braggart.

"Who's there?" Alexander said, looking into the dark corner. He walked the short distance to where she stood at the end of the room. "Georgiana," he said in surprise.

"Mr. Mayson," she said curtly, eyeing him with distaste.

"I didn't know you were here," he stated.

"Obviously," she said, her eyes meeting his in the dark.

A light rain had begun to fall outside, and it pelted the glass windowpanes. The conservatory was completely in the dark, though the moonlight shone from outside. They stood staring at each other.

"What are you doing here?" he asked. "All alone in the dark?"

"Is it normal for you to use the house of a prospective business partner as a brothel?" she asked, ignoring his question altogether.

He frowned. "A brothel?"

"That's what I said."

"You misunderstand," he said smoothly. "We came out here – " He stopped awkwardly as Georgiana narrowed her eyes but said nothing. He shook his head. "Why does it concern you?"

"My *friend* concerns me."

"Ah. Yes. Your friend. She concerns you." His eyes looked her up and down. "Are you perhaps jealous of the attention I give another woman?"

She shook her head in one quick movement. "You think you're quite something."

He shrugged. "I know what I am."

"Do you?" Georgiana arched an eyebrow. He remained silent. "Well, let me tell you what I see, Mr. Mayson. I see a man who's too arrogant for his own good. A man who is disrespectful of people's property and, most importantly, extremely bad-mannered where women are concerned." She looked up at him, daring him to say something.

"Come now, Ms. Gainsford." He grinned. "You can't still be mad at that kiss. Unless, of course, it was your first real kiss. In that case, all I require is a thank you," he said, a small smile on his lips.

"Thank you?" She was irritated by his words and his presence. "You really would be so delusional to think that after you accosted me in a public theater and took such liberties, I owe you a thank you."

His eyes were warm in the cool night. "You're welcome."

"Whatever plans you and my father are concocting, you have no reason to be in my circle of friends. So, I expect you to keep a wide berth of Madeleine and not become bothersome," she demanded.

"You have nothing to fear from me, mademoiselle," Alexander told her.

Georgiana scoffed. "I don't fear you in the least, Mr. Mayson. I detest the very sight of you."

With those final words, she swept past the man and rejoined her friends in the parlor. She tried to listen to what gossip Nathaniel was telling her, but the night dragged on as Madeleine giggled at every other word Alexander seemed to say.

She wasn't jealous at all. She knew him for what he was, and when this supper party was over, she would tell her friend exactly that. She studied him from across the room as Nathaniel droned on about a countess he had met in France and her penchant for bathing in champagne.

"Where on earth did you hear that?" she asked Nathaniel, laughing with him, but as he answered her, she looked over at Alexander Mayson with hooded eyes.

What did it matter if he was attractive? She had known attractive men before. His face was chiseled like a Greek god, and his wavy brown hair was kept tied in a queue, not powdered, which was unusual. He had full lips and dark blue eyes, and the longer she stared at him, the more intensely irritated she became.

When the evening drew to a close, only Nathaniel, Madeleine, and Alexander remained. It must have been well past midnight as each couple sat on the plush mint-green sofas, chatting before the fire.

"I have the most enchanting idea," Nathaniel told her. "We should go to Paris. Enjoy some time away from dreary London." He sniffed.

Alexander caught Georgiana's eye. She was about to refuse but then thought better of it.

"It sounds charming, Nathaniel," she said firmly. "Most charming."

"We should make a trip of it," Alexander said, coolly eyeing Georgiana. "I've not been for two years at least."

Nathaniel turned his attention to the other couple and stared at Alexander carefully. "We could do that," he admitted without much enthusiasm.

"Ah, here you all are." Jonathan came into the room. "Mayson, you stayed."

"The company was so agreeable." He came to stand before this host.

"It's getting quite late, Georgiana," her father told her. "I'm sure your guests are tired."

As her father made mention of the late hour, Nathaniel took the hint, kissed Georgiana on the cheek, and departed with a very sleepy Madeleine. Alexander remained behind.

"Mayson. Did you have a coat or a cane?" Jonathan asked.

"A hat," he corrected.

"Let me see to it," he said, as the servants were asleep, and he disappeared down the dark hallway.

Georgiana turned her back on him as she returned to the parlor. She studied the fire intently and sighed heavily when Alexander joined her.

"Come now, Georgiana," he said, using her name so easily that her eyes immediately flew to meet his. "The evening wasn't a complete loss."

She turned to face him. "Of course, it wasn't. My friends and I always enjoy ourselves."

"Friends like Nathaniel?"

"Nathaniel, yes. And Madeleine."

"I wonder how good a friend Nathaniel is," he said lowly. "To invite you to Paris. I wonder what your father would say."

Georgiana looked away. "He would not allow it."

"That's a shame. Because I could think of many places in Paris I would like very much to show you," he told her lowly.

She met his cool blue eyes. "What a loss! I shall have to find a way to bear it. Your devasting charms will have to be used on someone else," she said, her tone rich with sarcasm.

"Hmmm, I wonder," he said vaguely.

Jonathan returned with a tricorne hat in his hand and handed it to Alexander.

"It was a pleasure, Ms. Gainsford," he said, giving her a slight bow. "Mr. Gainsford."

Georgiana was relieved when the arrogant man was gone from their house. She picked up the candle to take upstairs to her room when her father's voice stopped her.

"Georgiana." Her name was said in a command and so she placed the candle back down and joined him in the parlor.

"Yes, Father."

He looked old and tired, and she would have liked to ease his burden and be a support to him, but she knew he wanted nothing from her.

"Were you pleasant to Mr. Mayson this evening?" he asked her.

"I treated him as a guest at the party, though he's a stranger to me," she answered honestly.

"Good. We might be entering into a business agreement and it will include a great deal of money," he told her.

Georgiana sighed inwardly. Money. Of course. What else mattered to him? Certainly not his daughter. "Yes, Father."

"I see that young flirt Ms. Mortier was at the supper party." He sniffed. "You know I don't care for her, Georgiana. I believe I told you that on more than one occasion."

Georgiana was suddenly tired. She didn't want to have this conversation once more. "You did."

"Yet once more you chose to go against my wishes," he said briskly.

"Surely my friends are my friends, Father. And Madeleine is a widow. So how she chooses to spend her time away from me cannot reflect on me," Georgiana said, bristling with anger.

Jonathan shook his head and scoffed. "You speak like the ridiculous child you are. Of course, it reflects on you! I've heard it said she has had several lovers in the span of a year. She's a slut! And if you allow her in your company, people will think the same of you."

"Do not your business associates do the same? Do not they take lovers and mistresses and most of them are married? So, is not their behavior, their sin, worse?" she said heatedly, her cheeks flushed.

"Stupid girl! You speak of men. Businessmen. They have money and prestige and can engage in such affairs. Your friend cannot!" He sneered.

Georgiana said nothing. The argument would only become more heated and wake Cook who slept on the ground floor.

He shook his head, looking over her form. "I've heard your beauty complimented on more than one occasion, and I must say it's the only thing to be complimented. Your head is filled with nonsense, you are wayward and disobedient, and I almost pity the poor man who will be tied to you for life!"

Georgiana swallowed against the tears she willed not to fall. "Anything else?"

"Go to your bed."

She nodded at her father. There was nothing more to be said.

Upstairs in her bedroom, tears fell down her cheeks. Her father disapproved of almost everything she did, but tonight he had been quite cutting. She was dreadfully tired, and she could not stop herself from weeping.

She removed her dress and drew on a clean white chemise and lay in her four-poster bed, wrapping her arms about her knees. He had called her disobedient, but other than her friendship with Madeleine, she had always tried to abide by his wishes and rules. He wasn't exactly strict, but his coldness was brutal. She had not ever received an embrace from him, and except for a pat on the shoulder, that was the extent of his physical demonstrations.

As for being stupid, she imagined her father was intelligent. He was the director of the East India Company and a member of Parliament, so he was respected and somewhat feared. However, she had been educated by governesses throughout the years and spoke French, played the pianoforte, and could sing exceedingly well.

Her father had made sure she had all the talents a young lady needed to attract a good husband. Anything Jonathan Gainsford did was only to enhance Georgiana's status to help him, never for her alone.

She thought again of the colonies and the threat of being sent there. Once she was there, she knew she might enjoy herself. Backwater and savage it might be, but at least she would live with her Aunt Arabella, who was snobbish but motherly, and her Uncle Richard, who was kindness itself. She only dreaded the voyage there, which was very long and arduous.

She thought suddenly of Alexander Mayson and closed her eyes. She could still remember that kiss in the dark hallway and his hands touching her. It embarrassed her that such an arrogant, conceited man should have been the one to touch her so and claim her first kiss.

He was correct in that. She had never been kissed before. Her father had eyes and ears everywhere, and she would never want to give him cause to do what he had once threatened to do: place her in a convent. He had only threatened it once when Georgiana disappeared one night at sixteen to attend the theater. She had returned early in the morning, and her father had enacted his punishment. No food for two days.

He allowed her to attend the theater and other events now because he knew she should be seen to attract a husband. He disliked Madeleine but he allowed her to accompany Georgiana as a sort of companion.

Moonlight streamed into her room as she drifted off into a fitful sleep.

Alexander looked over at the sleeping head of Philippine de Froissy. She had returned the evening before, and when she sent him a note, he had arrived at her house after the supper party. Their lovemaking had been rushed and passionate, and she had smiled slyly afterwards. She knew he had missed her and had been eager to take her.

But as Alexander looked about the richly decorated room in blue and gold, that was not it. He had always enjoyed Philippine's lovemaking, as she was passionate and giving. But he had not been thinking about her at all. He had been thinking about the green-eyed temptress who seemed to loathe the sight of him, which amused him immensely.

Georgiana Gainsford.

He laced his hands behind his head. The lovely woman surrounded herself with dandies and flirty widows, but she was all too innocent for her own good. He remembered that kiss at Haymarket Theater in exquisite detail. She had been surprised when he pushed her up against the wall, but she had also been intoxicatingly innocent. Her mouth had been so sweet and tender, and he could tell she was unused to such attention.

He took a strange satisfaction in being the first man to kiss her, and her luscious mouth was meant to be kissed. She was meant to be loved and appreciated. But she was not for him. A young unmarried virgin meant one thing, and it was the one thing he would not do anytime soon. Marriage.

He looked over at the sleeping woman beside him and caressed her naked back. She moved in sleep and made a slight sound. He pulled her tightly against him, kissing the back of her neck even as she murmured his name.

Chapter 4

MADELEINE LOOKED OVER AT her friend and frowned. "But, darling, what do you mean I shouldn't see him? He's by far the most interesting man I've met in London in the last year."

Georgiana had invited her friend to a nearby tea room in London where they served the brew to customers. She would have invited her to her home, but her father often came home for lunch and she didn't want to run into him after their row last night.

Georgiana tried to think of the words to tell her friend. "He's very – "

Madeleine waited and said nothing.

"Well, he's – "

Again, Madeleine said nothing.

"He's very arrogant," Georgiana said firmly.

"But, darling, that's what I like about him!" Madeleine smiled. "A man who knows his own mind."

"He's doing business with my father," she said stubbornly.

"Ah." Madeline nodded. "That's what's bothering you."

"Certainly. I don't want anyone who's doing business with my father near me or my friends," she said, irritated.

Madeleine placed her cup down. "Did something happen with your father? After the supper party?"

"Last night," Georgiana said softly. "He seemed almost venomous, Madeleine. I think he hates me."

Madeleine covered her friend's hand with hers. "He doesn't, darling. He's just old and mean. I've never understood your father, honestly. He has a beautiful daughter whom he should love and cherish. Instead, he's cold and withdrawn and ignores you."

"Oh, yes. He mentioned my beauty last night," she said, eyeing her coffee cup. "He said that's the only thing I am to be complimented on. He said my head is filled with nonsense and," she met her friends' eyes, "he pities the poor man who will be tied to me for life."

"Georgie!" her friend said softly, her eyes filled with compassion. "The man is a monster!" She took both her hands in hers. "He is! He tries to break your spirit down. I can't fathom it. Honestly, I can't."

"He wants me gone." Georgiana shook her head. "Married and off his hands or shipped off to the colonies, hopefully never to return."

"Well," Madeline said. "Imagine if you do ever marry, it might be to some earl or duke and then you'll have that power through your husband. Something your father can never have."

"Are you trying to convince me to marry a peer of the realm?" she asked her friend.

"Heavens no! I've never been as happy as when I was widowed." Madeleine sipped her tea.

"Well, that's because your husband was old enough to know Henry the Eighth personally," she said with a sparkle in her eye.

Madeline laughed. "Silly girl!"

They had just ordered another pot of tea when the bell over the door twinkled lightly. Two men dressed fashionably in dark plum, brown, and gold entered the room. They were shown a table nearby and ordered a pot of tea as well.

"Don't look now, Georgie, but your archnemesis is in the room," Madeline said, clearly trying to bite back a smile.

Georgiana frowned, "Who?"

Georgiana glanced over her shoulder and saw the two gentlemen who had just been seated. Alexander Mayson.

"Oh, lord," she said aloud, not meaning to, and bit down on her bottom lip.

Alexander, who was facing the two women, said a word to his companion and then walked to their table.

"Oh, God, he's not coming over here, is he?" she whispered to her friend just as he joined them.

"Mademoiselle, madame," he acknowledged them both cheerfully. "A pleasant morning, is it not?"

"It was," Georgiana said softly.

"You both look exceptionally lovely," he complimented them both. "That color is a favorite of mine." He indicated Georgiana's lemon-colored gown.

Georgiana smiled but said nothing to the compliment. She refused to be swayed by his sweet words and phrases.

"I'm here with my friend, Perry Thornhill." He indicated the other man. "Would you like to join us or would that be too impertinent?"

"No, thank you," Georgiana said at the same time her friend responded with, "We'd love to."

Georgiana looked over at her, and Madeleine shrugged.

"Come along." She prodded her friend kindly as Alexander moved back to his table. "At worse, they'll pay for our tea!" she whispered as the two stood up and joined the gentleman.

Alexander introduced the women to his friend Peregrine Thornhill, whom everyone called Perry. He explained that they had been at Cambridge together.

"What did you study at university, sir," Georgiana asked her new acquaintance who had sandy blonde hair and brown eyes.

"The law," he explained. "I must make my way in the world, as I'm the third son of a baron."

"I see." Georgiana nodded. "You won't have any money or title handed to you."

"Precisely." Perry smiled lightly. "And though I do imagine that would be nice, I would not like it to happen at the death of my brothers. So, I find my own way and the rewards will be all the sweeter."

"I think that's commendable," Georgiana said sincerely.

Alexander was listening to Madeline speak. She was as delightful and pretty as she had been at the supper party. But though she was flirtatious and welcoming, he found himself watching Georgiana. When she spoke, it was as if the whole world melted away, and he could see his womanizing friend was not immune to her charms.

"Although if any of us here are to be commended," Perry began smiling, "it's my friend Mayson. He has quite the past."

"Indeed?" Georgiana's eyes went from warm and lively to cool and remote as she looked from Perry to Alexander. "In what way?"

"Mayson here was a privateer! He roamed the seven seas for king and country," Perry said, pride in his friend clear in his voice. "Made quite a killing as I hear tell."

"That's fascinating," Madeline said, her eyes wide with excitement. "Tell us of it!"

"Privateer?" Georgiana cut in abruptly as her eyes surveyed Alexander. "Isn't that really no better than a pirate?"

"A privateer is authorized by their government to attack foreign shipping," he explained simply, their eyes meeting.

"A pirate has no such authority."

"So basically, you're given leave to attack other ships and do what? Legally steal from them?" she wondered. "That sounds like piracy cloaked as a privateer."

"Well, I guess that depends on if you think being a pirate is a good thing or a bad thing," he told her.

"You own a shipping line. Do you not?" she asked, looking down at the tea that had been poured out for her.

"I do."

"If Spain's privateers board your ship and steal your goods, hmm. One might say you've received some sort of comeuppance," Georgiana said lightly.

"Do you think I need comeuppance?" he asked lowly, meeting her eyes.

He suddenly had a moment's flashback of pushing her up against the wall and kissing her. His hands pressing into her and drowning in those emerald-colored eyes –

His reverie was broken when his friend cleared his throat, and everyone stared at him as he focused on Georgiana. Georgiana pulled her eyes away from his as he picked up his cup and took a long drink.

"I have an idea! You both must join us this Friday," Madeleine said in an excited voice. "It will be such an event!"

"What event is that?" Perry wondered.

"Jonathan Gainsford, Georgiana's father, is hosting a large ball at Clyvedon Hall in London. It's such an event. There will be dancing and food. You both must come," she said happily, not realizing that Georgiana was anything but pleased at the suggestion.

"I'm assuming we need an invitation," Perry said, reminding her.

"You'll come as my guest," Madeleine said simply. "What could be simpler? And Georgiana you can invite –"

"I've received an invitation, madame," Alexander interrupted her. "Gainsford invited me himself yesterday."

"There you are!" Madeleine threw up her hands. "We'll have such fun!"

When the women excused themselves, Perry and Alexander remained behind at their table. The loss of the brightly colored women was palpable, and they each seemed lost in their own thoughts.

"What absolutely charming women," Perry told Alexander as he added sugar to his tea. "Most charming. Especially the young mademoiselle."

Alexander didn't answer his friend but agreed.

"Did you see her eyes? And those lips." Perry grinned, looking down at the tea. "I could definitely do with something stronger than tea."

"I would steer clear, Perry," Alexander warned him. "Her father is intent to see her marry. He told me so himself."

"Come now, man," Perry said pleasantly. "Could you imagine being married to her? What glorious nights! She'd be with child in three months' time, I'd wager."

Alexander didn't know why but a strong wave of anger flooded through him at his friend's words. He shrugged it off as he paid the bill, and together, they left the teahouse.

"She doesn't seem to care for you much," Perry noted wryly.

"Really? I hadn't noticed," Alexander said nonchalantly, though he had.

"I think she's the first female I've seen that hasn't fallen for those Mayson charms," Perry recalled, grinning at his friend.

With that, Alexander and Perry parted company, as they were headed in opposite directions.

Alexander watched his close friend walk down the street for several seconds before he turned on his heel and headed to his appointment. Perry was correct in one regard. Maybe that was why he found Georgiana so fascinating. She didn't seem to want anything to do with him, and that was a rarity. He had always been able to charm women, even as a young lad. Serving wenches and bored widows had fallen onto their backs just as easily, no matter their station in life. But this one, this emerald-eyed beauty, had wiped her mouth to erase his kiss and seemed to want only his absence.

He walked along the street, humming softly to himself. He looked forward to seeing the beauty again.

Georgiana stood on the small dais and made a circle so everyone in the room could see and admire the dress. Flanna had accompanied her for the dress fitting, and her father was seated in the corner of the room, dressed in purple satin, sipping a cup of chocolate. His face was stern and unreadable. Her dress for the ball was made of satin with large vertical gray-blue and beige stripes. It had a square ruched neckline and elbow-length sleeves. Small bows decorated the bodice of the gown, and the overall effect was feminine and charming.

"I don't like the bodice," her father said sternly. "It's too low."

Madame Melier was older than her father and was dressed in all black. Her grey hair was pinned up. She was stern and uncompromising but was one of the most expensive and respected dressmakers in London. Her father used her services for that exact reason. He wanted people to know that he paid a fortune for his daughter's gowns and had money to spend on such frivolities.

"It is the fashion, monsieur," Madame Melier stated.

Jonathan gave the woman a passing glance. "My daughter is searching for a husband, not a protector."

Georgiana's face went warm, and all three women looked at Jonathan. The word "protector" was a term used when a woman was seeking a male protector in an exchange of sex for money. It was not a word to be used with a young unmarried woman such as his daughter.

"How much higher would you like it, monsieur?" asked Madame Melier quietly.

He surveyed his daughter. "Her bosom should not be too prominent," he said and pointed a finger at her. "Let men get a look but not too much of one."

"*Oui*, monsieur. It will be done." She nodded.

Jonathan seemed satisfied. "Your work is exceptional, madame."

"*Merci*, monsieur."

"The dress will be ready by Friday?" he asked.

She nodded and disappeared into the back room with Flanna to arrange packages for items that were ready to be taken that day.

"I was pleased to see young Mayson stayed behind for your supper party last night," he said, placing his chocolate cup aside.

"I think he was quite taken with Madeline," Georgiana informed him, stepping down from the platform.

"Hmph," her father grumbled. "Madeleine." Georgiana said nothing. Her father continued. "Perhaps you might pay him some attention. He's a good-looking chap, and the business deal might be sweetened – "

"Sweetened how?" she asked coldly.

"A pretty face and some kind words go a long way, Georgiana." He picked up his hat. "You might remember that this lifestyle you enjoy so much is not free, and quite the opposite, it's expensive."

"I'm sure your tailor is just as expensive as my dressmaker," she said tartly.

Jonathan gave her a cold look. "You have such a willful, ungrateful tongue," he said, shaking his head. "You inherited nothing of your mother's sweet disposition. Nothing." He picked up his ebony cane before departing.

Madame Melier joined her immediately with Flanna following behind. "*Ma petite*," the older woman said, shaking her head. "Do not pay him any attention. He does not appreciate you and that is most unfortunate."

Georgiana shook her head. "I'm not going to. The dress is lovely," she said, running her hand down the length of the skirt and relishing the silk texture of it.

"You will look enchanting, *no?*" She looked at Flanna to agree.

"You'll look lovely, Georgeen," Flanna said, smiling at her young charge.

Georgiana was alone in the house except for her servants. Her fingers moved across the pianoforte's keyboard as she practiced the scales before she began a melody. She enjoyed the piano, as she could practice and let her mind wander.

Oftentimes when the servants were moving about the house at their assigned tasks, she would come into the large drawing room and practice for an hour or two. She kept abreast with the scales and her father's favorite works, as she never knew when she would be called upon to perform at one of his parties.

She didn't mind playing because she enjoyed music very much, but her father viewed her talent as yet another tool in his pocket to pull out when it was needed to impress his business associates. Her father liked Heinrich Schutz, while she preferred Arcangelo Corelli's compositions.

She recalled her father's words at the dressmaker and knew that he wanted her to be nice to Alexander Mayson for their business arrangement. She had been rude and curt to him at the teahouse and that was unnecessary. She could be polite and treat him as a business associate of her father's and nothing more.

She stopped playing and looked down at the white and black keys. Her fingers caressed them and moved along their cool surface but didn't cause the hammer to strike the strings.

She stopped playing and walked quietly to her room. She must take a short nap. She wanted to be refreshed for tonight. She had told her father that she was going to the theater again. Though he disapproved of her friends and excursions, he allowed it. But she was not going to the theater. She was going somewhere much more exciting and daring. She could hardly wait!

Georgiana studied the scenery from the coach window and fidgeted nervously with a lace handkerchief in her lap. She was dressed charmingly in a sage gown, with elbow-length sleeves, lace at the edges, and a square neckline. Her hair was pinned up with a dash of powder on it.

She extracted a pot of rouge from her small beaded bag and opened the can in front of Madeline and Nathaniel, who were seated across from her. She placed a dot on her two cheeks and one on her lips.

"Can you rub it in, Maddie?" she asked innocently. "I don't have a mirror."

"Are you sure?" her friend asked her. "You look quite – " She stopped as she struggled for the right word.

Georgiana frowned. "I look quite what?"

"You look very – " Madeleine stopped and focused on Nathaniel for help.

"You look like one of those prostitutes," he said simply.

"Nathaniel!" Madeleine admonished him.

"*C'est vrai.*" He shrugged. "Is this what you want?" he asked her, uncrossing his turquoise silk-encased legs. "You know where we are going. Someone will mistake you for one of them and try to –" He glanced back at Madeleine.

Georgiana licked her lips. "I'm going to a pleasure garden. I might as well look the part."

Madeleine contemplated her innocent friend and then nodded. "You'll you be fine, my darling. We won't let you out of our sight. If Nate isn't with you, then I will be."

"Exactly," Georgiana said, and when they passed under a lantern as the coach moved along, she caught a glimpse of herself in the windowpane.

Who was that woman? Her hair was powdered white with a hint of pink, and her cheeks were red as if she was flushed. But her lips. Her lips were lush and ruby as if she had been kissed and made plump by the attention.

She sat back in her seat and stared at her two friends, her eyes wide with delight. "Have you been to the gardens before?"

Nathaniel grinned and sat back in his seat. "Many times, *ma chere.*"

"Maddie?"

"Yes, darling. I've been as well," Madeleine said dismissively.

"What is it like?" she wondered.

The two friends said nothing for a moment.

"It's an experience," Madeleine told her vaguely. "But you'll see soon. There is music, dancing, food. All the young people of London come to the gardens to enjoy themselves."

The coach swayed as it made a turn and they neared their destination.

"Stay close to me, Georgie, don't wander," she told the young woman.

"I won't," she promised.

***

As Georgiana stepped from the coach, she looked about herself and the structures that surrounded her. Cupid's Gardens was a pleasure garden in Lambeth on the Thames shoreline.

The Gardens had originally been purchased by Thomas Howard, Earl of Arundel, in 1643 and leased to his gardener, Abraham Boydell Cuper. In 1678, Arundel had completely rebuilt his house on the north bank, and Cuper's son was prompted to develop the land in Lambeth as a pleasure garden.

He had leased another seven acres from the Archbishop of Canterbury and decorated the gardens with many of the discarded busts and statues from the demolished Arundel House. The completed gardens were long and narrow and extended south from the river. There was a lake on the western side, and serpentine paths were laid out between the trees and bushes.

Madeline had told her that its arbors, walks, and several remains of the Greek and Roman antiquities made the place quite special and unique. It had become known as Cupid's Gardens not long after. The guests of the garden included royalty, the upper class, and anyone else in London who wished to partake in food, drink, and the romantic atmosphere of the waterside garden.

Though her party had come by coach, many people arrived at the pleasure garden by the river. Georgiana looked out over the water of the river Thames and saw several barges making their way to the garden. Music could be heard nearby, and she grinned at the sound of it.

"It's wonderful!" she said excitedly to her friends. Nathaniel had already met friends of his.

Madeleine pulled her about the shoulders. "Come along, Georgie," she said as they walked into the gardens.

The gardens at night were something to behold. Large torches lit the way as the two women walked along the vast green lawn. The orchestra grew louder, and she could almost identify the music. Was it –

"Madeleine, dear!" A man came towards them dressed in a vibrant pink with a large wig powdered white. He kissed her friend warmly on the cheek. "We haven't seen you for some time," the handsome man said, his eyes moving with interest over Georgiana's form. "Quite the beauty."

"Don't even think about it. She's only to look at, not to touch," Madeleine said tartly.

"Hmmm. What's the point in that?" he said before calling out to someone else and leaving their side.

"What did you mean, Maddie? Only to look at," Georgina asked, confused.

"Well, darling, you did want to come and I tried to persuade you, but the gardens are – well, they are often a place for people to meet," she said vaguely.

"Of course. Like a museum or an art gallery." Georgiana shrugged.

Madeleine smiled kindly. "Yes, dear. Like those places. But the people that come here are sometimes seeking something more."

The orchestra came into view, and the music floated around them. She felt like she was a cloud in the sky. It was Heinrich Schutz!

"Listen to the glorious music out here in the garden!" Georgiana cried exuberantly. "It's like a fairyland."

Madeleine shook her head. "Let's get some champagne."

Madeline had not wanted to tell her young friend the truth. A problem that persisted in plaguing the gardens was the presence of local prostitutes and their clients. It had become such a problem that guards were posted at various areas about the gardens, but a willing client could easily place a coin in the guard's hand to keep him silent.

Madeleine returned with two glasses of champagne, and being quite thirsty, Georgiana drank the liquid in one gulp.

"Darling!" Madeleine said, shaking her head. "Go slow! It's still quite early, not yet nine!"

Georgiana watched as the people walked by in groups. The men were dressed in their satin and silk, and the women looked dazzling in their brightly colored frocks. Their wigs were equally dazzling. Some wigs were high and bold, while others dangled down past their frock coats. It was exciting, and she smiled at those who passed by.

"Everyone looks so lovely," Georgiana said dreamily. "Shall we walk on?"

Madeleine nodded.

The large torches burned brightly against the night sky, and the acres of formal gardens with their long sweeping avenues were enchanting. Madeleine handed her another drink, telling her to sip it slowly as they walked along together.

"It's like another world, Maddie. So unique." Georgiana sipped her drink. "Don't you think?"

"I do, darling." She nodded.

Looming before them was a grand Chinese pagoda at the edge of the long avenue that Madeleine longed to show her. Floating paper lanterns drifted along the small waterway that followed the grand lawn up from the Thames and into the garden.

Georgiana grinned lightly as she took another sip. "We're far away, Maddie. No one can join us. It's just you and I here."

Madeleine made a little snicker. "Yes, and you, my dear, are not having any more champagne."

They passed by four men who were dressed in wool and looked to be of a different class. Their Cockney accent drifted towards them, and Georgiana could hear their words.

"Oi! What a face!" the one man said to his friends as Georgiana passed them.

Georgiana ignored them but was secretly pleased with the attention.

"Pay them no mind," Madeleine instructed her.

They made their way to the Chinese pagoda, which was very large, and several couples remained under the structure, talking and laughing in the night.

"That's the pagoda," Madeleine said, taking her friend by the arm. "It has several stories you can walk up. Let's go see it, shall we?"

Georgiana nodded in agreement. The night sky was so dark, and the champagne had made her feel warm and pliant. She wanted to feel like this always. She looked about the lawns and shrubbery, and everything felt pleasant and kind. She was floating in a daze.

When they came upon the pagoda, it looked foreign and oriental in a strange, fascinating way.

"Madeleine!" someone called out to her.

"I'll stay right here," Madeleine told Georgiana. "You can go inside and take the steps up to the different tiers. I'll join you in a minute," she said and waved to her friend. "Marie Louise!"

Georgiana admired the strangely shaped building and mounted the small steps to the next floor. It was only a small circular room with no one about. The small steps at the side led to the next story. She took the steps again, and the room was a bit smaller this time, but no one was about.

It was only a little over six feet tall, and each room was only ten feet by ten feet and becoming smaller.

As she made her way to the very top floor, her feet making no sound upon the wooden steps, she heard a strange sound. It was a grunting noise that sounded like a man and another sound more a moan and then almost a sigh. She frowned.

When she came upon the next room, she realized she was not alone. There was a man with his back to her, and his breeches and hose were down about his ankles. He was grunting and thrusting vigorously into a woman whose legs were wrapped tightly around his waist. Her back was up against the wall as he continued to thrust into her. Georgiana bit her lip as the woman's breathy sighs filled the air.

"Oh yes," she cried. "Harder. Harder!"

The man suddenly stopped and ordered the woman to "get onto your knees," which she did as she was commanded, and the man squatted behind her and grabbed her by the hips.

Georgiana covered her mouth in shock and disbelief and quietly took a step back until she had left the room completely. She pressed her back against the wall of the circular stairs. Her cheeks were flushed, and she felt strange and disoriented. She had once seen a stallion and mare mate, but seeing a man and woman couple before her was –

She heard the noises again above her and moved swiftly down the stairs. She didn't know how many floors she went down before she suddenly ran headfirst into another person coming up the stairs.

"Mademoiselle, be careful." His hands touched her shoulders lightly to steady her, though she couldn't make out his face.

Georgiana frowned in the darkness and then instantly recognized his voice and shrugged out of his light hold. "You again?"

Chapter 5

ALEXANDER LOVED THE PLEASURE garden for all the reasons most did not. It wasn't that they failed to see its beauty; it was just that most people preferred to use the garden as an excuse for a cheap tumble. He had nothing against the coupling of a man and woman, but the garden really was something spectacular to be seen at night.

He also loved the pagoda, and though he had never been to the Orient, the architecture was something to behold. Whenever he traveled to Cupid's, he always liked to climb the stairs of the pagoda and look out over the gardens on the top floor.

Tonight was no exception. He had left Perry somewhere long ago. He was no doubt caught up in some wench's skirts. He looked up in earnest at the pagoda and walked along the avenue past the shrubbery and trees. He passed by several people chatting happily on the bottom floor and mounted the stairs.

He was coming to the second floor when a woman ran headlong into him. He put his hands on her shoulders to steady her when she almost spat out the words, "You again."

He frowned in the darkness. He had not done anything to her. He had merely said, "Mademoiselle, be careful." Nothing to warrant her disgust.

But then the moonlight shifted and the small, long windows along the stairs revealed her face. Oh, my God! His heart thudded suddenly. Why did she look like that? Why did she have such an innocent sweet face painted up like a harlot? The rouge on her cheeks stood out starkly against her pale skin. It caused him to panic and then delighted him. She looked the same and like a stranger.

But if that wasn't bad enough, she had placed rouge on her lips, causing them to appear redder and lusher, and all he wanted to do was pull her into his arms and taste her. How was she even here of all places and why?

"Georgiana," he said softly.

"Alexander," she said boldly. He had never heard her say his name before, and his heart thudded heavily inside his chest.

"What are you doing here?" he asked her, his eyes taking in the pale green gown and lightly powdered hair.

She notched up her chin an inch to meet his eyes. "What do you think? Taking in the air in the gardens."

"You shouldn't be here alone."

"I'm not alone. Madeleine is downstairs."

"Still, things can get – wild here – "

"So, I gathered."

As she spoke, the heavy sounds of grunting and moans above them filled the air, and they appeared to be at their mutual climax. Georgiana blushed and looked away, but he was watching her face and the delicate breasts rising over her neckline, and he felt a surge of desire.

"Did something happen?" He was concerned.

"No." She tried to move past him.

"Tell me." He would not allow her to move past him, and the space along the stairs allowed only one person to move down in single file.

"I came upon them –" She refused to meet his eyes.

The sounds above them had stopped, and she looked up at the ceiling to the room above. The couple soon joined them and moved past them down the stairs. She noticed the man winked at Alexander and seemed pleased with himself, while the woman looked satisfied. Alexander grabbed Georgiana's hand and pulled her into the room that was only a few steps away.

"You shouldn't be alone in the gardens," he warned her. "You shouldn't even be here."

"I already told you," she said coldly. "Madeleine is downstairs."

He looked over her face and her clothes as if assessing her and took a step towards her. "Why are you here? Why the pleasure gardens? I'm sure your father would never approve. You should stay in safe places like the theater."

"Safe places like the theater?" she echoed his words. "I believe my last theater attendance was not so safe. Thanks to you."

"It was only a kiss," he told her, shrugging.

"That I didn't want!" she argued.

"Come now, Georgie," he said, walking towards her as she took a step back. "Don't be coy."

She bristled at the use of her nickname that only her closest friends used. "Don't call me Georgie."

"Isn't that your name?"

"It's a nickname that I don't give you permission to use."

"A kiss is such a small thing," he said softly. "I could take so much more. Is that what you want? Is that why you're here? You want a lover?" He had her backed up against the wall, and without a word, he drew a thumb over her lips. "You don't need any rouge. It only makes men want to taste you."

"And what if they do?" She boldly met his eyes.

"You think you can take a lover so easily? You don't even know how to kiss," he taunted her.

"I do!" She felt the champagne in her blood. It made her daring and reckless.

"Show me," he said simply.

"Why should I?" She shrugged. "I've already kissed you."

"No. I kissed you."

"Is there a difference?"

He grinned in the dark. Why was he playing this game? Why was he taunting her? He could feel his heart beating in his chest and his blood roaring in his ears. Why? He knew in a moment. He wanted to feel her in his arms. He wanted her sighing in his ear. He wanted her.

"There's a difference," he assured her.

She was contemplating it. He could tell by the way she gnawed on her lower lip and her gorgeous emerald eyes darted to his and then away.

"I – " she began, and he waited to hear what she would say.

Why had her friends even brought her here? The men became boisterous and loud the drunker they were. He had been the one to come across her but she might have met someone more intent on doing her real harm. He would never take more than a kiss from her. It would be indecent to harm such a lovely little thing.

"Very well," she said simply.

"I'm waiting," he said just as easily, though his heart pounded.

She moved away from him to stand in the middle of the room. He watched her as she seemed to be getting up her nerve. She turned back to him, and her eyes had completely changed. She looked confident, self-assured, and so alluring. She took a step towards him. Her eyes looked almost black in the dark room but he knew the green fire in them. Then almost timidly she moved to reach him and kissed him lightly on the lips without touching him at all.

"Devastating."

Georgiana frowned. "Devastating good? Or devastating bad?"

"Well." Alexander pondered his words. "That depends on whether you are my lover or my grandmother. As my Gran, it was perfect." He bit back a grin as her face screwed up with irritation. "Don't worry, sweetheart. It happens."

"Just stand there," she said, demanding his obedience.

"Yes, ma'am." A surge of desire flooded his entire body at her words.

Georgiana looked him over and felt again the warmth and honey she had experienced in that dark hall. She had tried to forget him and how he made her feel, but that had been difficult. Now in the pleasure garden pagoda, with the champagne dripping through her veins, she felt free and in control. What did a kiss matter? He was right. It was just a kiss. And she was going to make damn certain that she wiped that smug, arrogant look off his face for good.

She took a step towards him and looked into his eyes. They were a deep cobalt blue in the dark, and she watched them carefully. His chiseled face and sensuous lips were easy to want to kiss.

As she put a hand on his chest, she heard a soft intake of his breath and tried to hide her excitement. How she would make him rue the night he had kissed her in the dark hall. Her hand moved under his jacket to the shirt he wore without a waistcoat. She could feel the solid planes of muscled flesh underneath, and she pressed into him. He was watching her so intently, and she knew she was shaking some of his resolve. Good!

She pressed lightly into him. Her other hand moved to his hair he kept tightly tied and to the nape of his neck. He seemed so serious now. She had done it. She had wiped that arrogant smirk off his face. She could stop now. She didn't need to kiss him, but she wanted to. She liked being in control.

She leaned in and touched her lips lightly to his deepening the kiss once, then twice. She didn't realize she had moaned and sighed until his arms came around to crush her against him.

"Georgiana –" he groaned and literally picked her up off her feet and pinned her aggressively against the wall deepening the kiss with his tongue as his hand threaded into her white powdered hair.

Lost. He was absolutely lost. It didn't matter that this woman was completely off-limits. He could never have her. The price to pay was not one he would ever render. But her sweet kiss and the taste of her mouth and her breasts pressed against him was too much.

It had started as a game. Taunting her to kiss him knowing that she had no experience and that she would kiss him as she had done. But something had changed in her, and now he was drowning. Drowning in a silly game of his own making. Drowning in the kiss of this little virgin who had never been kissed before that night in the theater. A man could easily drown in the green sea of the eyes of this Circe.

That's what she was. Circe, the Greek sorceress who lured men to her island. Men who were driven mad by their desire to touch her. That's what was happening here. He was being driven mad by his desire to touch her.

"Georgiana!" came the voice of Madeleine from far below. "Georgiana, are you there?"

They both pulled apart and looked at each other without saying a word. And then –

"Fuck," he whispered.

He was shaking, trying to catch his breath. Neither of them said anything as they stood in the pagoda room. There were sounds far below in the gardens, laughter and people calling to each other, but it all seemed so far removed. Madeleine called her name again, and Georgiana took a step back.

"Don't go," he said almost longingly.

Georgiana turned to him, and what he saw on her face shocked him. She was smiling, and her face was filled with glee.

"Don't worry, sweetheart. It happens," she said before moving swiftly down the stairs to meet her friend.

He sighed and almost sagged against the wall. Jesus! He had a raging hard-on. He grinned, remembering her smile and words. So, the green-eyed Circe wanted to play. Well, she was most fortunate. Because he was very, very good at this game.

"I'm sorry, darling," Madeleine said, tucking Georgiana's arm into hers. "I saw two old acquaintances, and we were chatting about our time in Italy two summers ago. How was the pagoda? Did you enjoy it?"

Georgiana was about to respond when Alexander emerged from the shadows of the structure, watching her quietly. Madeleine had her back to him and did not see him.

"The pagoda? It was very nice." She nodded coolly, and then meeting Alexander's eyes in the dark, she told her friend, "But nothing of significance."

Alexander bit back a smile as the two women walked in the direction of the Thames. If he moved along the outer edge of the garden along the waterway, he knew he could beat them there and meet them as if he had just arrived. The little green-eyed witch wouldn't give him away.

As he was putting his plan in motion, he thought of the event that had just occurred. He had been so certain she disliked him, but she had been like a different woman this evening. Warm and compliant and so delectable. It had been so difficult not to give in to his desires. But he would not. Georgiana Gainsford could be played with but never to the full extent. He would never marry. He had no need to at the moment.

"Madame Mortier!" he called out to her as they came upon the river. Georgiana narrowed her emerald eyes in scorn.

"Monsieur Mayson!" Madeleine smiled at seeing him. "You've just arrived?"

"I have," he said, meeting Georgiana's eyes as he spoke the bold lie, daring her to contradict him.

"Have you really?" Georgiana eyed him coolly. "You should see the pagoda. We've just been there."

"Ah, the pagoda," he said as he fell in step with them both. "I have such lovely memories of the pagoda."

She refused to rise to the bait.

Madeleine's name was called by a man nearby. She waved happily and then turned to Alexander. "Mr. Mayson, will you be so kind as to accompany Georgiana for a few moments? I see some friends of mine I'd like to say hello to."

As Alexander nodded, Georgiana grumbled about "not being a child."

She watched as her friend became animated with a handsome older man and she scoffed at Alexander. "Rather leaving the wolf in charge of the sheep," she said sarcastically, looking him over.

"Am I the wolf?" he asked innocently.

"If the coat fits."

"And you're the sheep?" he said in disbelief when she said nothing. "I wonder how many innocent young sheep try to seduce a wolf?"

She turned to him, her heart beating faster. "I was *not* seducing you."

"No, little temptress," he said, running a finger under her chin to tip it up to meet his eyes. "You don't even need to try."

She jerked her head away from him.

"Shall we continue where we left off?" he asked lowly as they walked along the river. "It seems you like playing with fire."

Georgiana sniffed lightly. "You aren't fire, you're just a man."

He assessed her abrupt attitude and nodded. "Ah, I see. It never happened? You drank too much champagne? You didn't know what you were doing?" He ticked off several items that he thought might be the reason behind her complete switch of character from only a few minutes before.

"Hmph," Georgiana said. "None of that is correct."

They moved along the river bank and passed by several couples dressed in silk and satins who nodded at them in turn. They stopped where the river lapped softly along the bank, and the smell of the River Thames was heavy in the air.

"Well then?" he wondered.

"You stole a kiss from me, and I stole one back." She looked up into his face even as he gazed at her and then away. "That's all."

"Is that how you think it works?" he wondered. "Kissing is only the beginning."

"I've no wish for anything more from you," she said tartly.

He studied her lovely face in the dark when suddenly a woman's voice called out to him.

"Alexander!"

Alexander turned. Coming towards him was his good friend Perry and on his arm was Philippine de Froissy. He groaned. Her red hair, which she dyed regularly, burned especially bright in the dark night, and her face was pink from the night air. She looked fetching in a dark blue gown, and her wig was grand and magnificent, dusted with light blue powder.

"Dearest." She came towards him and kissed him on the cheek, but her mouth lingered near his.

Perry nodded to Alexander and eyed Georgiana with interest.

"And who do we have here?" Philippine asked as she directed her gaze at Georgiana, who returned her stare.

Alexander introduced them, saying nothing about his relationship to Philippine de Froissy, who nodded in Georgiana's direction.

"A pleasure mademoiselle," she said prettily. "I was taking in the sights and stumbled upon Perry, who is too uncouth and ill-mannered. Yes, you are, Perry," she directed at him. "He said you were here somewhere. You should have told me. We could have come together." She giggled. "As we so often do."

Georgiana looked over at the woman who laughed lightly and Perry, who seemed to find amusement in the words.

"If you're going to leave my bed so early," Philippine whispered to Alexander but loud enough for Georgiana to hear, "at least kiss me goodbye."

"If you'll excuse me," Georgiana told the threesome and turned back to return to the lawns of the garden where she had last seen Madeline.

Damn her! Madeleine had sworn so faithfully that she would stay beside her and now she had left her—twice! Madeleine was a harmless flirt but really. Everyone here seemed intent on consuming the most drink and being more than flirtatious. It was unreal.

A shattering of fireworks exploded into the air above her, and as the colors lit up the sky, someone stumbled into her. The man made an attempt at a bow, but he fell over into the dirt at the amusement of his friends who laughed loudly at his expense. The crowd was crushing, and more than once, someone came into her path, avoiding her, but once or twice, a hand grazed her body, and she felt certain it was not all accidental.

"Hello there." An older man smelling of alcohol came upon her and grabbed her about the waist. "You must be new here! You are a pretty little thing."

"I beg your pardon." Georgiana pulled at his arm as he winked at her.

"Ah! I understand!" He snickered. "You like a rough tumble."

He had pulled her along the dark edge of the lawn just as Georgiana elbowed him in the gut. He yelped.

"My God, she's a she-wolf! Attacked me for wanting a good time," he said as Georgiana picked up her skirts to move away from the tiresome fellow.

She had made a slight turn back to the main portion of the gardens when a man completely cloaked in the darkness of the trees and the night came towards her. She felt a moment's panic. Lord, she was surrounded! As he came closer, she sagged in relief.

"I never thought I'd be happy to see you," she told Alexander as he caught her roughly by the waist and pulled her along the dirt walkway. "What are you doing?" she said hotly, trying to evade his tight grasp. "Let go of me."

"I want to take you over my knee and give you a beating but I won't. What I will do is bring you back to the lanterns and the light. You need a guardian angel or a jailer." He shook his head.

"Angel? You? Don't make me laugh." She pressed her hand against him. "What sort of angel drinks like a dockhand and fornicates with every woman in London," she flung at him.

"Not every woman," he said, looking her over.

"And besides, this isn't my fault," she fumed. "Madeleine promised so faithfully that she would stay beside me. And Nate! I haven't seen him in hours!"

"You didn't need to run off after meeting Philippine," he reasoned.

"Ha! I don't need to stay and make small talk with your mistress." She glared at him. "It's unthinkable that you should even introduce us."

He didn't bother to deny the title she had given his mistress, as it was the truth. But it bothered him that she should think so little of a woman who had not done anything wrong.

"She was once married. He ignored her and was often cruel. She finds comfort now in the arms of others. What is so wrong in that?" he asked her.

Georgiana frowned. "Why do you speak to me like this? I don't think ill of her. I don't know her. Your behavior bothers me."

"Why is that?"

"You have the morals of an alley cat. I find that so distasteful. You should be more circumspect," she pointed out.

"Next you're going to tell me to marry?"

"Marry?" She laughed sharply. "Why on earth would I want you to marry? So, you can torture some poor woman for the next thirty years? I think not."

"Come now, Georgiana," he cooed, pulling her into the warm light of the lanterns. "You can't hate me forever. I'm actually quite nice. And you know me to be a good kisser."

"I don't hate you, Mr. Mayson." Georgiana looked over at him and then back up into the sky at the fireworks. "Frankly, I don't think anything of you."

"So brutal."

"I don't mean to be. Truly." She nodded, walking along the same green lawns that she passed when they had first arrived.

He played the seducer. "I wonder how it can be that you think nothing of me, when I'm consumed by thoughts of you."

Georgiana rolled her eyes. "I wonder how many women you've said that to."

Alexander shook his head. "Only you."

"Only me tonight," she added.

"For such an innocent little thing, you've a wicked sharp tongue."

"Perhaps you deserve it."

"Perhaps I do."

"Darling Georgie!" A very drunk Nathaniel stumbled into them and tried to right himself. "I'm in my cups, *cherie*." He looked over at Alexander and then said, "Be careful, Georgie, the man is an absolute scoundrel!" He narrowed his eyes at him and then moved along.

"Even a drunk recognizes you," she said, arching an eyebrow at him.

Alexander nodded. "How about this? I shall behave myself and act as your squire. We can drink more, eat, and be merry, and if we can't find the flirtatious Madeleine, I will see you home."

Georgiana looked him over. She knew better than to wander the gardens now that it was dark. It seemed that everyone here had another reason for visiting the gardens. Madeleine had no doubt deserted her for her gentleman friend, and Nathaniel was too drunk to know his own name.

"Very well. And in return I will be sociable and pretend not to know you for the rogue you are," she said with a curt nod.

"I'm wounded, madame." He took her by the arm. "Come. Let's find some vittles."

They walked back through the crowds, which was a crush of couples, people in groups who were laughing, talking, and enjoying themselves. They passed a man playing a violin, and the larger orchestra could be heard somewhere far away.

"Roasted chestnuts!" She saw the vendor's handmade sign, and they walked up to them.

Alexander handed the man a coin in exchange for two handfuls of chestnuts wrapped in newspaper. They were warm and flavorful, and Georgiana relished the meat-like contents of them.

"Heavenly." She munched on another.

"How about some ale?" he asked and returned shortly with two mugs.

Georgiana glanced up. The fireworks were no longer painting the night sky, and instead the inky black sky twinkled with stars. It was such a beautiful night, and Alexander was behaving himself as he said he would. They walked together in the farthest portion of the garden where several steps descended into a sunken garden with a large pool in the center.

"One moment," Alexander said. "Stay right here."

He was gone for a minute, and he returned holding two tin plates of savory meat in gravy. Her stomach rumbled at the sight and smell of it.

"Come." He led her down the stone steps and along the sunken pool, which spanned a large area.

They sat down together on the grass as Alexander watched her consume the meat. When she finished, she licked her fingers, and he felt such a strange pull and tug that he picked up his mug and almost finished the entire contents.

"That was delicious, thank you," she acknowledged. She stretched out her feet and stretched out on the grass. She admired the inky night sky, feeling drowsy and relaxed. "Where are we?"

He looked down at her. "In the pleasure garden," he confirmed.

"No!" She tugged on his arm and pulled him a little.

He realized she wanted him beside her so he moved to lay down next to her. Their arms touched as they both watched the night sky beside the large fountain.

"Now, where are we?" she asked again.

"London."

She shook her head. "Nope."

He smiled. She was a drunk little child. "Paris."

"*Non.*"

He paused. "Constantinople," he said slowly, drawing out the five syllables.

She was silent for a second and then squealed, "Yes!" in an excited voice. "Constantinople. Have you been?"

He nodded. "I've been to many places on earth."

He studied the profile of her nose and lips and realized how very much he wanted to pull her underneath him and kiss her senseless.

"Ah, yes, the privateer." She nodded, stretching her arms above her head.

"At your service." He placed a hand over his heart.

"And your favorite place?" She turned her head to stare at him.

He thought about the question. "Italy is very beautiful. Turkey and India are as well."

"You have been everywhere." She twirled a long curl of hair about her finger.

"I've been to many places." He admitted.

"You don't travel anymore?"

"Occasionally I'll travel to the colonies for work, but that's half a year gone from London. Two months there, two months back, and a few months to conduct business," he acknowledged.

"The colonies." She sighed.

"It's not so very savage as some would believe – "

"Yes, my aunt and uncle live in Massachusetts."

"The New World," he said, his eyes filled with life.

"I like the Old World." She said, meeting his eyes. "I like London and its people and its filthy streets and its beautiful parks."

"The good with the bad."

"Exactly." She met his eyes in the dark.

"How do you feel?" he asked her.

She grinned. "I feel very unrestrained. I feel free and pliant."

"There's another word for that."

"Oh, yes?"

"Drunk."

Georgiana frowned. "I like you much better like this."

"Like how?"

"I don't know. I can't exactly say. Just that here with you now – I like it. It's peaceful," she said honestly.

Alexander admired her delicate profile. If she only knew how he desired nothing more in this moment than to pull her underneath him and press her legs apart. He groaned inwardly and flung himself on his back.

But she was right. The little green-eyed temptress was right. Underneath the stars, with her lying next to him, it was peaceful. It was peaceful and perfect.

Chapter 6

GEORGIANA FELT SOMEONE TOUCHING her shoulder and calling her name. Why didn't Flanna leave her be? She was tired and wanted to sleep. But they called her name again, and when she opened her eyes, Alexander was staring down at her.

"Where am I?" she said, startled to see his face above hers.

"We're by the fountain. I think you've slept long enough, Sleeping Beauty," he remarked dryly. "It's time to get you home."

"What time is it?" She sat up.

"It must be at least one in the morning, I reckon," he remarked and watched as she touched her hair to make sure it was in place. "Maybe later."

"Do I look all right?" she asked him.

Alexander surveyed the woman before him. Her cheeks had a slight pinkness to them that was most becoming, and her hair softly framed her face and fell down her back.

"Here, let me," he said, pulling her hair back and securing it with a comb.

"You did that remarkable well," she said coolly.

"I've had practice."

"No doubt."

"Remember, you're supposed to be sociable and I'm to behave," he reminded her.

She nodded. "You're right. And you have behaved very well."

He had tried to behave, as she called it, but it had been difficult. She was such a luscious combination of innocence and sensual awakening. He wanted to be the man to truly awaken her, but that was not possible. As a young unmarried woman, Georgiana Gainsford could not be trifled with.

He already knew her father wanted her married, and the thought of her marrying another man frustrated him. He pushed the thought from his mind as they both stood up and began to walk back towards the coach in front of the pleasure garden.

"This has been such an interesting evening," she marveled as they walked together.

"I'm glad you've enjoyed it," he said.

"Especially you," she remarked. "You were very surprising."

"Was I?"

"Yes. I enjoyed our time tonight."

"As did I."

Alexander spotted his driver chatting with another man and gave him a curt nod. Once they were inside the coach and seated side by side, Georgiana's eyes slowly closed. She rested her head against his shoulder and her arm draped down almost into his lap.

Seated beside her in the dark, he was conscious of a delicate scent of lavender and rosemary that clung to her and the intimacy of her head on his shoulder. Her breathing was soft in his ear, and he could still feel that kiss in the pagoda. He realized he was dangerously attracted to her. As a man with no desire to marry, he must distance himself. A woman so lovely and innocent was dangerous. He could not have her.

"Georgiana." He touched her shoulder.

"Hmmm," she said softly.

"We're almost to your house, love." The affectionate term slipped from his tongue.

"Are we?" she asked sleepily.

He absently brushed the hair back from her face. "Almost there."

"It's been so nice this everything," she murmured. "Makes me forget."

"What do you need to forget?" he asked lowly.

She said nothing as the coach slowed to a still. She blinked and looked adorable in the darkness.

"We're here. At your home. Will you be all right? Should I ring the doorbell?" he asked solicitously.

"No!" she said sharply. "No, I'll go downstairs and enter through the servants' staircase."

Alexander frowned. "Servants' entrance? Why would you do that?"

"Because my father – he doesn't like – " she began to explain to him how it was but stopped abruptly as she felt his warm gaze on her. She could explain it all to him and how it was between them, but instead she said nothing else. "It doesn't matter. Thank you, Mr. Mayson. For seeing me home."

Alexander felt the shift in her manner, and he could tell there was something serious that she was not going to share with him, nor would he press. "It has been a pleasure, Ms. Gainsford. The evening would not have been the same without you," he said sincerely.

Watching her go down the steps to the servants' entrance, he felt a strange sensation. He had enjoyed the evening more than he cared to admit, and it was entirely due to the time spent with Georgiana. He felt a sense of loss, and when she disappeared out of sight, it was as if he had lost something precious. He rapped twice on the coach roof, and the driver took up the reins once more.

When Georgiana entered the house, it was dark and still. She felt as if she could hear her own breathing. Downstairs the grandfather clock struck the hour, and it was two in the morning. It was very late, but she had often come home at this time when attending the theater.

She removed her heeled shoes and kept them in her hands as she took the stairs off the kitchen to the second floor. Once in her room, she pulled off her dress and other garments and was soon in her chemise. She looked down into the street but it was empty. There was no carriage and no Alexander Mayson.

She pressed her cheek against the cool pane of glass and closed her eyes. The night, which had only been a few hours ago, seemed like a lifetime had passed. So much had happened and yet nothing had happened. She had spent time with Alexander, and he had been surprisingly solicitous and agreeable. But that kiss inside the pagoda. She cringed, remembering the couple upstairs, their moans and sounds of passion ringing in her ears.

But only a few minutes later, she had wanted to do the same and in Alexander's arms no less. She had wanted to feel his mouth on her body and be wrapped in his arms, and that annoyed her. The man who collected women like shillings. She had seen with her own eyes twice as the man tried to seduce her friend Madeleine and then his French mistress Philippine hanging on him like a cheap frock coat.

She was stupid to even desire the man. She may be innocent in the ways of men, but she had heard Nate and

Madeleine talk, and she knew that some men liked nothing more than to add to their collection. Well, she would not be another snuffbox added to Alexander's collection. It didn't matter what she felt. The man was a cad and a scoundrel.

If her father chose to do business with him, that was all well and good. But anything else between the two of them would be nothing more than Georgiana being cordial to her father's associate. She pulled back the bedsheets and moved between them.

It just irritated her beyond belief that he should be so handsome!

Alexander didn't sleep for an hour after he arrived home. He stripped off his clothes and lay in bed, watching the shadows on the ceiling. There were no sounds at this hour, and the cook and maid he kept had long gone to bed. He wanted to rest, but his mind wouldn't stop working.

He kept seeing flashes in his mind of Georgiana that night. Lying by the fountain in the grass and looking up at the stars, her profile delicate and perfect. Georgiana walking along the Thames and then eyeing him with equal parts of distaste and mistrust.

But most of all, he remembered her in his arms, soft and warm, with the scent of lavender filling his senses. He wanted so badly to press up her skirts, pull her legs apart, and fill her to the hilt. She was such a lovely woman, and her eyes filled with equal parts fire and animosity, always assessing him.

He wanted to rock into her again and again until he emptied himself inside her. He breathed out heavily. He hadn't wanted a woman this much before, and it surprised him. He would visit Philippine again tomorrow. He must stop thinking about the little virgin. She would bring him nothing but trouble, which he tried to avoid at all costs when not at sea.

As he drifted off, he could hear Georgiana's sigh and moan as he kissed her in the dark room in the Chinese pagoda.

"Truly I'm not angry," Georgiana told her friend as they walked together through Hyde Park the next morning. Georgiana was dressed in a seafoam-blue gown, while Madeleine wore a dark brown frock. "I'm disappointed if truth be told. Nate abandoned us the moment we set foot there and – "

"Honestly, Georgie," Madeleine began. "I didn't want to take you there. At night, after dark, and with too much drink, people use the garden as a sort of – "

Georgiana turned to her. "As a sort of outdoor brothel?" she finished.

"Why? What did you see?" Madeleine asked her with wide eyes.

Georgiana shook her head. "Not much and it was dark, but in the pagoda – I heard a man and woman – "

"Yes, yes. Exactly that," her friend finished for her, not wanting her to continue. "And I know how fond you are of Nathaniel, but, my darling, I'm afraid he's very uninhibited where that is concerned."

"Uninhibited?" Georgiana frowned. "What does that mean? In what way?"

"Nothing." Madeleine waved a hand at her. "He likes company is all."

"No more than any man, so you tell me," she answered.

"Yes. And so, my darling, I'm so sorry I left you. Were you terribly angry? Did you leave right away?"

Georgiana thought about the words. Didn't she remember asking Alexander to stay with her?

"No, not right away. I saw the fireworks."

"Oh, good!" She nodded. "That's excellent."

"And speaking of using the garden as a brothel, where did you go off to?" Georgiana asked her coldly, raising an eyebrow.

Madeleine walked a bit ahead of her. "That Italian gentleman, he's so charming –" she began.

"You didn't!" Georgiana said, scandalized by her friend's actions.

"Well, that garden is tempting and too much drink – and he's such a good lover," Madeleine prattled on, while Georgiana rolled her eyes.

"You should be more prudent, Maddie. What if you catch something?" Georgiana asked, concerned for her friend.

"Oh, my dearest! I'm very selective in my lovers," she assured her friend, pulling her along. "And that's why I never sleep with a Frenchman."

"Why no to a Frenchman?" Georgiana asked.

"Oh, because!" Madeline lowered her voice as a couple passed them. "Frenchmen are the worst! They'll bed anything. And I've heard the most disturbing things about Scottish men. But I mean, imagine bedding with them. You might as well bed a sheep!" she whispered and they both laughed at her suggestion. "They're savages!"

As they made their way into the park, a couple was walking towards them. Georgiana's breath caught in her throat. Coming towards them was Alexander Mayson dressed in deep grey and Philippine in bright pink. Her eyes darted to her friend, but she remembered that Madeleine liked Alexander and thought well of him.

"Madame Mortier." Alexander was the first to greet them. "Mademoiselle Gainsford."

Georgiana said nothing but didn't need to as Madeleine smiled at the handsome man.

"Monsieur Mayson! What a lovely surprise!" she greeted him.

He introduced Madeleine to Philippine, who smiled brightly on her lover's arm. Georgiana eyed Philippine with interest. The cut of her pink dress was daring and made of expensive silk. She wondered irritably how many dresses Alexander had purchased for her, and the jealous thought surprised her.

"Mademoiselle," Philippine spoke to her, and she realized she had been staring at the woman. "It is good to see you again. Did you enjoy the pleasure garden last night?"

Georgiana didn't meet her eyes and instead looked at the dress she wore, admiring it. "It was interesting."

"I have all my dresses made in Paris," she said, seeming to guess Georgiana's thoughts.

"Does that not take time to have them shipped over?" Georgiana wondered.

"I like to have the best." She nodded and then said lower, "So does Alexander. He is so picky on what I wear and what he then has to take off me." She made a simpering smile and moved to stand beside Alexander.

Georgiana thought instantly of the red-haired woman and Alexander entwined together in a lover's embrace, like that couple in the pagoda, and she felt uncomfortable. She could feel Alexander's eyes on her, but she refused to meet them. She instead listened to Madeleine speak about the king as a cool wind picked up.

Philippine gave a nod to them and moved down the path as the three remained.

"I believe I will see you both at the ball at Clyvedon Hall," he mentioned the upcoming event, his eyes remaining on Georgiana's.

She inwardly groaned. Who had invited him? That's right. Her father had. Another evening spent trying to avoid the handsome man collecting his snuffboxes of women. Could he just beg off?

"You mustn't feel obligated, Mr. Mayson, in attending the ball," she said coolly. "We don't want to bore you."

"Bore me?" He smiled lightly. "Nothing could be further from the truth, Ms. Gainsford."

"Well, I suppose you must put in an hour or so to make certain my father sees you," Georgiana reminded him.

"Indeed." He nodded as Madeleine trailed off in the opposite direction of Philippine.

"Honestly," she said when they were alone. "Don't feel you need to attend the ball."

"Why?" he asked. "Don't you want me there?"

"I don't see why you would want to be there," she countered.

"I could think of several reasons."

"One of them being . . . ?" she asked.

"Seeing you, of course."

"Of course," Georgiana said, tired of the conversation. "It was very nice seeing you again, Mr. Mayson."

He took a step towards her. "You speak as if – " He seemed to be trying to find the words.

"Yes?" She frowned.

"As if we didn't just spend the entire night together."

Georgiana looked behind her and then to the side to see the two women far enough away. "Don't say it like that! You make it sound as if I was – that we were . . . You make it sound as if we were lovers." She whispered the last word. "We aren't. Your lover is right there." She jerked her chin in Philippine's direction.

"Certainly, Philippine and I have an understanding. And it suits us both for the time being. But things change," he said simply.

"No doubt with you they do."

He took another step towards her. "Answer me this one question, and then I shall take my leave."

"Very well."

"How long after you undressed last night and climbed into your bed did you think of that kiss in the pagoda?"

She narrowed her eyes and lied to his face. "I went to bed right away. I didn't think of you at all."

"Liar."

"If you are having trouble sleeping because you're thinking about me," she said haughtily, "I regret to inform you that I do not suffer from any such maladies."

"You are fortunate." He nodded. "I was haunted in my dreams by a witch with eyes like emeralds and lips begging to be kissed."

Georgiana caught her breath in her throat and felt her heart skip a beat.

"Nothing to say? No sharp retort from that wicked tongue?" He grinned again.

Suddenly Georgiana felt emboldened, and his words and his smirk made her want to lash out. "No sharp retort, but just remember, Alexander, you stole a kiss from me in a dark hallway in a theater." She licked her bottom lip. "And in a pleasure garden in a pagoda, I stole one back."

In the middle of the park with people nearby, she knew he could do nothing. And she relished that thought.

"So, by all means, keep torturing yourself. Think about my wicked tongue and my kissable lips that you can't have now or ever again." She smiled, turned from him, and then glanced over her shoulder.

Alexander lay upon the bed, panting in exhaustion. After being taunted and teased by the little green-eyed witch, he had brought Philippine home and pounded into her. He had ripped her favorite gown in an effort to suckle her breasts and torn one of her garters off.

He had pushed her onto the bed, spread her legs wide, and poured his seed into her. When it was over, he was satiated, but something was missing.

"*Mon cher*. We must talk." Philippine rose from the bed and pulled on her dressing gown. "I don't think we should continue seeing each other," she said simply as she pulled up her long hair and pinned it back.

"What has happened?" He frowned, sitting up.

"You tell me."

"I'm at a loss."

"*Mon cher*. We started this as something enjoyable for us both. And it has been. You're a wonderful lover. But while I never minded that some men are attracted to other women, which is common, I don't want to be taken while you're actually thinking and wanting someone else," she said bluntly.

"Philippine – " he began, shaking his head.

"Do you want to know what I saw at Hyde Park today?"

"What did you see?"

"I saw a young woman, lovely and poised, doing her best to ignore you," she said softly. "And except for the time when it was absolutely necessary for you to make eye contact with myself or Madame Mortier, you were staring at the beautiful mademoiselle as well."

"I didn't realize."

"I know, my dear. And I wouldn't mind that. All men look at pretty things. But these last few times together, you are not here. You are with her," she said softly.

"Philippine, you're wrong." He pulled her down to sit beside him as a sense of panic flared inside him. "It isn't like that. She's lovely. She's attractive. As you said, men like pretty things."

"What color are her eyes?" she asked suddenly.

"What?" he asked, frowning at the question.

"Her eyes. Mademoiselle Gainsford's eyes. What color are they?" she asked lightly.

"They're green." He thought of her eyes. "Emerald green. With a fire inside them when she's angry or irritated or maybe that's just how she is with me – " He stopped.

She nodded. "You see?"

"Because I know the color of her eyes?" He scoffed.

"Most men would not have even got the color right. Let alone compare them to a jewel," she said, rising.

"I'm not in love with her," he said, looking at Philippine as she stood beside the bed.

"No." She shook her head. "Not yet."

Stupid, Georgiana thought when she returned home. What a stupid thing to do! Why taunt the man? Why bother him in such a manner, provoke him? She didn't want his attentions, and he certainly didn't need hers. He had a lovely mistress on his arm, and there was no need for her.

She had just stepped into the hallway when she heard voices and recognized one of them as Mariah Gower's. She didn't dare eavesdrop. Her father hated low-class habits such as that. But as she moved past her father's door, she couldn't help but hear a giggle.

"Jonathan!" She heard Mariah half moan the name.

"Mariah! My own true love!" he said in a voice Georgiana had never heard.

"We must be married, Jonathan," she said breathlessly. "We must marry before I can –"

"Yes, yes," he said in agreement. "Very soon."

She was stepping onto the staircase when the couple emerged from the parlor. Mariah was buttoning her bodice up, and her father looked uncomfortable.

"Georgiana," her father said curtly. "Come greet Madame Gower."

Georgiana stepped back into the foyer and greeted the woman as her father dictated.

"Georgiana, you look tired. Are you all right?" she asked kindly.

Her father looked her over quickly but said nothing.

"I had a restless night," she explained. "That's all."

"Ah." Mariah nodded. "Well. Make certain you get that rest. Beauty is only here for a short time."

Georgiana said nothing, knowing the dig about fleeting beauty was directed at her.

"I'll see you both Friday at the ball." Mariah smiled brightly at Jonathan and gave Georgiana a cool look before departing.

Georgiana fumed as she entered her room. That tart had been buttoning up her blouse when she emerged from the parlor. Then she dared to tell her beauty was here for a short time. Ha! As if she didn't know everyone aged.

She didn't want to go to the ball on Friday. It was a ball that her father hosted every year at Clyvedon Hall in London and a most talked about event of the season. For the past six years, Georgiana had acted as mistress of the event, greeting guests beside her father. But this year, she felt more than ever that the widow Gower was scheming to make herself the new Mrs. Gainsford and usurp Georgiana in all things.

Why should she mind? Much like her father, Mariah was a selfish woman who only had thoughts of herself. She wanted to have the manor home, the husband, and all the money and trappings that came with it. The sooner Georgiana was married and off their hands, the better.

Well, she was never going to marry. She would make certain that she used up as much time as she could before she was shipped off the colonies, but she would never marry to please her father. Never!

Chapter 7

FLANNA EYED HER MISTRESS lovingly. The gown fit her perfectly, and the dainty lace covered her breasts so that both her father and fashion could be served. She stepped out of the gown, and Flanna hung it in the armoire for the evening.

"You look lovely, dearie," Flanna said, nodding to her young charge.

"I'm not looking forward to tonight," she told Flanna.

"Why ever not? Your father has this ball every year. It's the talk of the season, and Clyvedon Hall is such a grand place." She grinned. "And you, its princess."

"I don't think he needs me this year," she added. "Not that he ever did. He has someone else on his arm."

Flanna took her hands in hers. "You mustn't pay any mind to your father or Madame Gower. Obey him by all means, as the good book says, but be yourself. You have so much life ahead of you."

Georgiana nodded distractedly.

"Now rest and take a nap, as it's still early yet. I'll bring you some bread, cheese, and tea when you wake, and then we will journey to the Hall. How does that sound?" She pulled the coverlet over her.

"Thank you, Flanna," Georgiana said, her eyes on her dear caregiver before she slid deeper into the cool bedsheets and drifted off to sleep.

Clyvedon Hall was owned by a former director of the East India Company who was a great friend of Jonathan's. For the past ten years, Jonathan had held a grand ball at the Hall, and it was a social event that most desperately wanted to attend. He enjoyed the use of the Hall, as the mansion was impressively situated near St. James's Palace and The Mall.

The house was built of red Dutch bricks that had been specially imported from Denmark; it had been built for the director's wife who had died shortly after its completion. The house was filled with marble floors, and the curved staircase that dominated the entrance was formidable. Though it was grand, Georgiana always felt the house was cold, lacking in any sort of warmth.

As she stepped into the foyer with her father and Mariah, the older woman gasped.

"My dear, what an extraordinary place!" Mariah said as they moved into the large sitting room off the main foyer.

The room always reminded Georgiana of a museum. The floors were tiled with black and white squares, and gold hung over the doors, the tapestries, the tables, and the chairs. It was a room that spoke of extreme wealth and privilege but seemed cool and aloof.

"Should I speak to old Clyvedon?" Jonathan said as he gazed at the middle-aged widow. "See if he would sell it to me?"

Georgiana shook her head. Her father was wealthy, but could he afford such a place as the Hall? She had not thought he could afford such an extravagance.

"Jonathan! Surely not! The expense of such a house!" Mariah dimpled and put her eyes down.

"But if it would please you," he whispered.

Georgiana felt slightly queasy as she listened to the fortune hunter playing her part to an older man who seemed oblivious to her designs on his purse. She moved away from the couple and down the hall. Closer to the kitchen, several servants were moving about. It was only five in the afternoon, and most guests would not begin arriving for some time.

She walked into the large dining room that her father preferred to be used as a buffet room. Several long tables were already set up, with cream-colored linen draped over them. The chandeliers were being lit, and the gold that decorated the ceilings and doorways glittered.

In the room opposite the dining room was the expansive ballroom. The parquet floors were polished with a high sheen to them, and a small dais was placed at the edge of the room for the orchestra. Last year, she had danced several in a row with a young man whose name she couldn't remember. Her father had been so excited at the dances and the young man. He had thought to receive a proposal from him, but he had instead returned to his native land of Sweden.

She wandered upstairs and looked into several of the bedrooms. There were at least twenty rooms, each decorated in a different color scheme. Her favorite room overlooked the back gardens and was decorated in a pale blue that reminded her of the sea.

The large grandfather clock struck the sixth hour, and she knew she should take her small bag upstairs and make certain her hair and person looked ready for the evening. They would host at least several hundred people that evening, and many of them were her father's business associates.

A knock fell upon the door, and soon after, her father entered. He rarely came to her room, and she looked up in surprise, turning away from the vanity table and mirror.

"I'm going to have Mariah greet the guests with me," he told her.

Georgiana nodded. "Very well."

"She'll make a lovely hostess." Jonathan smiled, dusting off his jacket arm. "She's a fine woman."

Georgiana said nothing.

"You should make more of an effort, Georgiana," he said suddenly. "She's to be your new stepmama."

"I'm not aware that I've been rude or disrespectful to her," she countered.

Jonathan sighed. "Mariah is a very delicate woman. She senses things. She knows you aren't fond of her."

"No, Father, I'm not. But I don't think she likes me either," she said honestly.

"Ridiculous! The woman is a lamb," he said softly. "A gentle, kind woman. Your forward ways frighten her."

"Such a gentle kind creature, she should join a nunnery instead." Georgiana knew she would anger him, but she was tired of the charade and tired of everyone coming before her with her father's affections.

Jonathan shook her head. "I cannot fathom you, Georgiana. You have such a wicked tongue. I expect you to behave and be polite to my business associates this evening."

"As I've always done," she said, her tone cold.

"I expect you to behave like a lady. You represent me, don't forget that. I'll have none of your trickery this evening." He gave her a cold look and then left her room.

Georgiana turned to look at herself in the mirror. Now she would not even greet the guests as she had done for so many years. The items she had brought with her were arranged before her on the vanity table, and she picked up the pot of rouge. She dipped her finger into the red substance, placed two dots on her cheeks, and rubbed them in. Anger and frustration welled inside her, but she refused to let any tears fall.

She smeared a bit of the red substance onto her lips and then pressed her lips together. She stood up. The dressmaker had added the delicate lace about the bodice to conceal her breasts, which her father found so distasteful. In a flash of anger, she ripped the lace from the bodice, crumpling it in her hand. There. Since Mariah was the innocent lamb and so very beyond reproach, she would play the wolf.

Coming downstairs, she felt an anger in her breast that seemed to choke her. She hated her father. She had behaved impeccably as always. She had been his hostess and his paper doll so that everyone could see how well he had raised her. She had performed like a monkey on the street at his command, and what did she get in return? Tossed aside like rubbish. Pushed aside by the harlot, talked to as if she was a servant and ignored and unloved.

A tray of champagne glasses was sitting inside the buffet room. She took one and downed it in one gulp. She didn't savor the taste or even the bubbly beverage. She just wanted to drink. She took another glass and downed it as well.

She looked about the room. Much could be said about her father, but he was not stingy with his purse when it came to showing off his wealth. The meats were varied, each on silver plates with a small card indicating what it was. The dishes included braised beef, fillet of beef with tomatoes, collops of lamb and asparagus, cutlets of lamb and spinach, medallions of chicken, duck with carrots, and pigeons with olives.

The vegetable dishes were equally varied; celery with cream, cucumber with eggs, roasted potatoes with cheese, spinach with brown gravy, glazed turnips, oyster and celery salad. Her stomach growled at the delicious foods, but she moved into a small room off the buffet one, which was decorated with white flowers and was solely dominated by sweets.

When she was younger, she had always loved this room. It was filled with sweets and pastries, and she had stuffed herself until she was sick. Along the tables, they were decorated with various tarts of apple, apricot, blueberry, and cherry, all dusted with sugar. Coffee eclairs, cream buns, lemon cheesecakes, and bread pudding were laid out upon the table, and Georgiana smiled at the delicious sweets before her.

A footman came by and placed a large silver carafe of coffee at the edge of the table as Georgiana spotted the freshly made banana fritters and took one. She relished the taste and moved away from the dangerous room.

The chandeliers glittered high above the large ballroom, and as she walked through the room, her heels echoed on the polished floor. The musicians had begun to arrive and were setting up their instruments; one had begun to play scales on his violin.

She glanced at herself in the mirror and saw the satin dress with its gray-blue-and-beige vertical stripes. With the lace now gone, the square ruched neckline was lower than she was used to, and her breasts pressed against the neckline when she took a deep breath. She smiled at the rouged cheeks and lips. She dared her father to say anything. She would not change a thing!

She felt a warmth that was likely from the two glasses of champagne she'd had, and she liked the feeling. It was a delight. She went out onto the terrace that overlooked a small green lawn and a gazebo far at the other end of the property. She heard voices inside and knew the guests had begun to arrive.

The smell of grass was heavy in the night air, and when the orchestra began to play, the music drifted to her. She wanted to stay out here in the cool air and not bother with anyone.

"Georgiana!" came the cry behind her, and she turned to see Madeline in a dress of purple with the same color ribbon threaded through her powdered hair.

"Hello, Madeleine," she said simply as she kissed her cheek.

"Darling, there's something different about you," she said, looking her over. "What is it?"

"Well, it could be my rouge, or my neckline being more in fashion and less like a child's, or perhaps it's my determination to enjoy myself tonight and not give a damn about my father and his idiotic mistress!" she said with passion, the drink giving her false bravado.

"Did you have another argument with your father?"

Georgiana said nothing.

"Well, if it's any consolation, you look very daring," Madeleine admitted. "Dazzling, in fact."

"I look as I should. I've put some color in my cheeks, and my dress is one that anyone my age would wear," she said resolutely.

"Quite right." Madeleine nodded as she followed her friend back into the ballroom.

The orchestra was now complete with fifteen musicians, and the music that filled the room was light and airy. Several younger men eyed her with interest as she passed them. Nathaniel walked into the room in a maroon-colored satin jacket and breeches, with a deep rose waistcoat and lush lace at his elbows.

"All the saints and the gods, you look good enough to eat," he said, pulling Georgiana to him and kissing her cheek.

"I'm not speaking to you," she told him tartly.

"Oh." He caught her about the waist as she eyed his pale face and beauty patch. "You can't blame me, Georgie darling. The garden was like a smorgasbord! Everywhere I turned, there were delicious little morsels for me to taste!"

"Is there a male version for a harlot?" she asked him. "Because if there is – "

"Besides wasn't our dearest Madeleine able to accompany you to protect your – "

"Nathaniel!" She swatted his arm.

"I wouldn't be half as bad if you agreed to marry me," he reasoned.

"Really?" Georgiana asked. "That would stop your wandering eyes?"

"They do more than wander, darling." He grinned, kissing her on the cheek.

They moved along to the buffet table.

"You do look quite fetching, Georgie," he remarked in a serious tone. "Truly you do."

"Madeleine said the same thing. Why? Because I have a bit of rouge on and lowered my neckline to join all the other ladies here," she pointed out.

"You seem dangerous tonight," he said softly.

"Dangerous?" she repeated, scoffing. "That's an odd word to use."

"It's the right word to use," he said seriously. "But dangerous or not, I shall have your first dance."

"Of course, you shall."

"And claim several after that," he teased.

"You only get one," she teased back as she sampled the beef with tomatoes and licked her fingers indecorously.

Alexander entered the foyer of the grand house, wearing a greyish-blue jacket, a waistcoat trimmed in silver, and black trousers. His hair was pulled back without a wig. He handed his tricorne hat to the maid in the entryway. There was a crush of people in the first room he came to, and Jonathan Gainsford waved him over.

"Mayson! It's good to see you." He nodded in appreciation. "You are most welcome to our little soiree."

"Little?" said the gentleman he was speaking to. "Eh, gods, Gainsford! There must be three hundred people, maybe more."

"It's a trifle," Jonathan told the man. "You must try all the dishes that have been prepared and drink and be merry this evening."

Alexander moved along. Madeleine was dressed in a fetching purple gown, but Georgiana was nowhere to be seen.

He nodded to his friend Perry who was chatting with a brunette as he picked up a glass of champagne. He noticed Nathaniel take the dance floor with a woman on his arm. His heart skipped a beat. Georgiana! She looked radiant in her gown and powdered hair, yet she defied fashion and wore no wig.

The couple moved through the minuet steps as they touched hands and then moved back from one another. She looked feminine and desirable, and he realized she was wearing rouge again on her cheeks and lips. In the low candlelight, her neckline was lower, and though it was the fashion, the globes of her breasts pressed against the fabric, and he felt suddenly so thirsty he consumed the glass of champagne.

When the dance had ended, the couple left the dance floor, and he followed them. They entered the terrace, and he was able to stand just inside the room but still be able to hear their conversation.

"Georgie darling, if we did marry, it would solve so many problems," Nate told her.

"But I've no wish to marry, Nathaniel," she countered. "You know that. I'm not going to switch an overbearing father for an overbearing husband."

"I would be the most attentive of husbands." He bowed over her hand. "I would make so little demand on you."

Georgiana rolled her eyes. "I imagine you would be. Out all night at the brothels, spending money on drink and women."

"But I would come home to you every night," he assured her. Her lips twitched in a smile, and when another song began, his eyes lit up as well. "Come, dearest, let's have another dance." He put out his hand.

"I'll sit this one out. Go find Madeleine," she told him. "She was longing to dance."

"Your wish, my command." He bowed slightly and was gone.

The ballroom was awash with candlelight, which made the room warm and inviting, and she longed for another glass of champagne. She wanted to feel as if she was floating. She wanted to feel as she had that night at the pleasure garden—

"Are you thinking of the pagoda," the voice said as she spun around.

Her fingers still grasped the terrace wall behind her as she stood staring into Alexander's handsome face. Alexander's eyes wandered over her dress; her breasts edged over the neckline. He desired nothing more than to place a kiss on each globe.

"Certainly not," she said heatedly.

Her rouged lips emphasized their shape and color, and he wanted nothing more than to pull her into his arms and hear her breathy sighs in his ear.

"I've been torturing myself," he admitted lowly.

"Why would you do that?"

"It's not willingly, Georgiana. But when I close my eyes and see those kissable lips," he said softly, "those lips that were made to be kissed, how can I not desire them again?"

"Didn't we go over this already?" She arched an eyebrow at him. "You can't have them now or ever again."

"What, never?" he questioned.

She shook her head. "Never."

"Doesn't that seem like such a very long time?"

The champagne sang in her blood. The bubbly liquid made her reckless, and she wanted to taunt this man before her. She wanted to tease this handsome devil and make him squirm. She wanted to, and she would.

She leaned in until her lips were close to his ear. "Never does seem like a long time. And isn't that just too bad for you?" she whispered, and then without stopping to think, she nipped his neck lightly with her teeth.

His hands were suddenly on her shoulders and he pushed her away from him. When she met his eyes, they were so dark, almost black in the night.

"Do you think you're safe here?" he growled.

"Safe? Safe from you?" She smiled lightly. "You won't do anything. You know you can't."

"Why can't I?" he whispered back.

"For all the reasons you already know." She moved away from him.

"Are you back to playing the temptress?"

"The green-eyed witch?" she returned.

"You play it well."

She smiled at him in the dark.

"Dance with me."

Georgiana nodded, meeting his eyes in the dark. "Of course. Anything to please you."

Anything to please you. Those words echoed in his ears.

Alexander clenched his right fist, willing himself not to jerk the little witch into his arms and – No. That would not do. The little temptress was right. He could do nothing. Francesca Caccini's "Romanesca" filled the air and was so graceful that Georgiana sighed as the instruments played their parts.

Dancing with Alexander, she felt as if the eyes of everyone in the large ballroom were on them as they moved together. She could feel his eyes hot upon her, and she met them once and then turned away.

Heavy applause from somewhere in the house, followed by a roar of laughter, alerted Georgiana that her father must have started a card game. He was exceptionally good at the game Hazard and rarely lost. She had often heard him tell the story of the night he had gambled against a lord and won a beautiful coach and four horses from him.

Pulling away from Alexander, Georgiana moved into the next room, and sure enough, her father was seated with several gentlemen, playing cards. She did not like to play cards. She saw no point in spending hours at a game and losing money when it was primarily chance and a bit of skill.

"Darling," Madeleine said with Nathaniel in tow. "I have the most wicked idea for the young people to do while the old men gamble and the couples dance."

Thirty or so young people had joined them in the foyer, and Alexander was among them.

"Do tell."

"How about we young people play an exciting game of chase?" she said, her eyes wide with excitement.

"Chase?" Georgiana frowned, but Alexander was already anticipating the next words.

"Darling." Madeleine smiled wickedly. "The men count to hundred and the women hide. The men give chase."

"Is that all?" she asked innocently.

"Well," Madeline looked at Nathaniel and then at Alexander, "that depends."

"On what?"

"What the man wants when he finds you." She giggled as she looked about at the young people surrounding her.

The words seemed to be electric, and she found herself staring at Alexander. Let him try to find her! She had been coming here for years and knew all the nooks and crannies of the Hall.

Nathaniel pulled Georgiana into his embrace and kissed her on the cheek. "I'd want a kiss from you, dearest Georgie."

"Drunkard!" she said, pushing him away playfully.

"I can think of a few things I'd want," Alexander said, his eyes fixated on Georgiana.

"Then I guess you'll have to find me," she said coolly. "Which won't be easy. So good luck."

The young people stood at the base of the staircase, while the men were told to go into the billiards room to count to one hundred.

Madeleine chuckled and Georgiana did as well and turned to her friend.

"They'll never catch us," she said resolutely.

"My darling, you are so obtuse sometimes," her friend said, shaking her head. "The object is not to try so hard. My goodness. Every woman here wants to be chased and *captured.*"

Georgiana noticed all the young women about her were tittering and had a nervous anticipation about them. She didn't want to spoil the fun. No one would find her, least of all the scoundrel Alexander Mayson. Alexander with no morals and too sinfully good-looking to be believed.

Someone began to count in the billiards room, and the women raced along the ground floor, turning into the library and the conservatory to hide.

She took the stairs quickly, taking care not to trample her dress. She would not let that arrogant Alexander find her. At the stairs, she made a sharp left and then a quick right. Instead of the opulent rooms of the guests, she moved upstairs to the rarely used servants' quarters, where no one would be.

The servants traveled on the Continent with the former director, and the long hallway of simple bedrooms faced her. She turned to the first door and opened it. It was a simple room with a chest of drawers, an armoire, and a bed.

The bed was covered with a cream-colored blanket that looked white in the darkness. A window seat had been fitted with a cushion. She took the seat just as she heard a door open and close in the hallway. Her heart pounded inside her chest, and then she shook her head. No one from the party would have found her. It must be a servant looking for a moment's reprieve.

She was admiring the front lawns of the house as shoes echoed on the stone floor outside. They barely registered before she realized they had stopped. When the doorknob turned, her heart beat faster. A figure entered the room and closed the door behind him.

"Ah, here she hides in the tower like a princess locked away," Alexander told her, a slight grin on his face.

She stood up and accused him, "You cheated!"

There was no way he could have found her.

"Cheated? How is that?" He took a step towards her.

"You didn't stay in the room to count!"

"Stay in the room to count? How would I know where you had gone if I had done that?" He grinned.

"No scruples! Not even in a game," she threw at him.

"Least of all in a game." He stood before her. "So, what is my prize?"

"For cheating?" She scoffed. "Nothing."

"Don't be a sore loser."

Georgiana raised an eyebrow. "I'm not. I didn't lose to you."

"Didn't you?" He nodded. "You like to be safe and be able to tease and torment me in places where you know I cannot act."

"That's not true."

He put his finger to his lips and then drew a line across her breasts.

"You're unspeakable!" She backed away from him.

"And you are what men call a cocktease."

"Despicable!" She felt her cheeks flame. "Are you going to let me pass?"

"Are you a prisoner?"

She glanced over his tall frame and then to the door.

"Do you think I'm going to chase you through the mansion?" he asked, raising an eyebrow.

"Of course not." She smiled at him, relaxing.

"Then what are you waiting for?"

"Nothing." She moved past him, and he made no move to stop her. She opened the door, and still he made no move to follow her. She shrugged. She was being ridiculous.

"Georgiana," he called softly to her. She turned back to see him grinning in the dark. "You should run."

Chapter 8

GEORGIANA FILLED WITH FRIGHT and then supreme delight. She shouted with glee, running through the door and slamming it shut to give herself more time.

"No!" she cried out, laughing as she raced down the hallway. Her shoes echoed on the stone floor.

Her steps were quick, but his were slower and methodical. She knew he could catch up with her easily. She made a series of turns and entered the second floor of the house, knowing he was right behind her. The doors facing the hallway were the guests' rooms. If she could make it inside, she could lock herself in.

The delicate strains of the music could be heard far below and the sound of people laughing somewhere nearby. Her heart was beating fast inside her chest from the excitement, and she gathered up her skirts to quicken her pace.

Then in one swift movement, Alexander caught her about the waist and pulled her into the very bedroom she was trying to get to. Standing before her, he faced her, but coolly behind his back, the lock clicked into place.

"Didn't run far enough," he said, his voice soft.

She still had a smile on her face. "Don't you think you've gone far enough with this?"

She knew they were in the plum room decorated for its deep purple color. The room was ornate with a large four-poster bed dominating the space.

"Ah, Georgie." He tsk-tsked. "You're such an innocent that you don't realize how far I could go."

"But you won't!" Her chin came up a notch as he took a step towards her.

"You think to tease me in public with no consequences, but everything has consequences, Georgiana." He suddenly shrugged out of his jacket and flung it onto a nearby chair.

"Wh-what are you doing?" she almost squeaked.

"Tonight, I'm going to go as far as I can without doing any true damage," he told her simply.

"What does that mean?" she whispered.

"It means you like to play with fire, and tonight you're going to feel the burn."

"Alexander."

"Georgiana."

"You're going to rape me?" she said, her eyes wide with fear.

"Rape?" Alexander almost looked offended. "This is the opposite of rape. You're going to beg me not to stop."

"I won't. I never would."

"You will," he assured her.

He pulled her into his arms, and she fell against his chest. He relished the feel of her curves under his hands, and he placed a warm, wet kiss on the tops of her breasts.

"Oh, God," she said in a breathless voice.

Alexander grinned in the dark. "Now, tell me once more how I'm never going to kiss you. Tell me that these lips that I've dreamed of will never be mine."

"They won't be," she agreed.

He covered her lips with his, taking his time even as his tongue delved into the sweetness of her mouth. He moved his hand down her cheek, farther down her neck as he deepened the kiss and she moaned lightly. Lifting her into his arms, he pushed her onto the bed and covered her body with his own.

"You've teased me for too long, but even now, I'll never do any lasting harm to you." His dark blue eyes met hers. "That would be unthinkable," he told her honestly, though she had no idea what he was talking about.

Her chestnut hair gleamed and her eyes glittered emerald green in the dark as he watched her.

"You are so lovely, Georgiana," he said softly. "I want you so badly."

As he had dreamed about so often, he moved between her legs, pressing up the many layers of skirts, petticoats, and chemise to reveal her pale, silk-encased legs. Delicate curls guarded the entrance, and not thinking beyond the moment, he flicked his fingers past the curls and into the warm, wet core of her.

He wanted to taste her and relish her sighs, but he didn't want to frighten her. She was trembling, and when she closed her eyes, she bit down on her bottom lip. Lightly stroking her with his fingers, he could see her soft cheeks pinken and hear her breathy sighs.

"Georgie," he whispered. "Moan for me."

The sensations that crashed into her were overwhelming. She could only feel his fingers inside her and the deliciousness that surrounded her. She moaned lightly as Alexander gathered her into his arms, kissing her once, then twice as her fingers bit into his shoulders.

"Alexander." She sighed even as he kissed her temple.

"Do you want me?" he whispered huskily into her ear. "Do you want me as much as I want you?"

She nodded. "I do."

Though he had taken off his jacket, he remained completely clothed. He hadn't wanted to take off anything else. He didn't want to make it easy. He didn't want to take anything from her that could not be reversed. He could still feel the insides of her walls gripping his finger, and he knew she was a virgin. He wouldn't take that from her, but God, he wanted to. He wanted nothing more than to lie naked with Georgiana and feel her skin against his and have her milk his cock until it was empty.

"Georgiana." He sighed into her ear.

Her body arched into his, and he was drowning.

Why had he done this? Why had he pushed himself into this? He had wanted to tease her back, but this was not a game he could win. He was drowning in those emerald eyes and fighting such a losing battle. How long could he keep the tight rein of control over himself? How long could he be in this bed with Georgiana before he succumbed? Dammit all!

He wanted her so badly. He knew he should leave. He should pull away from her and stop this before things escalated beyond saving. He should do it now.

Suddenly the door opened. It happened so quickly. Alexander was facing Georgiana, but Georgiana's face was clearly seen by the intruder from the light in the hallway. Mariah Gower had stepped into the room for a brief second. Mariah's eyes gleamed with devious pleasure as she spied Georgiana and the back of the man before closing the door quickly.

"Oh, no," Georgiana whispered as Alexander looked at the closed door and then back at her.

*****

Georgiana was seated before her father's large desk in his study. After Mariah discovered her with Alexander,

Jonathan had ripped her from the party and sent her home. She was told to wait for his arrival, which she had been doing for three hours. When he finally arrived home with Mariah Gower, Georgiana was seated in the study, still wearing her dress.

Entering the study, her father came to stand before her, and without a word, he slapped her hard across the face.

"You disgusting slut!" he said coldly as Georgiana held her cheek and tried not to let the tears fall.

"My dear –" Mariah began to say, trying to calm her fiancé down, though Georgiana saw a small smile on her face.

"No, Mariah, no!" he barked. "I'll not have you defend her. You told me earlier that Georgiana had behaved badly and needed to leave the party. Now," he directed to her. "Tell me plainly what you saw."

Mariah sighed heavily. "I was looking for a place to lie down when I came upon Georgiana in one of the rooms – "

"Yes." He nodded, glaring at his daughter.

"She was on the bed with a man, and her skirts were bunched up about the waist and her legs spread," Mariah said breathlessly. "I – I was so shocked that I backed out of the room before I could confront the man!"

"Legs spread like a common dock front hussy!" Jonathan spat out.

"I'm afraid that's true, my dear." Mariah nodded. "It is what I saw."

"You are no better than a harlot on the street," Jonathan cursed her. "With your cheap rouge and your breasts pushed forward for every man to ogle you. You disgust me!"

Georgiana remained silent.

"Who was the man?" Jonathan ordered. "I'll have his name!"

"I'll never tell you his name," she said defiantly, and her father struck her again.

"It must be that Nathaniel Lindsay." Mariah recalled the man. "They're thick as thieves."

Jonathan snorted. "Absolutely not. I've heard the rumors about him. He doesn't fancy women."

Georgiana frowned at her father's words. What did that mean?

"Well, daughter, you have your wish." He nodded at her. "You are to leave in two days' time for the colonies. I have arranged it. I'm sure my sister has absolutely no idea the sort of slut I'm sending her."

Georgiana raised her chin up a notch. "I'm sure she doesn't. And I'm sure if I had to do it all over again, I would do it exactly the same."

"You are nothing but a cheap whore! Get out of my sight."

Georgiana slammed the door to her room, pressing her fist against her mouth to stem the urge to sob and scream at the same time. She should have known. This was all her fault. She had pushed Alexander to the edge, and all she did was harm herself. She was an absolute fool. A stupid, silly fool!

She went to sit by the window and pressed her cheek against it to cool the flesh where her father had slapped her. She closed her eyes and tried to block out the scene in the bedroom. She had trembled in his arms and been so ignorant. Alexander must have known and laughed at her. He had known all along what she had just discovered tonight. Once alone and in his arms, Georgiana had been ready to sell her soul to feel his hand and mouth on her. Perhaps her father was right. She was disgusting.

I'll never do any lasting harm to you, that would be unthinkable, Alexander had said. But it was a lie. He had touched her, and already she yearned for him. His warmth, his passion. She wanted him still. Arrogant Alexander. With his handsome face and seductive ways. He would never be hers. That was a fool's dream.

Tears fell onto her cheeks. She wasn't crying for herself. She was a fool and deserved what was happening. Alexander was right. She had teased him and been burned in the end. She was crying at the injustice of it all. Now she would be shipped off to Massachusetts and would probably never return to England.

She would marry some colonial doctor, and that would be that. She wiped her tear-streaked cheek and thought angrily of Alexander. A flash of hate flared inside her. He must have known. He had known that she would react to his intimate attentions, which she cringed thinking about. Though she had teased him, he should have known better. He should not have taken it so far. And now, now she was banished, and what would happen to him? Nothing. She hated him almost as much as she hated her father.

She stayed by the window for another hour, and when the sun began to rise, she returned to her bed.

Alexander had never meant to go as far as he had. He had played a game with the little green-eyed minx, but then it had turned so serious. He lay upon his bed, wearing what he had been wearing earlier, having not changed a thing. He had replayed the night in his head over and over again. He had not thought to bed her that night. But once the delectable Georgiana was underneath him, the thought of her warm pussy surrounding his cock had been so difficult to fight.

He sighed heavily. Once the game had been decided, he had heard the women outside the door giggling and whispering to each other. When the chosen man began to count, Alexander had eased open the door to take a peek.

Georgiana had taken the stairs quietly, not once looking behind her so he had followed her easily to the servants' quarters. She had seemed so sure that no one would find her that she had not been in a hurry as she made her way to the chosen hiding spot. She had been intent on playing the game. She had seemed shocked to find he discovered her and almost disappointed. She wanted to win more than she wanted to play.

Or perhaps for her it had been a battle of wills. But for Alexander, the chance to catch the beauty unaware and in a place she could not run was too much not to at least try. When he told her to run, he had watched her run daintily down the stairway. She didn't move too fast, but she was trying so hard to get away from him. How could that be? It had been so easy to take her about the waist and deposit her in the closest room. But everything had changed inside that room. In the dark, her breasts had been heaving from the run, her cheeks flushed, and he wanted her. He would have to taste her.

If nothing more, he wanted to kiss her lips again and feel her pressed against his chest. But he had been earnest. He wanted to go as far as he could without taking her virginity. He wanted to hear her moan in his ear, feel her arch into him and return his ardor. But there were two things he hadn't planned on. He hadn't planned on Georgiana wanting him so much that it almost sent him over the edge.

And he hadn't planned on the interruption. As he was struggling to tear himself away from her and not do untold damage, the door had flung open and Georgiana had been horrified. Alexander had turned to look over his shoulder but it had been too late. The intruder was gone.

So as not to be seen leaving the bedroom together, he had given her a chance to collect herself, and after several minutes, he had left the room. But when he combed the Hall to speak with her, she was gone. In a flippant manner, he asked Jonathan where his charming daughter was.

Jonathan gave him a withering look but it was not directed at him. It seemed to be directed towards his daughter. "She is unwell. She has returned home."

He deducted that the person who had seen them together had told on Georgiana and that she had been dragged home. But his identity did not seem to be known to anyone. He had waited patiently for several hours to be summoned before Jonathan Gainsford. Georgiana had been compromised. Badly. And she would name him and he would face her father's wrath.

But the minutes turned to hours, and he waited. And waited. And nothing happened. He was not summoned. Finally, as the sun began to rise, he realized Georgiana would not name him. She would never name him. And suddenly the despair of being captured like an animal in a trap turned to anger. Why had she not named him?

***

Her father was gone very early in the morning, and the servants seemed to already know what had occurred the night before. She was branded as surely as if she had some mark on her forehead, and no one dared to say anything to her.

She dressed warmly and left the house behind. She wandered in the park, purchased several books at the local bookstore, and had tea alone. She had to pack and ready herself for the trip. Her father would not pay for any new clothes, as she was leaving in disgrace. She knew that if Mariah chose, she could gossip about her indiscretion, but she doubted she would. Not that Mariah wouldn't love to see Georgiana's name besmirched. But that would also besmirch Jonathan and she was too close to being the next Mrs. Gainsford to do such a thing.

Besides, Georgiana was being sent to the colonies. Mariah had gotten her wish. The wayward daughter was being exiled, and everything would soon be hers. She placed the teacup down as she stared down into the empty cup. She could almost laugh if the situation wasn't so ridiculous. Exiled to Boston. Because she had made the unfortunate mistake to be enticed by Alexander Mayson's charms.

She had paid for her tea, but there were few people inside and she wanted to enjoy what might be the last tea she ever had in England. The bell over the door tinkled, and Alexander Mayson entered the establishment.

Damn! she swore inwardly.

She pressed through the doors and was on the street. He had not seen her yet, as she was seated at a corner table, so she picked up her books and moved quickly through the room and into the street.

"Georgiana!" he called, but she ignored him.

Alexander was at the root of all her problems. If he hadn't been constantly battling her and trying to push her, they would not be where they were today. She picked up her step, passing into the street to cross. A coach almost trampled her as they dodged her. Alexander pulled her to safety away from the coach, but she was not pleased. The driver shouted something to her about watching her step.

"Get your hands off me!" she said, sharply.

"You're welcome for saving you," he said, irritated, and then frowned. "Georg – your face! What happened?"

Georgiana had forgotten about the red bruise on her face left by her father from the night before. She touched a gloved hand to her cheek and then turned from him. "It's nothing."

He studied her carefully. "We're not even going to talk about last night?"

Georgiana turned back to him. "What is there to talk about?"

"What is there to talk about? Are you joking? One moment we were in the room and the next you were gone. I looked everywhere for you," he recalled. "I couldn't find you."

"It was my fault. I admit it. I teased you and now I'm paying the price," she said simply.

"What price?" he asked, his hand reaching out to touch her but he stayed it.

"It doesn't matter," she said coldly.

"Georgiana – I didn't mean for this to happen. I lost my head. We both got caught up in something. This is my fault more than yours," he admitted.

"There at least we agree," she told him, meeting his eyes.

"Why didn't you tell your father it was me? I compromised you. It's not just your burden. You weren't alone. You shouldn't bear this alone."

"I don't need or require your help," she said, coldly moving away from him and starting down the street

He caught her by the arm and pulled her into a small green park that was nearby in the center of the square. She allowed herself to be pulled into the green without making a fuss because she was tired. But she was still angry at him and blamed him for his actions.

"Last night . . ." He seemed to be searching for the words. "I got carried away. I admit it. You were so desirable. I wanted – " he began awkwardly. "There's no excuse, but it's true."

"You don't need to do this. As I said, you may be to blame but so am I. It doesn't need to be melodramatic," she assured him.

"What price are you paying?" he asked again, touching her arm.

"It's not your concern." She pulled her arm away from him.

"I'm making it my concern," he said stubbornly.

"My father has decided – " she began and then stopped.

"What? What has he decided? Is he sending you to the country? Is he placing you in a nunnery?" His eyes were full of concern.

Georgiana rolled her eyes. "A nunnery? No."

"Georgiana, tell me. If he's placing you somewhere against your will, I'll do the right thing. We'll marry. I'll marry you," he said firmly.

Georgiana's heart skipped a beat and then she stopped. "How amusing! I'm not trading one overbearing uncaring man for another," she said passionately, turning from him.

"I care. You're not letting me right this wrong." He moved to face her.

"Marriage to you?" She scoffed. "That's not righting anything. That's another wrong. And you'll forgive me, but this conversation is absurd. If you feel guilty about what happened, please don't. I have my share of blame, and now as you so aptly put it – I must pay the consequences."

She began to walk away from him, and he felt a strange sense of loss and overwhelming panic. He caught up with her easily, but she moved away from him.

"Georgiana." He stopped her once more. "You aren't alone. This is me and you here."

"No, Alexander. There's only me. And trust me, I'll never make the same mistake with another man ever again," she said, her jaw firmly set.

"What does that mean?" he asked warily.

"It means you taught me a valuable lesson. So yes, I suppose I should thank you." She inched up her chin.

Georgiana, stop – "

"There's nothing more we have to say to each other," she said curtly. "Goodbye, Alexander."

When she returned home, she had a severe headache. Her trunks had been brought down from the attic, and they stood in the middle of the room as a reminder of what had happened and what the consequence would now be. She would soon be on a two-month journey to a faraway place where only two people in that world knew her.

She sat down on the window seat and leaned her head against the windowpane. She couldn't pretend that night had not happened. Even now when she closed her eyes, she could feel his mouth on her and his fingers – she shivered. So much had happened the night before that she hadn't really taken the time to ponder it.

The delicious memory of Alexander lying on top of her and causing her emotions to run rampant had been exquisite and short-lived. She had trembled in his arms and wanted everything he could give her until Mariah flung open the door and the dream turned dreadfully wrong.

Everything after that had been a nightmare. Her father had found her not long after in the ballroom and had grabbed her arm, tearing her away from the party. Her arm was still sore. He had flung her into the coach and had not spoken a word to her until the study. After calling her several names and slapping her twice, he resolved that she was dead to him. He urged her to pack all that she wanted to take with her because she might never see England again.

Georgiana sat in her room. Everything that belonged to her was in the one small room. It was scant. Her dresses, corsets, undergarments would go with her. But what else did she have? A silver-handled brush and comb, as well as a mirror. Two bottles of perfume. Several necklaces and rings she had inherited from her mother. Her mother. A small painting of her mother that had been given to her father before their engagement.

A dozen or so books, ribbons and combs to place in her hair, and not much else. Twenty-four years in this house and everything that was hers was in this one room. She moved away from the window and lay down on her bed. Tomorrow. Tomorrow she would pack for her trip. Tomorrow she would be ready to travel to the colonies.

Tomorrow she would forget once and for all that she had teased a young man named Alexander and that he had taunted her back. She hadn't lost her innocence that night in his arms but she had lost something far more precious.

She had lost her heart.

And she willed herself that she would never ever give another man any part of her.

Alexander paced the floor several times, thinking of his conversation with Georgiana. Sweet, kissable, lovely Georgiana. She was going to suffer because of him, and he couldn't allow it. He would not allow a young vibrant woman to be sent to the country or a nunnery because of him. He should have known better. He had always kept away from wide-eyed virgins for this exact reason. With divorced women and mistresses, there was an understanding. There was an exchange of favors but no strings to tangle into one's life.

But since that night at Haymarket Theater, he had been bewitched, and with one glimpse into those emerald eyes, he had become smitten. She had not seemed to enjoy his attentions, but then that night in the pagoda, everything had changed. One kiss had been his undoing. And then for the rest of the night spent in her company, he had been enchanted by her.

Then the ball. He had been intent on seeking her out to tease her a bit, maybe steal a kiss, but . . . He sighed. It had all spun so out of control. The hide and seek game and then the chase. How could he not throw her on the bed and relish the feel of her body beneath his? How could he not want to feel her breasts, her lips, the very core of her? He was falling. She was inside his head. She was in his thoughts.

What should he do? Go to Jonathan and do the right thing. No matter the cost. He wanted her. He would have her as his wife, and she would be his. That was an absolute. The emerald-eyed witch would be his.

The four large trunks sat inside the foyer, waiting to be loaded onto the coach. Everything materialistic that had ever meant something to Georgiana was inside them. Flanna couldn't make the journey, as her mother was ill and she had to nurse her, but an older couple was traveling to the colonies on the same ship and would keep an eye on Georgiana.

Her father had come out of his study and stood surveying the trunks and his daughter.

"I'm sure your aunt has no idea what you are really like," he said emotionlessly. "Try to behave with some decorum. At least refrain from spreading your legs with those red savages."

Georgiana nodded to him as well. "But I wanted to sample men of all colors, Father," she said spitefully, wanting to hurt him as he had hurt her.

"Disgusting," he said with a sneer and turned away from her.

She closed her eyes. She was so tired of fighting with him. So tired of the coldness between them. There was no semblance of a father-daughter relationship but instead a cold animosity he had always directed at her even before her fall from grace.

"Goodbye, Father," she whispered to the closed study door as she turned to the coach.

At the docks, there was no one there to embrace Georgiana and see her off. Her trunks were loaded onto the ship, and she boarded it quietly with no fanfare. Mr. and Mrs. Allen were the older couple meant to keep an eye on her, and the other passengers included an elderly vicar, two sisters near the age of the vicar, and a newlywed couple.

The ship pulled up anchor, and she watched the land slip away from sight. In a moment, everything and everyone she knew was gone. She remained at the railing for some time and then went down below to her simple cabin. She crawled into the bed and fell into a deep sleep. She wanted nothing more than to wish the time away from England and look toward the colonies and her new life.

Alexander sipped his brandy as he read the newspaper. His club was quiet that evening, and no one was about. He enjoyed such moments. Though he didn't like to admit it, his thoughts were consumed with Georgiana. He had thought of her often since that night at Clyvedon Hall a few days ago. It was a new experience for him, and though he tried to push the emerald-eyed beauty from his mind, she would return there often.

He had thought about marriage to Georgiana, and the idea of it excited him. She would never bore him, and he would spend a lifetime making her happy. He had written to Jonathan to discuss Georgiana and a union between the two of them, but Gainsford had not responded immediately to his request to meet. When he did, he mentioned that his business venture was on hold and that he would connect with him when everything was in order.

Business venture. Of course! Gainsford didn't think it had anything to do with Georgiana. He thought he was moving forward with the business venture. Alexander decided he would visit the man in person and ask for Georgiana's hand in marriage. It was the simplest way to end all of this. No more consequences for Georgiana and they would be married as soon as it could be arranged.

Alexander sighed with relief. Georgiana would be his bride. Georgiana would be his. He smiled at the thought. He looked at the newspaper on his lap and then heard two men speaking to the right of him.

"I can't say I blame him," the one man told his friend. "It's everywhere. A scandal."

"A scandal is right." The other man shook his head as he lit his pipe.

Alexander was trying to concentrate on his newspaper and brandy, but the gossip of the two men intrigued him. Scandal? What scandal?

"Apparently she was actually in bed with a man," the first man said as he began to deal the cards between them. "Can you imagine? A young unmarried woman?"

"No longer intact, that's certain. Such a shame. She was quite beautiful but now . . ." The man picked up the cards he was dealt.

Alexander was listening intently now. His throat was dry as he strained his ears. They couldn't be speaking of Georgiana. Impossible!

"Has the man she was with been named?" the dealer wondered.

"Some say it's Lindsay."

"Nathaniel Lindsay? Out of the question," he said firmly.

"Why is that?"

"Come now." The man grinned. "You must have heard the rumors. Lindsay likes his sport with more pipe and less puss."

His companion laughed. "And what of the fallen beauty?"

"Georgiana?" the man questioned. "Gainsford was furious. He's packed her off to her aunt and uncle in the colonies. Poor dear. She'll probably never see England again."

Alexander felt the room tilt.

"You haven't heard the best part," the dealer said, looking about the room as if about to tell some great state secret.

"What's that?"

"Gainsford is to marry Mariah Gower."

"The widow Gower?" the man repeated. "Hmph! Good luck, I say. That's a woman who likes her gold."

"That she does." He nodded. "And apparently Gainsford has put in an offer for Clyvedon Hall."

"Clyvedon Hall!? I would never have thought old Clyvedon would sell the place."

"Gainsford made an incredible offer, so I hear."

"Must have."

Alexander felt shaken as the two men left the room. So Gainsford was no longer interested in the shipping line because he was purchasing a large estate to impress his new bride, Mariah Gower. And Georgiana. Lovely, emerald-eyed Georgiana had been shipped off to the colonies. So that was the consequence she spoke about. A strange sensation flooded his body, but he couldn't place his finger to name it.

He drank the rest of his brandy and frowned. The more he thought Georgiana out of his reach and in the colonies, the more he felt an emotion that was entirely foreign and new to him. And when he concentrated on the feeling, he knew its name. It was an overwhelming sense of panic. An intense feeling that something precious was falling out of his grip. And the feeling that flooded into him was panic. Pure, penetrating panic.

The trip had been an arduous one, and for much of the journey, Georgiana had rarely seen her fellow passengers. Mrs. Allen was seasick most of the trip, while her husband attended to her. The two sisters were German and kept to themselves, and the newlywed couple kept almost entirely to their room.

Georgiana had spent most afternoons looking out over the vast blue waters and her evenings playing chess with the elderly vicar. She was more than relieved to hear the crew tell the passengers that they would be at their destination the next afternoon.

When she walked down the gangway, her first glimpse of Boston was a mixture of sailors shouting to one another as the shipments were unloaded, seagulls squawking in the air, and the many people moving about the piers as they engaged in their business. Waiting on the pier was a slender man dressed in livery, next to an impressive coach. A large ginger-haired man stepped out of the coach, looking expectantly at the people coming down the gangway. His eyes eventually rested on her. He had a smile on his face as he walked resolutely towards her.

"Georgiana!" he called out to her as if he already knew who she was.

"Uncle Richard?" she asked the large man.

"Indeed, I am, my dear," Richard Wilkinson said as he swept her up into a warm embrace and kissed her cheek. "You are the spitting image of your mother, Lord rest her gracious soul. I daresay the society will enjoy having such a lovely woman amongst them."

Georgiana warmed at the compliment. "You're very kind. How nice to meet someone who speaks of my mother. I didn't know her well."

"Of course not, you were but a child when she died." He motioned to a slender man who loaded her trunks onto the coach.

"I was five," she agreed.

"Your Aunt and I were still in England at the time and spent many evenings with your parents so many years ago. Your mother was vibrant and lovely to behold. I know her passing was hard on Jonathan." He took her hand in his and assisted her into the coach.

Georgiana wondered at her uncle's words. Had her father ever been sad about her mother's passing? She always thought it had been the death of the son he had longed for that had been a huge blow, not his wife's death.

When they neared the residence of her aunt and uncle, he pointed out the building as it came into view. It was on a prominent road in Boston and decorated with colorful red bricks. Three sides of the building had oversized windows, and the three-story house was most impressive. A small half-circular gravel drive led up to the house.

When she stepped out of the coach, her uncle took her by the arm and steered her into his home. A tall thin woman with delicate features and a mop of black hair threaded with grey greeted her.

"Oh, my goodness! Georgiana! What a beauty you are," she said, coming towards her and kissing her cheek. "Doesn't she look exactly like . . . ?" She turned to her husband.

"Exactly like her." Richard grinned. "I told her as much."

"Well, you do, Georgiana." She nodded. "You look very much like your dear mother. I have tea laid out in the parlor. I knew you would be tired from your journey. We don't have anything planned this evening, but tomorrow there's a supper party and I can't wait to show off my niece newly arrived from London!" She clasped her hands over her small bosom.

"Thank you, Aunt Arabella."

"Oh, my dear, that's much too formal." She led her niece to the parlor. "Everyone calls me Bella. You must as well."

"Aunt Bella," Georgiana repeated.

"My, my." She poured out the tea as Georgiana and Richard each took a seat in the handsome parlor decorated in peach and brown colors. "I think we'll have gentlemen callers at our door before the week is out," she said, handing the first cup to her niece. "Don't you think, Richard?"

"Undoubtedly."

"And I think our younger women might be a bit jealous." She dimpled. "Such a beauty here will take all the attention away from them."

Georgiana looked down at her cup and then back at her aunt and uncle. "Did my . . . did my father write to you? Did he tell you I would be joining you here?" She knew they could not know about what had just occurred between her and Alexander, but she wanted to know what had been written about her.

Arabella frowned as she tried to remember and took a sip of her tea. "What did my brother say? It was several months ago."

"He said Georgiana needed a change," Richard recalled. "That she would be joining us in the next few months."

"Exactly," Arabella agreed. "A change. And, my dear, you couldn't have more of a change than Boston from London." She laughed lightly.

So, her father had not written disparagingly about her. She believed that. Anything about her reflected on him, and that he would not allow. Appearances above all else.

"But you'll see. Society is not so stifled as one would believe." Arabella looked to her husband for confirmation, and he agreed. "They'll be supper parties, card parties, dances, picnics when the weather improves. You'll enjoy yourself. And who knows? You might find yourself a Boston husband while here!" Her aunt raised her eyebrows and smiled.

Georgiana warmed to her aunt and uncle, but inwardly she thought, *Never!* Alexander Mayson was at the root of all her troubles, and she would never let another man into her heart.

Chapter 9

SIX MONTHS LATER

BOSTON, MASSACHUSETTS
1716

Arabella watched Georgiana over her teacup at the breakfast table. Her husband was engrossed in *The Boston News-Letter* and Georgiana was eating a breakfast of eggs, toast, and tea. The girl had not been at all what Arabella had expected. Her brother, Jonathan, had written her last year, but the letter had gone into more detail than Arabella had originally told her niece. Jonathan had written that he was saddled with a wayward daughter who enjoyed nothing more than gambling, dancing, and theater, and all of it involved late nights out and friends he disapproved of.

Arabella had bit back a smile and tried not to respond to her brother in a tone that inferred Georgiana sounded like an absolutely normal young woman. She had always felt sad that she had left her young niece in England to be raised by her cold brother. She had wanted to be a part of Georgiana's life, but her husband, Richard, had wanted to try his luck, and together they had grown wealthy and successful in Massachusetts.

Richard was a successful lawyer and a confidante to Governor Samuel Shute, who oversaw the Province of Massachusetts Bay. They had never been able to have children, but Arabella had watched her husband become an attentive, delighted uncle these past few months. He escorted both women to the many parties and balls, and as predicted, Georgiana was a huge success.

Her beauty could not be denied, but she was also intelligent, had a way with words, and was kind to those around her. She had watched her niece blossom in the New World and was not surprised when several men began to pay her particular attention.

"I noticed a certain gentleman paying you attention last night at the supper party," Arabella said to Georgiana as she buttered her toast.

"Yes," she admitted.

"Who was that, my dear?" Richard wondered.

"Oh, my love! You must have noticed," she said. "Mr. Hackett."

"Oh, yes. Elias." He nodded to them both but seemed disinterested.

"He paid her particular attention at the party and then the dance before that. And didn't he make certain she had punch to drink at one such event, I can't remember which one," she prattled.

"That's all true, Aunt," Georgiana admitted. "He's been attentive to me."

Arabella smiled. "But you could do better. Much better."

"Agreed," said her uncle.

"Better?" Georgiana frowned. "I'm not looking to marry."

"No?" Richard spoke up. "I thought all women dream of marrying."

"No, Uncle. I've no wish to marry at this time," Georgiana explained to them.

"You will find your mind changed when the right man comes along." Her aunt smiled.

A fleeting thought filled Georgiana's head of Alexander holding her in his arms, but she dismissed it immediately. "But Elias Hackett is a nice man. I will say that for him," she told her aunt and uncle.

"He's very somber," Arabella told her.

"He's very religious," Richard added, turning over his newspaper. "Almost a Puritan."

"Exactly so. He'd be a dour husband," Arabella said to her niece. "You are right to not set your cap for him."

"I think the word I've heard is that Hackett is quite sweet on Georgiana here," Richard told them. "Not the other way around."

"I don't view him as anything beyond a kind gentleman who travels in the same circles we do." She explained to them both.

Richard waved a hand. "That's no matter anyway. Every place I've taken you to, you have men at your feet. So, finding one that you do like will not be the problem. It will be finding the right one."

"Just so," Arabella chimed in.

"Are you so keen to have me gone?" she half teased, half asked.

"Gracious no!" Arabella said quickly, followed by her husband.

"Put it from your mind, my dear niece." He patted her hand. "You are welcome with us as long as you remain in Massachusetts. You need never leave."

"And certainly our house is big enough," she added. "Come, Georgiana. Finish your breakfast so we can make our appointment with the millinery."

Georgiana went upstairs to retrieve her hat and gloves. Her spacious room overlooked the garden that was filled with red maple and oak trees. Georgiana had been with her aunt and uncle for six months, and she felt like a new person. She felt respected and admired, but most importantly she felt a warmth and love that she had never experienced with her father. Her aunt cared about her comfort, and she was admired wherever she went in Boston.

News traveled very slowly, and though there were whispers about why Georgiana had come to Massachusetts, most regarded it as a chance to spend time with her aunt and uncle and possibly find a husband. Her reputation remained intact, and she had plenty of male admirers.

Though she found the men handsome and agreeable, she kept a distance and vowed that none would find their way into her heart. Beyond a name on her dance card, none of the Bostonian men were given a second glance. However, one man seemed very taken with her.

Elias Hackett was a tall slender man with serious brown eyes and black, inky hair. He was a quiet man except when he once consumed too much liquor and spoke for forty-five minutes straight about his mother living in England and the cesspool it had become. She often found his eyes upon her, and when they were together at a party, he monopolized her time.

She enjoyed the innocent attention and found him harmless enough. He seemed captivated by her beauty and spoke often of it and her purity, which she did not correct him. But she did not fear Elias's attention, as she knew them to be purely sociable. He was a confirmed bachelor, and as he was nearing forty, it was understood that he would never marry.

She grabbed her hat and gloves and went downstairs to join her aunt.

Half an hour later, the two women were at the fashionable millinery shop, searching for a new hat. Georgiana noticed a small difference between the fashion in Boston compared to London. But much like London, the colonists dressed according to their occupation and social status. The wealthier colonists could afford more luxurious imported materials such as satins, silks, and brocades, while those with less money would purchase linen, cotton, or wool.

But she did notice that the fashion trends in Boston relied heavily upon styles brought back from Europe, especially London. At numerous events she attended, women who barely knew her would make her acquaintance only to hear the latest fashion on the style of dress.

Georgiana studied the different hats and liked the ones in more subdued colors and not so affected. She knew the satin and silk were imported and so very expensive.

"You'll see Boston tries to compare with London," Arabella noted to her niece. "Sometimes they succeed." She shrugged.

"Indeed," Georgiana agreed. "I quite like the different styles."

"You look very well." Arabella surveyed her and a newer dress her father had made a month before she departed. "I'm sure the company here hasn't seen such fashion in some time."

"Your compliments are too much, Aunt Bella."

Arabella squeezed her hand and kissed her cheek suddenly. "Knowing my brother as I do, I'm sure he was not complimentary enough."

That evening before their supper party at a friend of the Wilkinsons, Georgiana penned a long letter to her friend Madeleine. She had not had any news from England, not even from her father, who she had not expected to write. She assumed he was now married, and she hoped they would be happy together.

When they arrived at their destination, small groups of people were seated together, speaking quietly. Several card games were being played as she accepted a glass of warm cider from a servant. She was watching one card game when the solemn Elias Hackett joined her.

"Good evening, Mistress Gainsford," he said formally.

"Mr. Hackett. I've given you leave to call me by my first name, though you refuse to do so," she said, teasing him.

He nodded stiffly but declined. "I think the formality of the surname gives a deference amongst strangers."

"Quite right," she said rather than arguing the point.

"Though you and I are known to each other- " he began clumsily. "I mean, in the sense of knowing each other and spending time together..."

Georgiana bit back a smile as she sipped her cider. "Yes, Mr. Hackett."

"And though time has given us the respect of each other's confidence, I still find the use of the surname appropriate," he stated firmly. His wrists were bony and prominent as he moved them through the air as he talked.

She nodded, used to his odd speech, and thought nothing of the formal thoughts.

"Would you like me to read to you? I – I came upon a passage today in Proverbs that reminded me very much of you," he asked softly.

"Did it? Then please," she allowed him as they took two chairs that faced each other near the fireplace.

She heard several people laughing at a nearby table as she focused her attention on Elias.

He pulled out his worn Bible and caressed the front cover before turning the pages to the passage he sought. He read aloud: "*She is more precious than jewels, and nothing you desire can compare with her.*"

His eyes were on her in adoration as Georgiana tried to appear at ease.

"More precious than jewels and—and nothing you . . ." He stopped uneasily and seemed to be having trouble swallowing. "Well, I thought of you."

"That's very kind, " she told him, taking up her glass of cider.

"Ah!" He turned at the sound of the small piano being played. "Music! *My lips shall greatly rejoice when I sing unto thee; and my soul, which thou hast redeemed,*" he quoted again and Georgiana nodded.

She was used to his quotes and compliments. He was deemed an odd man by many others in their circle. He was very religious but had never married, and most thought he never would. Georgiana admired his quiet ways and polite manners. He came from a wealthy English family, but one would never guess. He wore black clothes adopted by the Puritans and never wore any jewelry.

She felt safe with him. He would never make her heart race or cause her blood to sing in her veins. He would never take her in his arms and make her forget everything right and decent. He was nothing like Alexander, and she was glad of it.

But recently it had been whispered that Elias Hackett thought to finally take a wife and that wife would be Georgiana. She didn't quell the rumors because it was ridiculous. He loved God far more than he could ever love a mere mortal woman.

Elias excused himself to speak to someone else he knew and was replaced by her aunt.

"Are you enjoying the evening, my dear?" she asked her.

"Very much."

"And your Romeo?" She nodded in Elias's direction.

"As always, more in love with God than he could ever be with me."

"That's no bad thing, Georgie." She had taken to calling her by her nickname. "All most women want is a good comfortable home and a little money. But I'm not sure he's the right man for you."

"I agree. But he's not asked me anything, and I don't think he will. He likes the company. I think he's lonely," she said with compassion. "I feel a little sorry for him."

Georgiana watched the thin, black-haired man close his eyes as the music drifted through the house and he was transported with it. She turned away from the music and the card table and gazed into the fireplace. How long ago had it been, that night in the pleasure garden? Six months ago? Together, they had looked up at the stars and the world had disappeared.

Where were they? Paris? No. Constantinople. She could hear his voice in her ear, and the words still echoed as if he had just said them. *Moan for me.* Such deliciously erotic words and she had done just that. She had felt the weight of him above her and her legs had been spread even as he—

She closed her eyes and stopped herself. Why torture herself like this? Alexander Mayson with his lopsided grin and his arrogant handsome face. She had wanted to shake his resolve. She had done so in the pagoda, but she hadn't. Not really.

Now tell me once more how I'm never going to kiss you. Tell me that these lips that I've dreamed of will never be mine. She shook her head. What a stupid fool she had been. She had been teasing and tormenting a handsome man who knew his way around women extremely well. She had started a game that could never be finished, and now she was paying the consequences in this small colonial town. Boston wasn't a savage backwater town, but it certainly wasn't London.

When another piece began on the piano, Elias came towards her. He looked pale in the candlelight but appeared in good spirits as he smiled at her. "I'm not sure if I told you but you look particularly lovely this evening," he complimented her.

She noted the glass of punch in his hand, which was laced with spirits. "I thought you don't drink alcohol."

"I don't usually, but tonight," he smiled, "I have made an exception. Tonight is a special night."

"Is it?" she asked, her eyes wide. "Why is it special?"

He took her by the hand and led her down the long hallway and into the small back parlor. "I have made a decision." He cleared his throat. "A momentous decision!"

"Pray tell, what it is, Mr. Hackett?"

"Can you not guess?" His eyes were wide with delight. "Do you not know?"

"I'm at a loss." And she was.

He licked his lips. "I have decided at long last to take a wife."

Georgiana frowned. "A wife? This is news!"

"My dear. The lord tells us it is not good for man to be alone. I will make a helper suitable for him, he said." He nodded vigorously. "And that is what you are, my dear. Extremely suitable. You are virtuous, kind, and beautiful." He said the last word in a whisper, ogling her breasts.

"Mr. Hackett, am I to understand you are asking me to marry you?" she asked, bewildered that he was contemplating marriage and with her.

No," he said sharply, shaking his head. "No, my dear. That is not the proper way. I must approach your uncle, as your father is not here."

"My uncle?"

"For permission, of course. And then," his face was a wreath of smiles, "then you will be mine."

"Mr. Hackett, I – " Georgiana looked wildly about her, but they were quite alone.

Georgiana was genuinely shocked. She liked Elias Hackett, though he was extremely religious, and she had never met another man so God-fearing. But his words caught her off guard. She had heard the rumors but had never believed them. She had never thought the quiet timid man would want to marry, and she had not encouraged him. She was truly at a loss for words.

"Mistress Gainsford." He suddenly bowed over her hand. "I find myself overwhelmed tonight with the drink and your beauty. I must take my leave. Please know I am earnest. Until next time we meet." He took her hand in his and kissed the back of it.

She could feel the warmth of his mouth on her hand, and a small amount of saliva remained on her skin, which repelled her. Georgiana watched as the man left the room, leaving her behind with a stunned feeling.

―――― *ele* ――――

"He proposed?" Arabella repeated, looking at her husband and then her niece. "He actually proposed? Richard! Come here!" she called out to her husband.

They had just entered the home of her aunt and uncle when Georgiana told her aunt the news.

"What is it?" He entered, concerned. "What's happened?"

"Elias Hackett has proposed to her!" Arabella told her husband.

"Hackett?" Richard wondered.

"Well, he didn't actually propose," Georgiana recalled. "His exact words were that he must approach you, Uncle Richard, as my father is not here to ask for permission."

"Hmmm," came Richard's cool reply.

"You don't approve?" Georgiana asked him.

"Hackett is well enough, my dear. He's solemn and quiet. Which, in itself, is not a bad thing. But I don't think he's a good match for you," he said simply.

"I entirely agree, Georgiana." Her aunt nodded. "He may be God-fearing and polite, but that won't make a marriage. He's not for you."

"He'll be coming to see you shortly, Uncle Richard. To ask for your permission as he said," she told him. Richard rolled his eyes. "I would not like you to give an answer right away. I want time to think. He's not a bad man. He's just not . . ." Georgiana searched for the right words.

"Not?" Arabella asked.

"He's never asked me much about myself. He's never asked about my life in England, my family, my likes, my dislikes. He's wholly absorbed in his Bible, and maybe I shouldn't expect – " She was looking for the right word.

"What, my darling?" Arabella wondered.

Georgiana couldn't put her finger on it and then she knew. Fireworks. Passion. Excitement. She wanted that. She wanted –

No! She wouldn't say his name.

"I would like some time to think on it," she said simply. "That is all."

"And you shall have all the time you want, Georgiana," her uncle said kindly and kissed her cheek. "A marriage. A husband. That's entirely up to you. It's a very important decision. If you don't want Hackett, then that's all that needs to be said. I tell you that, and I will tell him that."

"Thank you. Both of you. For your kindness to me," she told them sincerely before she slipped upstairs to her room.

Upstairs, Georgiana gave thought to the odd proposal. She had spent time with Elias, and he was a quiet man absorbed in his religious works. She was quite surprised he had chosen her, as they had very little in common. They never talked about much else beyond his biblical passages and his thoughts on them. She let him speak and quote, and she listened.

She had become a mute thing around him, and she viewed him as a calming acquaintance, but that was all. Perhaps that was exactly why he had chosen her. He thought her meek and demure, and that attracted him. She would give it some thought, but she knew he was not the man she would marry. She would have to be delicate and polite but kindly refuse his proposal.

True to his word, Elias Hackett came to the Wilkinson house the next day to speak to Richard. Richard was cordial but very clear that the choice of husband was entirely Georgiana's. He would not stand in his way nor would he bar the man from his niece but it was her choice.

"You understand that my family is extremely wealthy," Elias had stated, straightening his slim frame in the chair. "She would want for nothing."

"I understand."

"She would be a welcome addition to our family and the name Hackett. I think Georgiana Hackett has a lovely ring to it." Elias smiled. Richard said nothing. "I would – I would like a child with her within the year." He took out a handkerchief and dabbed at his mouth.

Richard realized with horror the man was drooling over his niece. By all the saints!

"Certainly, children and procreation are normal occurrences in a marriage," Richard added.

"Exactly. And she is so – so lovely," Elias stuttered. "Such beauty."

"My niece has been blessed with much favor." Richard nodded, standing up to alert the other man that the interview was at an end.

"I am looking forward to setting a wedding date in the very near future," Elias said, nodding vigorously. "And then the honeymoon. I have not yet decided if I prefer –"

"As I said, Mr. Hackett," Richard said, cutting him off, "my niece has yet to make up her mind."

"Of course! Of course! Women like to draw out these things to incite our passions." Elias giggled as Richard looked over the middle-aged man.

Richard doubted very much that many women had ever sought to inflame Elias Hackett's passions.

"Thank you for your time." Elias shook the other man's hand.

As Richard walked him out into the foyer, he heard Elias speaking lowly and turned to him.

"A spring wedding is best," Elias mumbled, mostly to himself, but looked up suddenly at Richard. "Or maybe summer? Summer when everything is –"

"Good day to you, sir." Richard closed the door behind him.

Picking up the mail that had been left in the foyer for him, he sorted through it quickly and saw a letter addressed to him from the governor. He sliced the letter open and groaned. Jesus! What a nuisance.

Seated at dinner that evening, Richard shared his conversation with the eager to-be bridegroom.

"I've left it up to you, my dear," Richard said as he enjoyed the warm squash soup on the cool winter evening. "Whatever you wish, we will support you."

"Thank you, Uncle Richard," Georgiana said gratefully.

"And as I was showing Elias out, the mail arrived," he said, pushing forth a letter. "From the governor."

"Troublesome news?" Arabella asked.

"More of a burden," Richard said. "There is a viscount from London coming to the colonies. The governor has asked that we avail him of our home, as we have the rooms and our home is quite exceptional. Those were his exact words."

Arabella beamed. "Our home is quite exceptional."

"And a viscount no less," Georgiana teased her aunt.

Richard picked up the letter and read it over quickly. "Viscount Lichfield. Does that name ring a bell, Georgiana?"

"No. It does not."

"Apparently he has business to discuss with the governor, and as our home is one of the most distinguished in the city, he asks that we supply him rooms for his stay." Richard shook his head. "Quite a bother."

"But no, my dear!" Arabella disagreed. "If this viscount is coming here for business and if the business is successful, then that reflects well on you. Doesn't it, husband?"

Richard touched her hand on the table. "You are correct, my dear. It will reflect well on us."

"How many people is the viscount bringing with him? We might need to prepare more than one room," Georgiana directed to her aunt.

"The letter didn't say," Richard noted.

"Then we should prepare at least another room for a valet or his wife." Arabella nodded. "An excellent point, Georgie."

"When is the viscount arriving?" Georgiana asked, picking at her food.

"He should be here in two weeks," he informed them.

"We should plan some events for him," Arabella pondered. "Perhaps a ball and a small supper party in his honor."

"I'll be happy to help you plan, Aunt Bella," Georgiana said, her eyes heavy. "I'll retire for the evening if you don't mind."

When she had gone upstairs, Richard looked over at his wife. "I'm not at all sure about Hackett." He shook his head. "He seems quite taken with Georgiana."

"I don't think he's the right man for her either," she agreed with her husband.

"Georgiana has a good head on her shoulders. She'll give the proposal much thought before she agrees. I've no doubt," Richard pointed out.

"Absolutely. Georgiana is no fool. She'll make the right decision."

The next evening, they attended a small soiree at a neighbor's home. Several young women she had met since her time in Boston nodded to her, and one young woman came to stand beside her at the buffet table. Sallie Elkin was the daughter of a young lawyer who was friends with Richard. She was fair, freckled, and timid. She viewed Georgiana as a wild untamed thing, and when she spoke, her eyes were always wide.

"Good evening," she said softly.

"Good evening," Georgiana returned.

She looked down at Georgiana's empty plate. "Do you not care for the venison?"

"I'm not that hungry," she admitted.

"I'm always hungry." She smiled, revealing her dimpled cheeks. "My mother says I eat enough for two boys."

Georgiana looked over at the two card tables set up and saw her aunt at one table and her uncle at the other.

"My father doesn't approve of cards," Sallie said in a whisper.

"No?" Georgiana said. "My father doesn't approve of anything but loves cards."

Elias Hackett rose from his place on the sofa and came towards them. "Mistress Gainsford, Mistress Elkin," he acknowledged both women. "Would you care to take a stroll with me?" he directed at Georgiana.

Together they walked through the small house and to a little garden that was no more than a patch of grass and a bush. It was nothing much to behold, but the air was refreshing.

"I've spoken to your uncle," he told her hurriedly. "I'm ready to set the date. I'll write to my mother in England. She's not well so she won't be here for the ceremony, but she'll give us her blessing."

"Mr. Hackett," Georgiana began. "You have not even asked me yet. Never mind my uncle."

"Well, your uncle was agreeable to the marriage," he interrupted her. "I spoke to him and we even discussed the month to get married." He reached out to touch her arm and shivered.

Georgiana frowned. "Are you unwell, Mr. Hackett?"

He cleared his throat. "You are so lovely, my dear, that when I touch your skin, it quite overwhelms me."

"Mr. Hackett. I did speak with my uncle, and he has told me that the final decision is mine. So, you must give me time. I won't take long to decide," she assured him.

"A simple church affair will be best," he spoke to her. "And our home will be the flat I currently reside in. It's very comfortable. It's in a boardinghouse run by a godly woman—"

"You won't want to move to a larger house?" she wondered at him.

"A larger house?" He seemed mystified, then he grinned. "Ah, yes! A larger house indeed. With more bedrooms and a nursery." He spoke the last word shyly. "I will have to ask my mother for more money for such an expense."

Georgiana wondered where the conversation was going.

"I told your uncle I want a child within the year," he said. "A child between you and I . . ." He licked his lips again. "You and I –"

Georgiana felt a little uneasy at his words and mannerisms but instead she said, "I think that any children in a marriage are in God's hands. No?"

"Oh, no! You're quite wrong there, my dear. A virtuous, good woman would be the exact tonic for children. You will ensure we have strong sons." He nodded and licked his lips again. "Strong sons," he murmured.

"We should get back," she said quickly.

That night, Georgiana tossed and turned. She dreamt of Elias Hackett pulling her into his arms and kissing her. His kiss was dry, and when she tried to pull away from him, he held her tightly against his slim body. When she heard him chuckling, she pulled away, only to see the man who held her was Alexander Mayson.

On his face was a sardonic smile, and his eyes held a quiet blue fire. He pressed her against the wall, and they were once more in the dimly lit theater hallway. He spread her legs apart as she wrapped them about his waist like that woman in the pagoda did. Her sighs filled the hallway. Then the scenery changed.

He was holding her down on the bed, and she was looking up at him. Why did he look so handsome and so exciting? Why did she want him so badly? And in a second, his features changed. It was Elias Hackett holding her down, and as he grinned down at her, spittle from his drooling lips fell onto her cheek. He was using his legs to press hers apart, even as she told him to stop. Stop. Stop!

She finally scrambled away from him, and when she looked back at the bed, it was once more Alexander's handsome face. He held out his hand to her. When she took a step towards him, he lashed out, and the bony grip that held her was Elias.

"We'll be married soon," he swore to her. "I want sons. Strong sons. Strong sons."

Strong sons, strong sons, strong sons echoed in her ear.

She woke up in a cold sweat and shivered in the night air. What did it mean?

Chapter 10

THE NEXT WEEK, AS Georgiana and Arabella paid calls and attended different private parties, the buzz among everyone was the impending arrival of the English viscount. The young ladies gossiped behind their fans and hoped he would be handsome and unmarried, and the men hoped over smoking and brandy that he would be good for business. Georgiana hoped to make a good impression for her uncle and that his stay would be comfortable and enjoyable.

Meanwhile, Georgiana had been thinking of Elias's proposal. She wandered about the house at twilight when the sun was setting and the rooms were orange and thought about her life. She missed London. She liked the simplicity of Boston, but she enjoyed the diversions London had to offer. She knew her aunt and uncle might return to England to visit but never to stay. Their life was in Boston.

Elias was also another colonist who now called Boston home and would not consider returning to England to live. She had asked him once, and he had been firm in his response. London was a den of sinners. She surmised that sin could exist anywhere, be it Boston or London. But it appeared Elias did not intend to leave Boston for London.

She was looking forward to the governor's ball that evening. Her aunt had confirmed that it was a lavish event that reminded her of the balls of London when she had been a debutante. Georgiana stepped into her gown, which was a yellowish gold that suited her hair color and eyes. It was the last extravagant dress her father had purchased for. The square neckline bore no lace and was daring even for England. Georgiana didn't care. She adored the dress, and its simple cut showed off her trim figure and breasts.

"That color is superb on you!" Arabella said admiringly.

Her uncle nodded, saying she was a "picture."

Her aunt had chosen a gown of silver and red, while her uncle looked dignified in a chocolate-colored jacket and breeches. When they arrived at the mansion for the party that evening, Georgiana could hear the orchestra playing and smiled as she was helped down from the coach.

"It's all so beautiful!" She admired the torches that lit up the drive and the flowers that seemed to decorate the mansion at every turn.

Governor Shute was not married but had an eye for the ladies. As he saw the threesome arrive, he nodded in their direction and first took Arabella's hand in his to kiss and then Georgiana's.

"The fairest in the land," he said fondly to Georgiana and winked at Richard.

"She's a jewel," her uncle said in agreement.

"She is that," Samuel agreed. "You ladies enjoy the refreshments and food. We'll have dancing later."

A footman passed by with champagne, and they each took a glass.

"It is a glorious evening, Georgie," her aunt said. "I don't think I've ever said it outright, but I am so glad you have come to us."

"As am I." She smiled at them both. "The best thing my father did was bring us together."

She sipped on her champagne and spotted her new friend Sallie, as well as Elias dressed in black, looking lost and forlorn. His eyes lit up immediately when he saw her. He rushed to her side, glowing with pride.

"Mistress Gainsford!" he said deferentially, nodding to her aunt and uncle. "What a pleasure to see you!"

"Mr. Hackett," Georgiana acknowledged him.

"I had thought not to come tonight," he informed them. "I was feeling a little unwell. My stomach gives me problems from time to time."

"Nothing serious?" Arabella asked him.

"No indeed. My mother has several recipes that soothe my stomach, which I will give to Mistress Gainsford to make for me once we are married," he explained in detail, and his words irked her.

She frowned and looked over at her uncle, who raised an eyebrow and looked distinctly at Elias and then back at her. She stifled a laugh and maintained a serious face in front of him.

When her aunt and uncle moved away, Elias stood next to her.

"Will you dance this evening?" she asked him.

"No, my dear. I think not. *Run from anything that stimulates youthful lusts. Instead, pursue righteous living, faithfulness, love, and peace*," he quoted to her.

She sighed inwardly. The dance barely allowed hand holding so she doubted it would stimulate anything, but she nodded at him.

She sipped the champagne until it was gone and picked up another glass. The music was a beautiful piece, though she couldn't name it. She looked through the sea of people and saw several familiar faces. Boston was not nearly as large as London's metropolis, and Georgiana saw the same people at many of the parties she attended. The candlelight shed soft light on the assembled group, and as she sipped her drink, she saw a man at the far end of the corner.

He was impeccably dressed in a suit of grey silk with embroidered silver thread and a simple powdered white wig with his hair pulled back. He looked remarkably familiar, and her heart skipped a beat. Alexander! She laughed a little to herself and looked down into the glass. Preposterous. Alexander was no more here than the King of France.

When she looked up again, the man had vanished into the sea of faces. She drew a finger along the edge of the glass. How many soirees and balls and parties would she attend this month? The next? What was the point of it all? What was she doing here? Maybe her father had been right all along. She should have married some Englishman and been content to live in the country somewhere, raising children and putting on weight.

"My dear, do you care for some air?" Elias asked her quietly. "We could speak privately."

Georgiana had no wish to be alone with him at this moment. She preferred to be looking up at the stars, imagining she was someone else in the world, but she allowed herself to be led. The garden here was much grander than any she had seen so far, with a small rose garden, a shrubbery, and a little maze. They walked through the maze and only made three turns before it was complete.

The lanterns outside were brightly lit, and they passed another couple out taking in the air.

"Most charming, is it not?" Elias nodded, and his face looked flushed.

"It is," she said as they each took a seat on the small wooden bench near the maze.

"I have thought much on what you said about a house for us, and I think that is correct," he agreed. "I will ask Mother to send money for something small yet adequate."

"Mr. Hackett, I have not given you my answer – " Georgiana began.

"Mistress Gainsford!" he interrupted her. "I know that you will make me happy. I have given it much thought, and your beauty is beyond compare!"

"I understand that, Mr. Hackett, but– "

"But, my dear," his voice turned serious, "I must speak with you of the most importance. This dress you are wearing, it's not suitable. The neckline is too – too . . . You can see far too much of your person." He swallowed visibly. "I understand in London this may be the fashion but in Boston . . ." He stopped. "Men will lust after you!" he said with finality.

Georgiana shook his head. "Please, Mr. Hackett – "

"No, they will! Men are the lowest creatures. Men are base and vile." He licked his lips as he looked at her breasts. "Women have the power to drive them mad. Drive us mad!" he said softly, and then suddenly without warning, he pulled her into his arms. "Mistress!" He groaned loudly in her ear and placed a sloppy kiss on her cheek as she tried to evade his touch.

"Elias!" she cried out in irritation and pressed against his bony chest to be released.

"I'm sorry. I seem to have intruded on a lovers' tryst," a cool voice came from the dark garden.

Elias sprang from Georgiana's side as he tried to compose himself before the stranger. "I – I lost my head for a moment. My darling and I were talking, and the moonlight swept us up." He shook his head. "I will compose myself, my dear, and return when I am more myself." He left quickly, muttering under his breath, "*For the mind that is set on the flesh is hostile to God.*"

As Elias rushed back to the house, Georgiana faced the interloper whose face was shrouded in darkness.

"Ah," the man said suddenly, coming into the lantern light. "Now I see why he lost his head. A woman so beautiful with emerald-colored eyes, one might even call her a temptress."

Georgiana stood up abruptly as the man came towards her. "It can't be you!" she whispered. Her heart thudded inside her breast. "It can't be."

Alexander's face turned into a mocking smile as he looked her up and down. "Did you think I had died? Did you want me dead? I assure you I'm very much alive, Georgiana."

"Why – why are you here? What are you doing in Boston?" She frowned.

"Ah, Boston. That's such a long story, and I have all the time in the world to tell it," he said.

Georgiana narrowed her eyes. Anger and hate for him flared inside her. He was the reason for her exile. "You don't need to play your games, Alexander. Just say you're here for business. What could be simpler?"

"What indeed?" He looked at her intently. "Perhaps I'm here to remedy what I would have done six months ago had you not slunk off in the middle of the night."

"Slunk off in the middle of the night?" she repeated furiously. "You dare to tell me that! You! After what you did that caused me to be exiled!"

"What did I do?" he said innocently.

"You know very well what you did!" She bristled, her cheeks heated and flushed.

"I'm at a loss," he said, his eyes wide.

"That night at the Hall." She looked around. "In the bedroom." She whispered the last part and Alexander was completely mesmerized by her lips."

"Oh, that."

Georgiana narrowed her eyes. "Oh, that? Oh, *that* caused me to be sent to the colonies for punishment when I was wholly innocent!"

"Wholly innocent?" Alexander bit back a laugh. "Didn't you bite me in the neck that night?"

Georgiana blushed deeper. "I don't recall - "

"Don't recall? Didn't you tease me that night and at the pleasure garden in the pagoda," he reminded her.

Georgiana shook her head. "I didn't say I –"

"You just said you were wholly innocent!" he pointed out.

"Very well. I teased you. It was in the wrong," she admitted.

Alexander nodded. "And that last night in the Hall, we did so little really – "

"You conceited ape! What you did to me . . ." She struggled to find the words.

"Yes?"

"You touched me . . ." She met his blue eyes in the night.

He waited.

"Have you forgotten?" she said, changing tactics.

"There are many things I've forgotten, Georgiana, but that night," he came closer to her, "holding you in my arms, hearing you moan in my ear, that's something I'll never forget."

"To speak aloud these things." She shook her head. "You're more arrogant than the last time I met you."

"I have changed in some respects," he admitted.

"The worst respects." She rolled her eyes.

"And here I travel all this way to Boston to find you in the arms of another man being made love to –" He waved a hand at the bench where they had been sitting.

"He wasn't!" Georgiana denied hotly.

"It looked as if he was," Alexander pointed out.

"No," Georgiana defended. "And since you seem so concerned with my affairs, Elias Hackett has asked me to marry him." She raised an eyebrow in defiance.

"I know."

She frowned. "You know? How do you know?"

"Apparently you and the reformed bachelor are all Boston cares about at the moment." He shrugged nonchalantly.

"That's absurd."

"It's the truth." He took a step towards her and caught a curl of her long hair lying over her chest and picked it up, his fingers brushing the tip of her breast.

"Don't." She backed away from him.

He nodded and moved past her, looking at the small, pristine garden. "I didn't know that you had been sent to the colonies," he said in a serious tone. "You recall that you never told me the consequence your father had placed upon you."

"Would it have mattered?" She faced him squarely. "What difference would it have made? I would still be here in the colonies, exiled, and you free to do as you wish."

"You're angry at me," he guessed.

She met his gaze. "I was. But then I realized much of this was inevitable. My father had given me an ultimatum long ago, and I never would do what he asked. So, I'm here, out of the way in Boston, and he can live his life as he pleases."

"What ultimatum?" he wondered.

"He wanted me to marry, and I don't think he cared much to whom, just that I did."

"Would he be pleased with Elias Hackett as a son-in-law?" he asked.

"At least Mr. Hackett is an honorable man with honorable intentions!" she flared at him.

He scoffed. "Honorable?"

"He's asked me to marry him. He wants me as his wife. All you ever did –" She stopped.

"All I ever did?" he pressed.

"All you ever did was try and seduce me with no thought of consequences. But then as a man, you have none," she recalled.

"I have consequences," he murmured softly.

"I doubt it. I must return to the party. I only came out here because Elias asked me to," she told him. She went to move past him but he grabbed her arm.

"Georgiana," he said.

She looked up into his face. "Alexander. We needn't be enemies, but I think the less time we spend in each other's company, the better," she said coolly. "You are here on business. I wish you much success." She moved past him and went back to the house.

Alexander watched her walk back into the house and felt an exhilaration he hadn't felt in six months. He had spent the last four months taking care of his family's affairs and readying himself to make the trip to Boston. He wanted Georgiana Gainsford for himself, and nothing on earth would stop that. Soon after he discovered she had been shipped off to Massachusetts, he had realized that he was consumed with thoughts of her.

Her eyes, her smile, her tartness, everything about her seemed to follow him wherever he went. He had tried to reconcile with Philippine, but it had been a disaster. They had slept together one final time, and he had groaned in frustration. He wanted Georgiana. He wanted her as his wife, and he would stop at nothing to make that happen.

Seeing her in the arms of another man had been torture. He knew Georgiana would attract attention wherever she went. She was such a unique and lovely woman, and it was inevitable. What he hadn't imagined was the pure hatred that had flowed into him at the sight. The strong desire to do bodily harm to the supposed fiancé had been so visceral it shocked him. He had never felt such a raw, intense emotion before.

The rake in him wanted to find a secluded room and force her into it. It wouldn't take long for him to part those slim legs and then she would be his. Then she would have to marry him. He wouldn't give a damn about the scandal as long as she was his. But he wouldn't. He would bide his time. He would seduce her. He would leave Boston after his business was concluded, and he had already decided that Georgiana would be with him.

***

As Georgiana picked up the ladle to pour herself a glass of punch, her hand was trembling. She glanced behind her but he was not there. Alexander Mayson! That man was at the heart of all her problems. She didn't like seeing him again. In his silk clothes and his powdered wig, he looked like a stranger. He looked so refined and removed. But underneath the clothes was a vibrant, handsome man who was too damn sure of himself. She drank the punch in one gulp, and it burned her throat.

The hell with him. Outside of this ball, there was no need for her to cross paths with him again. She resolved to do just that.

"My dear." Her aunt came into the room and helped herself to a glass. "Here you are. I've been looking everywhere for you."

"Mr. Hackett and I were in the garden."

"Oh, yes? Have you decided then?" Her aunt took a sip of the potent punch.

"Not quite."

"Well, come with me. We've quite a surprise for you. Your Uncle has a particular guest he would like you to meet," she said happily. "It's the viscount! He's come early!"

Her aunt pulled her along the ballroom floor, and standing near the orchestra was her uncle, the governor, and a man with his back to her.

"Ah, here she is!" the governor said fondly. "The jewel of Boston."

Georgiana warmed at the compliment.

"Georgiana, I would like to introduce you to our very special guest, newly arrived from London. Viscount Lichfield," he said smoothly. "Georgiana Gainsford, this is Viscount Lichfield."

The man in the silk grey suit turned to face her, and her smile faded from her face.

"Mademoiselle," Alexander said as he kissed her hand.

She struggled not to snatch her hand away. "Lord Lichfield," she whispered, looking at the people forming a circle around them.

What game is he playing now?

"Please. You must call me Alexander. Lord Lichfield sounds very formal here in the colonies." He smiled at those surrounding them.

"I can tell, Lichfield, with all the eligible ladies in the room, you will not lack for company whilst here." The governor winked as her aunt and her uncle smiled.

"At the moment, I only desire to dance the minuet, if Mademoiselle Gainsford would agree?" he asked politely.

"Of course, she will!" her aunt said, pressing Georgiana forward as she was about to decline.

Georgiana placed her hand on his forearm as he led her out onto the dance floor. She was not immune to the stares of everyone in the ballroom as they watched her being led out.

"Lord Lichfield?" she questioned in disbelief as the music began. "A viscount?"

"Afraid so." He nodded as she placed her hand in his as they stepped together in unison in the dance.

She wondered at his gall. "You think because you're in the colonies people don't write letters to England? That we don't hear news of what's happening there? How long do you intend this charade to continue?" They moved in a circle, facing each other, holding onto one hand.

"Not long."

She performed the steps as required, trying not to watch Alexander. He was nimble on his feet and held the beat well as many other men did not. He also looked different. His clothes looked expensive and were silk, and she never recalled him wearing a wig in London.

"Something has changed about you," she noted, watching him carefully.

"Do you think so?" He took both her hands in his as they moved around in a circle.

"I do." She felt the warmth of his hands as he held hers.

"What would that be?" They moved apart. He bowed to her, and she curtseyed to him.

"I'm not sure. There's just something different about you," she whispered.

He didn't say much more, but he relished the feel of her hand in his and watching her face in the candlelight. When the dance was over, he was sorry to relinquish her.

"Dearest." Elias came to her side once the dance ended. "You will forgive me for the garden. I had one drink this evening and it went to my head."

Georgiana smiled at his words but inwardly cringed. Why was he being so loud and talking about the garden? One sloppy kiss on the cheek did not reel her senses. "Mr. Hackett, please do not trouble yourself."

"I don't feel well," he said suddenly. "My head and stomach. I think something did not agree with me. They both ache."

"Let me walk to your coach," she said helpfully. "It will take you home."

"Such a comfort." He nodded meekly. "Already the model wife."

Georgiana hated to admit that she only wanted him gone so she wouldn't have to suffer his constant attention and whining.

When he was settled in the coach, she smiled kindly at him. "Rest yourself."

"Thank you, my dear," he said, touching her hand.

The coach moved down the lane and she turned back towards the governor's house. Alexander was leaning against a pillar. She felt a tug in her breast at his handsome beauty and narrowed her eyes as she came towards him.

"Did you need something, *Lord* Lichfield?" she asked him formally.

"Hmmm." He nodded. "As a matter of fact, I wondered, the Wilkinsons. Your aunt and uncle?" he asked her quietly.

"My Aunt Arabella is my father's sister," she confirmed.

"Ah, yes. I was just curious because the governor told me I would be staying in their home." He brushed a speck of nonexistent list from his sleeve. "I was most pleased to hear that their house is quite impressive."

Georgiana's eyes widened as she realized. "My God! You're staying with us! You know I live there too! Did you plan this?" She came up the steps to him to be on the same level. "Did you?"

"Plan what?" he asked, his eyes wide.

"Plan this! Stay in their home. Close to me –" She was rambling.

"Close to you? What am I going to do? Seduce the niece of the couple I'm enjoying their hospitality while also doing business with Wilkinson?" He grinned.

"I wouldn't put it past you."

"Honestly, Georgie. Their last name is Wilkinson. Yours is Gainsford. I didn't know there was a relation, and the accommodations were made by the governor, not me," he said simply. "And you will recall I didn't know you had been shipped here until this evening."

Though he had been able to discover she had been sent to Boston before he arrived, the arrangement to stay with the Wilkinsons, her family, had been entirely coincidental.

"I don't believe anything that comes out of your mouth," she said coldly.

"Are you going to lock your door at night to keep me out?" he said lowly, teasing her.

She felt her heart race. "I'll put a chair against the door at the very least."

"A chair? Do you think that will stop me?" he wondered, and she didn't miss his teasing tone and the grin on his face.

"You're wasting your time with me, Lord Lichfield," she said coolly, meeting his eyes. "If I accept Elias's proposal, then I am to be a married woman."

"That's very true, Miss Gainsford," he said, assessing her. "But – "

"But?" she asked sharply.

"You aren't married yet." He spoke the words one at a time and then turned back into the house.

Scoundrel! She hissed.

Returning to the ballroom, Alexander took up a glass of champagne and drank it down. It wasn't as strong as gin, but it would do.

Richard came up to him and patted him on the back. "Are you enjoying the society, Lichfield? I'm sure it's nothing compared to London."

"I wouldn't say that, some things are most comparable," he said warmly as his eyes rested on Georgiana, who had joined another partner on the dance floor.

"Georgiana, my niece." He nodded, seeing the direction of his gaze. "She's greatly admired here."

"With good reason," Alexander allowed. "She's quite lovely."

"She is. And though I have recently been approached for her hand, she has not accepted as of yet," he informed the man.

"Elias Hackett?" Alexander asked. "I had heard of the proposal."

"A good man," Richard said slowly. "Devoted to his church and God –"

"Admirable," Alexander agreed but felt Richard was holding back, though he did not elaborate.

"My niece and wife have spent the last week readying your room to make it comfortable and planning events for you to enjoy." Richard touched Alexander on the shoulder in a friendly gesture. "You have the choicest room in the house, one that overlooks the garden."

"That is most generous." Alexander nodded.

"And a ball in your honor next week," he mentioned. "Although we didn't expect you so soon."

"I arrived a few days early," he said. "The journey was not as arduous as anticipated."

Alexander was not immune to the hot looks directed his way from the young women and their mothers. As an Englishman, and now a viscount, he was a catch equal to the golden calf. Though he had no desire to be captured by anyone here.

Georgiana curtsied to her dance partner at the end of the dance, and another man quickly took the first man's place. The second man was younger than the first and seemed to be drowning in her emerald eyes. Alexander knew the feeling.

"What business brings you to Boston?" Richard asked.

"Import and export back to the king." Alexander nodded as Arabella joined him. "Expansion of my shipping line which I own."

"You are such a welcome addition to our little town," she told him. "I'm so happy my husband and I were able to accommodate you. You don't have anyone else in your party?"

"My valet fell ill before the journey and so I am a lonely party of one," he said.

"Party of one, but from the looks of the women here, you need not be lonely," Richard teased him.

They chuckled at the joke as Alexander bowed to them and moved along the room. How often had he thought of this moment? Once he discovered she was in Boston, he had made arrangements to travel here after his family situation had been handled. The arrangements with the governor had been secured when he asked to stay with a prominent family. He knew the chances of staying with hers were high.

He was not surprised to learn that she was on the verge of accepting a proposal, only the man himself was surprising. He was very dour and severe and didn't seem a match for the high-spirited green-eyed witch.

He had not expected her to welcome him with open arms but she was like a stranger with him. She was cool and aloof, and he knew she must have suffered from being so harshly removed from her home land and relocated to Boston. As he watched her move about the room, a familiar tug and pull filled him. He wanted her. He ached for her. How many nights had he woken in a similar state, damp from the sweat of another erotic dream?

Once, he had even disgraced himself by waking up to find he had ejaculated in his sleep. It was only once he had made up his mind to travel to Boston to make Georgiana his that he had found some semblance of peace.

Chapter 11

AS THE PARTY WAS winding down, Georgiana's toes were pinching from the dancing, and as much as she longed to stay, she wished for her bed as well. Her aunt and uncle, who wanted to stay, had urged her to leave. Alexander, hearing the conversation, had offered politely to see her home.

Georgiana turned and eyed him suspiciously. "There's no need, Lord Lichfield. I don't want to impose. I can see myself – "

"Nonsense!" Arabella nodded. "That's perfect! You can both go on home, and Georgie will show you where everything is, Lord Lichfield. We'll be fine and you'll be in safe hands."

Georgiana cringed at the thought of the short ride home with Alexander, but as she pulled her cape about her, she realized she was being ridiculous. The man was not going to pounce on her.

In the short ride home, she could feel his warm eyes on her, but he said nothing. As they exited the coach, the red brick home rose up to meet them. It was a handsome house even in the dark, and she was proud of it.

"Let me show you to your room," she said quietly in the dark foyer.

The servants were long asleep, and her aunt had asked her to help. Her aunt and uncle never had the servants wait up for them when they attended a party that would be late. She went up the grand staircase and into the hallway on the second floor. His soft footsteps followed her.

She opened the last door on the right, and he followed her inside. Moonlight streamed in from outside, as the curtains over the windows had not been drawn. She moved to close the curtains on the windows, plunging them into darkness.

"Oh," she said, staring at him from across the room. Her eyes darted to the large bed, but he moved to the fireplace and threw several logs on the fire that were beside it.

Besides the four-poster bed, the room had a writing desk and chair, a chest of drawers, and an armoire. It was a comfortable room, and soon, the fire began to burn brightly.

"Do you require anything else before I retire?"

"Stay with me awhile," he said softly, his words almost a caress.

"Why?" she asked warily.

"I want to talk," he said easily, his tone even and smooth.

"At two in the morning?" She narrowed her eyes at him.

"Are you tired?" he wondered.

"It isn't that," she explained, her eyes searching for his. "I don't want you to get the wrong impression."

"What impression would I get?" He frowned.

"I'm in your room. Your bedroom. At night."

"We were in a bedroom once before." His words were so simple, yet said so much.

"That won't be repeated," she stated firmly.

He nodded. "I see. I only wanted to talk with you, but since you are set against it," he shook his head, "I'll bid you a good night."

She gave him an assessing look and then took the seat before the writing desk and turned the chair to face him. "Very well. What would you have us speak of?"

She settled demurely in the chair. What wouldn't he give to take the few steps to her, cup her face oval-shaped in his hands, and taste her lips? His soul? Maybe. Her eyes glittered in the dark as she waited. Great. Now he had a hard-on that was best not to be seen.

He took a seat at the small bench at the edge of the bed, facing her. "Have you enjoyed your time here? It's your first time, is it not?"

"It is."

"Is it what you expected?"

"In some ways, yes. In others, no. I do miss London and all the diversions," she admitted.

"So many diversions." He nodded.

"And you? You want to tell me about this pretense of Lord Lichfield? Or did your shipping line become so lucrative you purchased a title?" she said tartly.

"I guess we never spoke of it," he realized. "I'm the second son of the Earl of Lichfield. My family never regarded me as that important, and it's the reason I became a privateer and then started the shipping line."

"Second son?" she asked.

"Not long after you left, my father and brother were traveling on the Continent and contracted some foreign disease." He shrugged lightly. "They were both dead within a week."

"Oh, Alexander." She came towards him and was suddenly seated beside him. "Forgive me. I was unnecessarily harsh. I had no idea. I didn't know your family background."

He looked down at their hands as she covered his with hers. "My brother left no issue. He was about to be married, but the marriage had not occurred. I inherited it all. The title, the lands, the wealth. All of it," he said unemotionally.

"I would give you my congratulations, but under those circumstances . . ." Her words trailed off.

"No, don't." He threaded his fingers with hers. "I was never close to my father or brother, but I never wanted them dead. I had made my way in the world, and this new one . . ." He shook his head. "It barely makes sense to me."

"Surely you can continue with the shipping line?" she asked softly. "You've built it up. It's the reason you're here."

"It is. And I do but I'm honestly not sure," he told her. "The estate is immense and requires constant attention."

She pulled her hands from his. "So, you have numerous decisions to make."

"Numerous," he said, watching her face in the firelight. "Where are we now?"

She frowned. "Where are we now?"

"Constantinople?" He smiled lightly. "Still there?"

She shook her head. "Florence."

"Florence." He nodded in agreement. "Do you like it very much?"

"I've never been," she confessed.

"You should go."

"On my honeymoon?" she asked suddenly.

"Ah, the honeymoon with Mr. Hackett."

"He did propose."

"Which you aren't honestly considering," he said frankly.

"Why do you say that?"

"Because you would have said yes already if you really wanted to marry him."

"I'm giving it much thought," she said, taking her hands into her lap. "It's a very important decision."

"It is. You should think about it." She stood up and he did as well. "Let me see you to your room," he offered.

"And then I walk you back to yours?" She bit back a smile.

"We could go on like this for some time."

"Eventually we'll get tired," she pointed out. "How long will you be staying with us?"

"Several weeks." He contemplated her. "Perhaps longer." They walked together into the hallway as he followed her. "The Lichfield estate is vast. So many now look to me for advice and guidance. It's very draining," he confided to her.

"From what I know of you, Alexander, I think you'll be very suited to the task."

He was taken aback by her words. "Do you think so?"

"I do. You seem extremely competent."

He felt a rush of warmth at her words. She thought well of him.

"This is my room," she said at the door two down from his.

"Tonight has not turned out as I expected," he said softly. "But seeing you again, Georgiana . . ." He couldn't find the words.

She nodded. "Good night, Alexander."

"Good night."

Once inside her room, Georgiana leaned against the door, her heart pounding inside her chest. She had tried to behave normally and not seem surprised, but she had been shocked to see Alexander that evening. Handsome, seductive Alexander. When she saw him, it brought back all the memories she had of him. That night in the pagoda when she taunted him. Their very last night together at Clyvedon Hall.

She could still imagine his body covering hers and his fingers inside her as she moaned so obscenely into his ear. She closed her eyes in shame. She had been consumed by him. She knew that had Mariah not come into the room that night, she would have given Alexander anything he wanted.

But she had come into the room, and they had been separated. She had been filled with bitterness at him, and the ship ride to Boston had been a tempest at sea and in her heart. But seeing him again, all these months later, there was no denying the attraction.

Her hand strayed to the doorknob behind her. There was no lock. She knew he would not sneak into her room in the middle of the night. Alexander might corner her in a dark room or garden, pull her into his arms, and kiss her, but she knew she must maintain distance. There was no future with Alexander. He was a fire in her blood, and she needed a calming force.

Alexander returned to his room, stripped down naked, and climbed into bed. Georgiana. How beautiful and self-assured she was here in Boston. He had not expected her to be so changed but she was. He guessed much of it had to do with the loving influence of her aunt and uncle and not the cold distance of her father.

The past few months had been scattered and erratic. His father and brother had died so unexpectedly, and now the entire estate fell on his shoulders. He had spent one month poring over the books of their estate and learning how it ran. The next month, he had felt as if he couldn't breathe for the weight of it all. The country was beautiful and serene, but he felt trapped.

He had dreamt of Georgiana almost every night, and when he woke in the cold mornings, he longed for her beside him. He had come to Boston to attend to several outstanding business items that needed his concern. He would be turning much of the shipping line over to a partner who would run it so he could focus on the estate.

But his true reason for coming to Boston had been Georgiana. He had longed to see her face and try to make right what had happened after Clyvedon Hall. The unexpected engagement was an irritating obstacle, but her good sense would end it.

He heard voices outside in the hallway. Arabella and Richard had returned.

Thinking of Georgiana down the hall, slipping into her bed, was torture. She was close enough to kiss and tease and far enough away that she might as well be in England. He groaned and pushed himself onto his side. He wanted her now more than he ever had before. He must plan and plot, and when the time was right, he would act. Alexander had come to Boston with one true purpose.

He wanted Georgiana as his, and he would have no other.

The next morning, Georgiana awoke to the sound of rain pelting her window. She had slept poorly and had dreamt of Alexander. It was not a dream that caused her blood to boil. She had been lost in the dark alleyways of London, and Alexander had come to her rescue. It had been a strange dream full of shadows and darkness, and when she had come upon a dead end, two strange men had been waiting for her. Alexander had swooped in to protect her against the deviants, and she had felt safe and protected in his arms.

Pulling on her wrap, she went to the window and looked out. It was an overcast day with grey clouds in the sky, and she wanted nothing more than to go back to her bed.

A knock fell on the door, and she turned with a start. Alexander! Her heart thudded inside her chest. She placed a hand to her hair and then went to answer the door. It was the maid letting her know that breakfast was to be served in half an hour. She closed the door and realized she was vastly disappointed that the maid had not been Alexander.

She must take care. Alexander was here on business and nothing else. She must be polite and cordial and treat him as a guest of the house. She must not forget the reason she was in Boston. She had teased and tormented Alexander, and he had responded. He was a rake and a cad and much better at this game than she was. She must always remember what sort of man he was.

She dressed in a simple pale blue wool dress suitable for the cooler winter temperature and went downstairs. Her aunt and uncle had not yet risen, and she found herself alone in the dining room. She helped herself to the porridge and coffee. She was just sitting down when Alexander entered the room.

"Good morning," he greeted her.

"Good morning," she answered in turn, looking over his brown jacket and cream-colored breeches. She didn't meet his eyes, and when he sat across from her, she could feel him staring at her.

"Did you sleep well?" he asked.

The words and the tone conveyed nothing, yet seemed so intimate. When she raised her eyes to meet his, he was staring back at her, but there was no grin or smirk on his face.

"Well enough. I woke up to the rain," she told him. "I don't mind the rain except that I wanted nothing more than to go back under the warmth of the coverlet."

Alexander said nothing to this, but his eyes seemed to smolder in the cold morning light.

"Ah, here you both are." Richard came into the room and helped himself to breakfast, followed by Arabella.

"Darling," Arabella said as she took a seat nearest her niece. "If the rain lets up, we should go to market. What do you think?"

"If the rains lets up," Georgiana agreed.

"Where are my two lovelies off to," Richard asked, placing his linen napkin on his lap.

"I thought Haymarket," Arabella told her husband just as Georgiana met Alexander's eyes.

"Haymarket," Alexander repeated.

"It's an open-air market that has been a part of Boston since the 1600s," Arabella explained. "There are all sorts of vendors, and the fish is the freshest to be found."

"We might be able to join the ladies after our business is conducted," Richard told him.

"Excellent. If the rain lets up, then we can meet at the market. What do you think, Georgiana? To be squired about by two handsome men? We'll be the envy," Arabella teased her niece.

Georgiana nodded and glanced down at her half-eaten porridge. They were finishing their breakfast when the knocker fell upon the door. A somber and pale Elias Hackett entered the dining room with his tricorne hat in hand.

"My own true darling," he said, coming to stand inside the room but his gaze was focused on Georgiana. "You'll forgive me. The drink last night, it quite went to my head. I came here immediately to apologize to you and to you," he directed at Richard.

Georgiana pushed aside her porridge and tried to smile. "Mr. Hackett. Don't trouble yourself. All is well."

"How many glasses did you have, sir?" Richard wondered.

"I had but one," he told them but shook his head. "However, my diet is very strict. I don't often imbibe. And last night the moonlight was so captivating, as was the company." His eyes once more strayed to the young lady of the house.

Georgiana felt embarrassed and looked at her aunt.

"We have just finished our breakfast, Mr. Hackett," Arabella said. "Would you like some coffee?"

He refused. "No indeed. However, the rain has let up, and I thought I might convince Mistress Gainsford to accompany me for a walk in the Commons."

"That's very thoughtful of you," Georgiana said just as Alexander spoke up as well.

"I think we should all partake in the fresh air," he said, smiling. "There is nothing like the smell of the earth after the rain. Don't you agree?"

"Don't you have your business appointment?" Georgiana reminded him.

"We can spare the time," Alexander remarked, and Richard nodded in return.

The women went to get their hats and gloves, and Alexander looked briefly at Richard before his gaze rested on Elias. Elias said nothing, but his movements were stiff and formal, and he was clearly not pleased to have his morning tête-à-tête with Georgiana interrupted. Alexander didn't give a damn.

Alexander wasn't letting the man take Georgiana into a secluded garden and try to seduce her. He saw the way he looked at her and recognized it well enough. There was nothing godly in it. It was filled with lust.

He had seen it happen before with his plainer-looking friends. Most women never gave them the chance, and the minute one did, they were all over them. He guessed that Elias may be able to hide behind his Bible and words, but the man lusted after Georgiana. It was very evident. He had witnessed it with his own eyes the night before when the man pulled Georgiana into his arms and sloppily kissed her.

He had said the drink caused the action, but he doubted it. Most likely the man had wanted to kiss her for some time and used the drink as an excuse. Coming upon them in the garden like that had been startling, and upon seeing Elias holding Georgiana in his arms, he had wanted to smash his face in. He wasn't often given to violent tendencies, but Georgiana brought out his baser nature.

When Georgiana and Arabella returned wearing their gloves and hats, the small group assembled in the foyer.

"It looks like you are the odd man out," Elias pointed out to Alexander as he took Georgiana by the elbow.

Alexander looked quietly over the man. Some time ago he would have had the man marooned on a small island to rot to death.

Pushing that from his mind, he smiled at him. "I'm certainly fine with that," Alexander said, taking his hat in hand. "Lead the way, sir."

―――*ele*―――

Founded in 1634, the Boston Common was almost a hundred years old. The park was a vibrant place for people to converge, and it saw its fair share of executions, sermons, protests, and celebrations. It served as a meeting place, a pasture, and a military training field. It had first been purchased in 1634 by Puritan colonists who paid a minimum of six shillings towards the fifty acres.

Not long after in 1640, it was ordered that no portion of the Common would be granted private use. The Common was made up of gently rolling scrubland and was slightly wooded with a handful of trees. The rolling hills and ponds made it a delightful park to pass the time.

The land was rough and rural, which was well suited to its use as a pasture. As this was its primary purpose, those who walked along the Common shared it with a village herd of seventy milk cows who grazed the field.

As the five people walked along the Common, Alexander walked behind the two couples, quietly keeping an eye on Elias. The man didn't touch her, but he spoke to her periodically, which irritated him. They were passing by a small mound when an older man began to speak loudly to anyone who passed him. The Common was a frequent site for hangings and executions of murderers, thieves, pirates, witches, and religious dissenters who spoke to the passersby.

"What is the root? Where did it all begin? Adam and Eve's temptation and fall," the Puritan spoke passionately to the gathering crowd. "People are sinful! Listen to me! People are sinful! Lust is a sin!"

The man was dressed all in black, which contrasted sharply with his white hair and beard.

"Adam and Eve – nay, *all* people are susceptible to temptation and sin," he shouted, drawing a small crowd around him. He seemed to be surveying the crowd, and his eyes suddenly fell on Georgiana. She met his gaze, and the older man narrowed his eyes. "Lust! Intense desire may lead to fornication!" He swung about him as he held his Bible in his right hand. "The lust of a woman is a sin!"

Georgiana knew he was talking about her, and she met his gaze. She didn't drop her eyes or turn away but stopped where she was to face him. She had done nothing wrong. How dare he choose to make her a part of his pathetic sermon!

"Ah!" Elias turned to stare at the religious man who was speaking so loudly and smiled. "Why, it's my good friend Fortitude!" He gave a nod to the man. "He's a most learned and God-fearing man! I'll return to you shortly, my dearest."

Elias made his way to the black-clothed Puritan, while Alexander took Elias's place beside her.

"You can't honestly tolerate him," he said lowly as they walked on.

Georgiana shook her head. "He's not flash and grand, but he's not as bad as you might think. He's very religious."

"Who are you trying to convince?"

She looked over at her aunt and uncle, who had moved on, and realized they stood alone together. "I'm not trying to convince anyone, Alexander," she said firmly. "You don't know him."

"That's very true, I don't know him. But I know that the thought of you married to the good pastor makes me want to give him a good beating," he said honestly.

Georgiana smiled lightly, though his words made her feel warm. "That only means you have a problem controlling your anger."

"Or I have a problem with any other man touching you," he said bluntly.

"Any other man?" She scoffed. "Does that pertain to friends and family?"

"Any man that could call you wife," he said softly. "Any man that could hold you in his arms as I did that last night—"

"Alexander, don't," she interrupted him.

"Do you ever think of that night?" he asked her.

"No, I don't," she lied. "Do you?" she asked recklessly.

"If you don't think of it, why should I," he said flippantly.

Georgiana turned back to see where Elias was, but he appeared to be arguing with the black-clothed Puritan and seemed to have forgotten about her entirely.

"Come," he said, taking her by the arm. "Let's join your aunt and uncle and go to market."

Once at Haymarket, they were surrounded by people both selling their wares and purchasing them. The onions were large and colorful. The ears of corn, squash, beans, and potatoes were all being offered for reasonable prices.

She watched as her aunt picked out several items, and when Richard made the payment, she placed the item in her basket. Georgiana looked on wistfully at the easy companionship between them and wondered if they had always been that way.

They came upon one vendor who was selling cranberries and wild berries and yet another vendor who had a wide assortment of various nuts of all shapes and sizes. She stared at the chestnuts for several seconds, not realizing she was doing so.

"Do you want the chestnuts, miss?" the vendor asked her.

Georgiana looked away from him just as Alexander came behind her.

"Do you want them, Georgiana?" he asked, delving into his pocket for the coin.

"No, it's just –"

"We'll take the chestnuts." Alexander nodded, and the vendor wrapped them up in newspaper and handed them to her.

Georgiana took the chestnuts and stared down at them. How long had it been? Not so long ago. Another night, another place, but with the same man. The fireworks shattering overhead and spilling their colors into the sky. The Chinese pagoda and his arms around her -

"Are you thinking of the pleasure garden?" he asked softly in her ear. "And of me?"

Georgiana looked down at the chestnuts the vendor had roasted. "Were you there?" She popped a chestnut into her mouth. "Was that you?"

"Brat!" He took a chestnut from her.

They passed another vendor with golden pears and purple plums, and Georgiana admired the ripe jewel-colored fruit. A finer vendor with costly goods was selling tea and coffee, and next to him, a vendor was selling rum. Finally citrus fruits and different spices filled the air.

"I love coming here," she admitted to him. "It seems so exotic."

"You see this market in every city in every place in the world," he said appreciatively. "People coming together to purchase and sell goods."

They came to the fish vendors, and Georgiana held her nose as they passed through them quickly while her aunt stayed behind to make a purchase. As Boston was located along the coast, seafood was a staple that was readily available. Bostonians had their pick of cod, herring, bass, sturgeon, mackerel, clams, and lobster.

Looking over the plentiful seafood, Georgiana told Alexander, "My aunt has asked Cook to make her special chowder." She munched on another chestnut. "You're in for a treat."

Together they passed along the live animal pens, which included chicken, geese, ducks, and pigs, and moved into the outer area of the market. Several smaller vendors were gathered, and Alexander excused himself. He returned with a handful of pink peonies wrapped with a white ribbon.

"For you," he said simply.

Georgiana didn't know why, but the sight of the flowers made her feel strange. "Thank you," she said softly.

The sounds and smells of the market filled the air, and she saw Alexander absorbed in the spices while the pink peonies she held made her smile. They were so lovely.

Alexander turned abruptly away from Georgiana. He had wanted to come along for the childish reason that he didn't want Elias Hackett walking in the park alone with Georgiana and making memories with her. But spending time with her was agony. It was the worst kind of torture.

Seeing her lips turn up and smile at something only made him want to taste her. Seeing her excited about the damn chestnuts made him want to purchase every nut in the city. And the flowers? The lush pink blossoms? He wanted to crush them in his hand and fling them onto a bed right before he laid her down upon it. It was a strange madness. She seemed immune to it. She had no idea, no idea at all how badly he wanted her.

It was better that way. At the moment, he saw no need to press the issue. He wasn't worried for one second that the solemn vicar was going to steal her away. She had probably been surprised by the proposal and not realized he was the absolute wrong man for her. She needed a man who would let her be her true, vibrant self and would let her shine and blossom like those peonies in her hand.

She deserved –

"Ah, here you are!" Elias Hackett came towards them. "You've purchased yourself flowers? That is a bit of a waste, is it not, my dear?" He smiled but with no warmth.

Georgiana looked at him and then down at the lush blossoms. "But I didn't buy them for myself. Mr. Mayson bought them for me," she said, smiling sweetly as Alexander stood nearby at the coffee and tea vendor stall.

"Mr. Mayson?" Elias repeated, startled.

Alexander came towards them, munching on an apple. "I did purchase the flowers for Miss Gainsford. Lovely blossoms for a lovely blossom."

Elias bristled at Alexander's words. "Well, if you want to throw good coin away –"

"But I didn't throw good coin away," Alexander said smoothly. "I spent money on flowers to put a smile on Miss Gainsford's face." He took another bite of the apple and walked on ahead as Elias's face grew pink.

Elias turned quickly to Georgiana, glaring down at the flowers. "You should not have accepted them, my dear."

"Not accept them? Why ever not?" she asked, confused at his words.

"It's unseemly! To accept flowers from an unmarried man," he explained.

"That's silly!" She smiled. "They are flowers. Nothing more."

"Nothing more?" he repeated. "Did you not just hear Fortitude's sermon in the park about sin and lust?"

Georgiana shrugged as they moved along the vendor stalls. "Your friend Fortitude seemed an odd sort. Why was he prattling on about lust and sin so early in the morning? Most tiresome."

Elias gasped. "My dear! You must not say these things! Fortitude is a respected member of the –"

"He's a sanctimonious old windbag!" she said sharply.

Elias caught up with her. "My dear!"

"He is! And I don't appreciate his gaze upon me as he spoke of those subjects," she said haughtily. "You should have spoken to him about that."

"I don't care for your tone, Georgiana," he said quietly. "You are not yourself this morning."

"But I am," she disagreed. "I feel quite invigorated by the morning air. Don't you think there's something quite lovely about the smell of earth after a rain? It really is something special."

"Very well." Elias calmed himself. "We won't quarrel over Fortitude. The man can be tiresome, as you say, but he's very respected in his circle."

Circle of one, no doubt, Georgiana thought inwardly.

"But the flowers." He stuck a bony finger up. "I must stand my ground over the flowers." He nodded to himself. "That's not the right thing. You should have refused."

"Why?" she asked sincerely.

"Because. Because it sends a message," he explained to her.

"What message would that be?"

"That you are open to receiving him. Open to his gifts and to – " He stopped. "Open to him."

She waved her hand dismissively. "That is preposterous."

"It's the way. A gift such as flowers might seem innocent. But they open the door. Next he will step inside that door and then there will be lust and – "

Georgiana heard him prattling on, and all she could remember was the door. He had stood in front of the door and locked it behind his back.

Didn't run far enough.

No, she hadn't. She had not run that far at all. But inside that room at Clyvedon Hall, so much had changed. The plum room with the fireplace burning low and Alexander.

You're such an innocent that you don't realize how far I could go.

And she hadn't. The arrogant Alexander, so sure of his charms and his handsome face, knew so well how to seduce a silly young woman.

You think to tease me in public with no consequences, but everything has consequences, Georgiana.

Oh, yes. How true that had been.

Tonight, I'm going to go as far as I can without doing any true damage.

Now she knew what he had meant. What he had done that night.

It means you like to play with fire and tonight you're going to feel the burn.

"Georgiana?"

Georgiana turned to see Elias staring at her intently, and she had been miles away. She had not heard anything he said. She had been far away in England in a plum-colored room, in the arms of a scoundrel.

"I'm sorry. I was thinking of a Bible verse that captured my attention," she lied easily to avoid any more questions.

"That's excellent, my dear!" he said happily. "Well, try and remember about the presents."

Chapter 12

GEORGIANA WAS LYING ON her bed with a copy of the book *Paradise Lost* beside her. She had been reading but had since lost interest in it.

A light mist had taken over the city, and she was alone. Her uncle and Alexander had gone to their meeting, while her aunt was paying calls. She was thinking of the morning's events and wondered at Elias's words. He had not defended her when his bombastic friend seemed intent on shaming her, and the words afterwards about the flowers had been vexing.

Why did Elias think that the simple flowers were a declaration of love? Alexander had done exactly as he had said. He had purchased the blooms to make her smile. It wasn't anything grander than that. But then Elias had continued.

The flowers sent a message, he had said. *That you are open to receiving him.* Georgiana bristled at the comment. What did Elias know of such matters? He was a confirmed bachelor. Everyone in town thought he would never marry. But he was a man. Certainly, he understood their nature more than she.

But no. She would not let him make Alexander out to be some villain for buying flowers. As she had said herself, it was preposterous.

She looked at the door to her room, and before she could talk herself out of it, she wandered down the hallway.

Opening and closing the door quickly, she stood alone inside Alexander's room. His room was the same as hers but decorated in brown and maroon. On the table lay his brush and comb and two bottles of cologne. She took out the stopper and smelled. The scent was woodsy with a hint of sandalwood.

One of his blue woolen jackets lay casually thrown over the back of the chair, and she picked it up and put it to her nose. It carried a slight scent she couldn't quite name. Cedar? Sage? She looked at his bed, which was slightly mussed. Perhaps he had sat down upon it after their trip to the market before going out again.

She opened up the first drawer. His linen garments were neatly folded and in place. Had he done that? Was he so meticulous? She thought he would be. He was always put together, not a hair out of place. His clothes were so well-tailored and costly. She sat down upon his bed. She had been in this room his first night here.

He had asked her to stay, and she had. To talk. Had she been concerned that he would pull her into his arms and kiss her as he had done in the pagoda? At Clyvedon Hall? He hadn't. Was she disappointed? Had she wanted him to? What silly questions. Why would she want that when she was considering another man's proposal?

She looked down at the coverlet, plucking at the fabric, when the door opened and closed unexpectedly.

"Georgiana?" Alexander stopped in the middle of the floor, shocked to see her. "Why are you here?"

Georgiana looked equally shocked to see him. "I – I was walking in the hallway and heard a noise in here." It sounded as if she was making the story up as she went along, which she was.

"A noise?" He placed his hat on the table. "What sort of noise?"

"It was very loud," she admitted, stalling for time as she stood.

"Very loud," he mused. "It might have been a large mouse roaming the halls."

"It might have been. Or maybe a skunk?"

"Or a squirrel?" he interjected.

"A raccoon!" she added.

"Definitely." He nodded. "A racoon."

"Yes."

"So did you see one?" He looked about the room.

"One what?"

"A racoon?"

"Oh, no. I didn't. But I did see its shadow before it snuck off," she said as their eyes met.

"What do you mean, snuck off?" He glanced furtively around the room. "Is it still here? In my room?"

"No! No." She shook her head. "It ran down the hallway."

"Ah. The hallway. But the door was closed when I entered." He motioned to the door.

"It was," she said, nodding. "I was frightened so I closed the door the minute it left. It was a very large racoon."

Alexander shrugged out of his jacket. "If you wanted a quiet word with me, you've only to ask, Georgiana."

"I don't!" she denied. "I mean, not quiet. We live under the same roof."

"We do."

"I was wondering." Her hand curled around the post of the bed. "The flowers –"

"The flowers I gave you this morning," he asked for clarification.

"Was there a particular reason you gave them to me?"

"Do I need a reason?"

"Did you have one?"

"I saw the flowers. They were pretty. I thought they would bring a smile to your face." He shrugged.

"And that's the only reason?" she pressed as he came to stand before her.

The afternoon light was shifting, and there was a soft yellow haze about the room.

"Is there something else that you aren't telling me? Something missing here from your questions?" he wondered.

"I was told I shouldn't accept them," she said firmly, but her fingers were wound together.

Hackett! He swore inwardly. *Bastard.* "For what reason?" he asked softly.

"To accept flowers from an unmarried man," she began. "It sends a message."

"Does it? I confess I must not be as learned as your intended. I saw the flowers and gifted them to a young woman of my acquaintance. That's really all there was to it." He shrugged easily.

"Of course," she said, feeling silly. "I'm being ungrateful."

"What message do the flowers convey?" he pressed.

"I can only tell you what Elias said, not what I think," she explained.

"Go on."

"He said . . ." She met his eyes in the yellow haze of the room. "He said that accepting them opens me to receiving other gifts - "

He watched a pink tint creep across her lovely cheeks. "And?" he prompted her.

"And opens myself to receiving you." She looked away from him.

Alexander watched her in the haze of the room. He had honestly only thought to gift her a small present. The ulterior motive in Elias's head no doubt stemmed from jealousy and the thought of the beautiful Georgiana in another man's arms. He had suffered from that thought himself. But that he wanted her could not be denied.

"Receiving me?" he repeated the words.

"I shouldn't have brought it up. It's quite silly. As you said, they're flowers, nothing more."

Alexander stood very near her and smelled a floral scent that clung to her. He ached to bury his head in her hair and fill his arms with her. "I distrust Hackett," he said suddenly.

"I'm sure you would."

"It's not for the reason you think," he countered.

"What reason do I think?"

"You think I might be jealous because he could be your husband if you fall on your head and forget yourself," he said softly.

She swatted his arm. "Stop that!" she said lightly.

"But that's not it. I don't distrust him for wanting a beautiful woman. For wanting you as his own, that's understandable," he began.

She felt her knees weaken as he called her a beautiful woman.

"But I think Hackett wants you as a trophy of sorts." He took a strand of her hair and rubbed it between his finger and thumb. "He doesn't want your mind or your fire, and if you marry him, you'll be miserable. And I don't say that because I'm jealous, that's a given. He'll suck the life from you like a leech and leave you empty."

"You needn't be jealous," she said quietly. "You have something he can never have."

"What is that?" His blue eyes looked cobalt in the yellow haze.

"My first kiss."

He felt his heart thud inside his chest. "I was your first kiss?"

"In the theater, in the hallway."

His palm brushed against the softness of his cheek. "That night, I think I was in a daze."

"You behaved badly," she whispered.

"I could do so much worse." His words were a caress.

"You did. At Clyvedon Hall," she reminded him.

"Even then." He shook his head and closed his eyes, filling his nostrils with the delicate scent of her. "Even then, I barely touched you. If you only knew how much I wanted to –"

"Then I guess we should both be grateful Mariah came upon us when she did." She nodded.

"Gratitude is not the word I would use." He wanted to kiss her. He wanted to tell her that Elias could be damned and everyone else on earth. He wanted her for his own. She must end her absurd engagement with the Puritan and –

A knock fell on the door. The maid told them supper would be in half an hour, and Georgiana stepped away from him.

"Why did you kiss me in the pagoda?" he asked her suddenly.

"Why ask me that now?" She frowned.

"I want to know." And he did.

"I don't remember," she lied.

"You do. Tell me."

She thought for a moment. "You are always so sure of yourself, Alexander. I wanted to shake your resolve. I wanted to wipe that smug look off your face. And I wanted to kiss you."

Jesus! he thought.

"And I was drunk."

Alexander smiled at that. "Blaming it on the drink?"

"Not blaming." She shook her head. "But here and now, I wouldn't kiss you."

"Ah, it's the light of day, is it?" He looked about the room. "Should I draw the curtains to make you change your mind?"

"That was then. The pleasure garden seemed so strange. Everyone was uninhibited. I got swept up in it."

"And then you fell asleep on me," he recalled.

"I did not!" she protested.

"In the coach ride home."

"The coach ride home?" She paused to remember. The warmth of the coach. His body next to hers. She had rested her head against his shoulder. Nothing indecent. So innocent and yet so intimate. "So, I did."

"I remember the scent of lavender and rosemary," he recalled that night. "I remembered it again at Clyvedon Hall."

She thought suddenly of the scent that he carried with him. Clean and masculine. Sage? Sandalwood?

"We should go downstairs for supper," she said, trying to change the conversation.

"After you, mademoiselle."

Once dinner had been consumed and they were seated about the fireplace, enjoying brandy and coffee in the comfortable parlor, a knock was heard on the front door.

"It's quite late for visitors." Arabella looked at the clock, which showed a little past six.

The four people waited for their guest to be announced, which turned out to be Elias Hackett.

"Good evening. Am I intruding?" he asked Richard, who shook his head and offered him a chair to warm himself by the fire. "I have come for a quick word with Mistress Gainsford, if that is not objectionable?" He looked to Richard and not Georgiana.

Georgiana frowned and looked back at him before she nodded and stood. "Of course. Let's go into the back parlor."

Alexander could say nothing about Elias's intrusion, which he deemed as such. If the man wanted a word with Georgiana, there was nothing odd about that. But he felt a strange sense of possessiveness overtake him whenever he thought of her now, and it seemed to intensify when Hackett was nearby.

"She'll be fine in the parlor," Richard said aloud, but Alexander had the sense he was directing the remark at him.

"Forgive me for intruding upon you, my dear, at this late hour," Elias said when the door had closed and they were alone.

"That's quite all right, I'm glad you've stopped in," Georgiana explained. "I wanted to speak with you."

"I wanted to let you know that my mother cannot travel, as she is not well, so I thought the wedding could take place in England – not ideal, of course – but then we could travel the Continent, visiting the churches of repute. She will want to attend the wedding," he said firmly.

Georgiana took a deep breath as she faced him. "Mr. Hackett. While I deeply appreciate your desire to take a bride and enter into matrimony when you never thought of doing so before, I regret to give you my answer now. Which is no."

Elias frowned at her words. "I don't understand. No to the marriage taking place in England? Or no to the honeymoon in Europe?"

"No to all of it, I'm afraid."

"But, my dear." He frowned at her. "You must understand. My mother wishes to be at our wedding, and the chapels and churches in Europe, it will not be a waste of time. They are quite renowned."

"Then you should visit them. But I won't be with you." She tried to say the words gently.

Georgiana's words seemed to finally be resonating, and he looked confused. "But you accepted! We are to be married. You will be my wife." He reached out to clasp her hand in his. "You accepted!"

"No, Mr. Hackett. I asked for time. I never gave you my answer until tonight," she said softly. "Please let's not make this more difficult."

He narrowed his eyes. "I'll be made a laughingstock. I have been jilted!"

"That's absolutely untrue," she told him. "You asked me to marry you but a short time ago. Very few people know."

"Maybe you told no one, as you were already set against me," he flung at her. "But I told several people."

"Then you should not have," she reasoned. "Because even when you did propose, I told you I required time."

Elias paused for several moments, and when he looked back at her, his eyes were cold. "It's that one, isn't it?" He tipped his head in the direction of the other room. "I knew it! I suspected it for some time!"

"I'm afraid I don't know what you are talking ab-"

"Oh, yes?" he said, raising his voice. "The debonair viscount? You know nothing of him?"

Georgiana shook her head. "He's a guest of my uncle's."

"And I was a perfectly respectable prospect – a learned man of the cloth before he came. Now I'm not good enough!" He swore, his face turning an angry red.

"Mr. Hackett, there's no reason for this. I was flattered by your proposal and found myself caught up in it. But you and I have nothing in common. And I saw that long before Alexander –"

A flare of triumph filled his eyes. "Alexander?" He made a sound. "You call the man by his first name? Such intimacy! Alexander indeed. And the flowers." He sneered. "A cheap whore purchased for the amount those flowers cost!"

"Mr. Hackett!" she said angrily and stood up. "You are completely out of line! You have called me a nasty name that is absolutely uncalled for and untrue!"

"Am I?" His bony hands curled into fists as he stood as well. "I've been cuckolded. Behind my back, you've been seeing him –"

"This is absurd!" Georgiana shook her head. "I'll not stand and listen to this a moment longer. I thought to give you the respect you deserve and refuse your proposal. But I see much like your beloved Bible, you are a wolf in sheep's clothing."

"What's that, madame? You dare to use the Bible against me?" He seethed. *"But you trusted in your beauty and played the whore because of your renown and lavished your whorings on any passerby,"* he quoted to her.

Georgiana's face felt aflame as he called her a name no gentleman would ever use with a lady. She had been polite, but she would not stand for his behavior a moment longer. "We have nothing more to say to each other. You should leave."

She swept past him and opened the door. But as she entered the foyer, Elias was behind her and had grabbed her arm in his bony hand.

"I may have been the innocent cuckold here and jilted by my intended bride, but at least I'm not a whore!" he shouted at her, and spittle clung to his lips. "Because that's what you are, Georgiana, you are a whore!"

The last word rang through the hallway, and Georgiana winced at the sound of it. The commotion caused her aunt, uncle, and Alexander to step into the foyer as well. Alexander looked at the two standing before him, and before he could second-guess himself, he took several steps to reach the couple and wrested Georgiana away from Elias's grip.

"Don't touch her again, Hackett," he growled.

Elias pointed a finger at Alexander and then directed all his words at Richard. "Do you see this? Do you? You have allowed this snake into the garden of Eden. You are harboring a snake at the breast in this den! This brothel! This whore of Babylon!"

Arabella clutched at her throat as Richard tried to calm down the man.

"Come now, Hackett. This is not worthy of you. Lord Lichfield is a guest in our home. He has business with the governor himself. You take things too far," he said kindly. "Tell us, has something happened?"

"Has something happened? Indeed, it has! My own beloved has refused me," Elias said almost piteously. "That's right! Georgiana has refused my proposal and now I know why! She has become the concubine of this - this pretender! This *lord* as he calls himself."

Alexander had positioned himself so that Georgiana was half behind him. If the crazed Puritan struck out, he would take the blow. He would make sure she was protected. "If your fight is with me, Hackett, then so be it. Do you want pistols at dawn? I'm certainly ready to defend the honor of Miss Gainsford."

Georgiana's hand tightened on his arm through the fabric.

Hackett looked horrified at the suggestion. "D-duel?" He scoffed. "Of course, you would resort to a barbaric scheme!"

Alexander waited but said nothing.

"A duel?" Arabella cried at the words. "Surely not, Lord Lichfield."

Richard agreed with his wife. "Let's have this settled here, Alexander. Many words have been said and they can be corrected, can they not?"

Alexander eyed Hackett with extreme distaste. "You have called your own self a cuckold, which is completely false. I am a guest of this house and nothing else. As to being jilted, you have not been. So, these two issues we can dismiss as easily as you said them."

Hackett watched the other man warily.

"But you made a comment here in this very hallway that I will not forgive," Alexander said coldly. "You made the mistake of opening your mouth and calling the young woman of this house a foul name. Now," Alexander eyed Elias, "before you is a choice. You will either immediately apologize to Miss Gainsford or I swear to you by all that you hold dear, we will meet on the dueling field tomorrow morning to settle this as men."

The grandfather clock in the hallway ticked loudly as no one said anything. Georgiana stood at an angle behind Alexander, and a few feet away from her aunt and uncle. As she looked up into Alexander's face, she saw that it was a mask of controlled emotion. But in his jaw, a muscle ticked. She had never seen him hold such control over evidently masked anger. It seemed to be just under the surface, barely held in check.

Meanwhile Elias, she knew, was angry at her for refusing his proposal and for being held accountable by this stranger. He was weighing his options, but she knew that either way Alexander would have what he wanted from him.

"Mistress Gainsford." He cleared his throat and turned to her. "I spoke in haste and anger. I ask that you accept my apology for the words that were said. It was very thoughtless of me," he said, his eyes focused on Georgiana, and then at the last minute, they rested on Alexander.

Georgiana's throat was dry. She didn't have anything else to say to the man so she gave him a curt nod.

Alexander moved quickly to usher Elias down the foyer and to the door. Arabella trailed beyond them and bid him a good evening before the door was shut firmly behind him.

"Well," Richard said with a sigh. "I won't pretend I'm sorry to see the last of him."

"Richard! What a thing to say!" Arabella chastised him.

"Perhaps we could all use a drink," he said, and Richard agreed.

But when they returned to the parlor, Georgiana was withdrawn as Alexander placed a small glass of brandy into her hand.

"My dear," Arabella began. "You must put it from your mind." She patted her shoulder as she sat upon the sofa. "You've made a decision and there's an end to it."

Georgiana nodded but said nothing. Alexander stood by the fire, looking so unreadable now. He was like a stranger to her.

"I think I'll retire for the evening," she said and left before anything else could be said.

When she was gone, Richard shook his head. "I can't say I ever warmed up to Hackett. I could see him taking a fancy to Georgie, but I never thought it would go beyond mild flirtation."

"You don't think he might speak about her?" Arabella said, concerned. "Sully her name in public?"

Alexander narrowed his eyes. "He won't. And if he does, I will call him out. Make no mistake."

Georgiana couldn't sleep. She moved to her right side, then her left, but the words that Elias had said echoed in her ears. She had thought to be kind and refuse him gently, but he had turned so nasty.

But at least I'm not a whore, because that's what you are, a whore!

The words had been so unexpected and venomous that she had been unsure how to take them and then had realized there was nothing she could do but leave.

But Alexander, he had been the most surprising part of the night. He had defended her honor and been ready to fight a duel for it. She wanted no man harmed on her behalf, but he had been ready to do so. That had been unexpected. She remembered him stepping between her and Elias, she assumed to keep her safe.

And when Elias apologized, it had been false and insincere but still. Alexander had forced it from him. She turned onto her side again. Alexander. What a strange man full of surprises.

The next morning, she accompanied her aunt to pay calls and then parted from her to visit the apothecary. It was a modest one, quite unlike the grand shop she visited in London with Madeleine. She thought longingly of her friend. She had not heard from her, and she wondered how she and Nathaniel were doing.

Inside the shop, there were various soaps, powders, and pomades for the hair, an assortment of tongue scrapers, as well as snuffs, wash-balls, hair combs, skin products, and medicinal elixirs.

She looked over the bottles with their handwritten names below. She smiled at some of the names that evoked feelings of exotic foreign lands and romantic blooms. The Orient Far, Honeysuckle Devine, and Rose Mine.

She had her favorite perfume from London that she had used for several years, but she thought to purchase something new this afternoon. She also wanted to buy her Aunt Bella a fragrance as a gift for her continued kindness.

"Is mademoiselle looking for something in particular?" the man behind the counter asked. His voice held a slight French accent.

"Is the Honeysuckle Devine popular? It's a gift for my aunt," she told him.

"*Oui*! That is a popular scent, as is the Rose Mine." He nodded, letting her smell the perfume she asked after.

"Yes, I'll take that." She nodded. "Can you wrap it and have it sent around?"

He nodded as the bell over the door chimed, indicating someone had entered.

"Do you wish to try something for yourself? A lovely mademoiselle must have a signature scent," he told her.

Georgiana smiled. "Must I?" Certain he told every woman the same thing, but she liked thinking of a signature scent.

"This one," he showed her a bottle, "is called the Orange Blossom of the Sun." He smiled indulgently. "Named after the Sun King in France. His favorite fragrance being the orange blossom."

He took the stopper off the bottle and allowed Georgiana to smell the citrusy scent. "The Sun King plucked the orange blossoms from his castle's own orangery, which was hand-prepared for him," the man explained.

"He was fortunate." She inhaled the clean, citrusy scent again. "I'll take this one as well. Thank you."

As the man moved along the counter to wrap the items she had purchased and send them to her Boston address, she looked at the different soaps and pomades on the shelves, but she felt someone following her. She turned her head to give him a glance when she saw that it was Elias Hackett. She took a quick intake of breath.

Of all the places to be in this town, he was here in the apothecary? What a most unfortunate coincidence! She would be cordial.

"Mistress Gainsford," he acknowledged.

"Mr. Hackett."

"A pleasant day, is it not?"

"Most pleasant." She moved on to look at the items that caught her attention but Elias followed her.

"I think I must once more apologize for my behavior last night," he said solemnly. "I spoke hastily. Harshly."

"It is forgotten, Mr. Hackett." Georgiana nodded lightly.

The apothecary clerk came back to confirm the address, and once she paid him, he informed her the package would be sent out that afternoon. She thanked him for his time, and when she turned to bid Elias goodbye, he was no longer in the store. She shook her head and took to the streets to resume her errands.

As she walked along the street, she had the distinct impression that someone was following her, and when she looked back, Elias Hackett was standing there, watching her. Not to be cowed by him, she turned and walked up to him.

"Mr. Hackett. Is there something you require from me? You appear to be following me," she asked bluntly.

He swallowed. "I think last night I jumped to a conclusion. I think that you want to marry me, but you just need time. Time to adjust to the state of marriage, time to –"

"No, Mr. Hackett. I don't desire any more time. I have given you my answer. So please, do not continue this," she said honestly.

"But that's not as it should be," he said strangely. "It's not the correct outcome."

"What is not as it should be?" She shook her head.

"I have thought of none but you since we first met. And I have thought often of you as my wife, and . . ." He stared at her breasts and then swallowed again. "I want you as my wife. To bear sons. Strong sons. Sons to be raised as God-fearing. How can you dismiss me so?" He frowned at her.

"Mr. Hackett, this is entirely inappropriate." She swallowed.

"No! It's not! *Let a woman learn quietly with all submissiveness. I do not permit a woman to teach or to exercise authority over a man; rather, she is to remain quiet,*" he quoted to her.

Georgiana shook her head. "I must go, Mr. Hackett. I have an appointment."

"I will force you if necessary," he snarled at her suddenly. "I will take what's mine by force!"

Georgiana took a step back. "Keep your distance from me, Mr. Hackett. I have been civil to you, but I won't tolerate being bullied or frightened. So keep your distance from me," she warned him.

Chapter 13

GEORGIANA WALKED QUICKLY AWAY from Elias, looking anxiously about the street to hire a coach so she could return home. Running into Elias twice in one day had made her realize that he was following her. She had thought seeing him at the apothecary had been innocent enough, but the second time revealed his true intentions.

I will force you if necessary . . . I will take what's mine by force!

A shudder ran through her. Should she even take the man seriously? Should she tell her aunt and uncle what he had said to her? No. Why worry them? He was angry. She had refused his proposal, and he was bitter. He would not do anything. What could he do? Force her to marry him? That was not possible. He was trying to frighten her.

She felt a sense of unease and looked back down the street. There was no one watching her, just people going about their business. But she had the strangest sensation she was being watched. When she finally returned home, she felt exhausted. The interaction with Elias had been strange and his words bizarre. When she closed the drapes over the window from the bright sun, she had the urge to sleep.

A sharp knock on the door woke her, and she startled up abruptly. She felt a moment of disorientation and then she realized she had fallen asleep.

"My dear, are you all right?" her aunt called out.

Georgiana put a hand to her hair and then stood to open the door. "I'm fine," she said when she greeted her aunt.

"No one had seen you since breakfast." Her aunt's face was drawn.

"I came home earlier than I had anticipated and fell asleep," she clarified. "That's all."

Her aunt nodded. "You're tired. Yesterday was so trying."

"It was."

"Come downstairs when you are ready. Supper is soon to be served."

But at dinner, she picked at her plate and didn't pay attention to the conversation between her uncle and Alexander, and while his eyes were upon her, she avoided his. She excused herself when they went into the parlor for brandy and coffee.

An hour later, she was seated by the window, looking out over the street. A chill had settled in the room, and she wrapped a large pink woolen shawl about her. She had changed into her chemise to get ready for bed but was not tired. She kept replaying the exchange between Elias and her the night before and then this afternoon.

Could she have handled it better? Could she have been kinder in her refusal? If she was honest with herself, she had never even meant to accept it but it had been flattering. Was she a horrible person for giving him hope?

She nibbled on her thumbnail as she watched a coach and two horses move slowly under the window and down the street.

The household would be settling in for the night, but she was not tired. She rested her head against the wall and wondered what was happening in London. What had happened to Madeleine that she had not written once since the time she had spent here? And why had no one else bothered to write her? It made her feel disconnected and forgotten.

A soft noise caught her attention and she looked up to see Alexander enter the room. He closed the door behind him.

"Alexander?" she whispered, her eyes wide. "What are you doing here?"

"Your aunt and uncle are still downstairs. I wanted to speak to you for a moment. You'll forgive my intrusion," he said quickly.

"You shouldn't be here." She clutched at her shawl, conscious that she was only wearing her thin chemise.

"You didn't seem yourself at dinner. Is everything all right? Are you ill?" he asked, taking a step towards her but keeping a distance.

"I'm not ill. I just – " She wanted to tell him about Elias, but she didn't want to stir up more trouble between them. She didn't truly think that Elias would do anything, and if she was wrong, then she would have caused more trouble for both of them. "There's nothing wrong. A slight headache."

Alexander looked at her for several long seconds. "You would tell me if there's something wrong? I would help you, Georgiana. You've only to ask."

"I know that but you needn't feel as if my honor is your duty to protect. Last night – " she began.

"Last night?" he repeated. "Last night was unacceptable! That *vicar* can't come here and speak to you like that. I won't allow it."

"Alexander – "

"I mean it, Georgiana," he said, his eyes consumed with fire. "I won't stand by and allow you to be insulted by such a man. Men are refused all the time. Engagements break for a variety of reasons. I've seen it happen myself. But last night – his behavior – the name he called you was above and beyond anything I would allow."

"I understand the sentiment behind why you did what you did." She nodded. "I just couldn't bear something happening to you. Not on my account."

"You were worried for me?" he asked softly.

"Of course!"

"That's some comfort." He nodded.

"How could you think I would not be worried for you?" She shook her head. "I don't want your death on my conscience."

Alexander smiled lightly. "My death? Your faith in my abilities overwhelms me. I'm rather adept with a sword. And looking at your past fiancé, I don't think I would need to be that good at all."

She dismissed him. "You're being flippant. I was being quite serious."

"I'm not such a monster as that, Georgiana," he said. "I would never require death as a conclusion to a duel. First blood is enough."

"Have you fought many duels?" she asked suddenly.

He shrugged. "One other."

"For a woman?" she asked, berating herself the moment she asked. She sounded jealous.

"Yes." He nodded. "And in that case, the woman's honor was settled quickly when the man was but nicked in the arm. In the case of last night, Hackett had the good sense to issue an apology before a duel was deemed necessary. But had he not, I would have met him on the field."

"I know you would have," Georgiana said. "And though I can honestly say a duel has never been fought over me, I do thank you for the gesture."

"I could do no less."

"But I can't help thinking for myself." She pulled at the shawl around her shoulders. "I handled everything wrong. Perhaps I should never have even given him hope."

"You did nothing different than a thousand other women before you." He shook his head. "But the man took it badly is all. In that, I can't say I blame him."

"Why is that?"

"The chance to call such a lovely woman as you their wife, that's quite an enticement."

Georgiana looked away from him.

"If you are sure there's nothing I can help you with –" he asked.

"There's isn't."

"I'll bid you good night then," he said formally and left the bedroom as quietly as he had arrived.

Several days went by, and nothing of note occurred. Georgiana felt foolish in the extreme. Elias had been angry in the moment and lashed out. She felt more relaxed when she realized her life was settling into a normal pattern once more. A small supper party the night before and a card party this evening at a friend of her aunt and uncle's house would be a nice change of pace. Georgiana had already picked out a blueberry-colored dress for the occasion.

She and her friend Sallie Elkin traveled to Haymarket to do some marketing. She had offered to pick up several items for their Cook, and her list was small but varied. She had already managed to procure the vegetables and now needed fruit for the dessert and then meat. She didn't mind that the task was normally performed by a servant, as she liked to be out of the house and of use.

As she moved along the vendor stalls, Sallie stopped to purchase some ribbons for her hair, and Georgiana admired the chocolate-brown and forest-green colors. Sallie was admiring a yellow ribbon and then picked a pink one as well. Georgiana moved on, keeping an eye on her friend so as not to lose her, when another vendor called out to her.

"I have some fine-looking pears, miss," the vendor said, and she moved to examine them.

She purchased several, and as she waited for them to be bundled up, her eyes strayed to the people around her. The coffee vendor scooping up his beans, the fishmonger wrapping his cod up in newspaper for his customer, and a woman selling dried flowers and herbs. She would love a dried posey of lavender, she thought as she placed the package in her basket and paid the vendor.

As she moved down the vendor stalls, another person brushed against her. She looked up, a little annoyed. There was plenty of room and no need to brush up against her. She had a sharp retort on her tongue as she turned but gave a start. Elias Hackett's angular face stared back at her.

"Miss Gainsford," he said. "It's a beautiful morning, is it not?"

Sallie, who was still perusing at the ribbons, would be no help to her at all. Damn her! she thought ungraciously.

"I saw you looking at the dried flowers." He smiled serenely. "Which one do you want? I must buy a gift for my fiancée."

Georgiana was startled at his words but refused to engage with him. "Good day, sir."

Without warning, he grabbed her by the crook of the arm and pulled her to the dried flowers stall. "But I want to buy you something."

They had taken several steps before Georgiana jerked her arm from his. "Enough," she snapped, her cheeks growing warm and red. "I've been plain enough, sir. Let me be!"

Georgiana turned away from him and was making her way back to Sallie when he caught up with her again. This time he grabbed her elbow in an iron hold, causing her to drop the basket she held.

"No, madame!" he hissed in her ear, causing several people to stare at them. "There is no such word, *enough*. You will be my wife."

When Georgiana struggled to be released from his grip, two vendors nearest them saw the interaction and stepped up to Elias. They shouted at him to release her, and several more people turned to stare at the tall slender man holding the woman. Sallie looked up to see the commotion, and Elias snarled at them all.

"You've no business to come between a man and his property! None at all!" he yelled at them. "She is mine! Mine!"

In a fit of anger, he pushed Georgiana from him, and she stumbled but then righted herself.

"What God has joined together let no man put asunder," he shouted at the vendors who were all staring at him.

Then with a final dark look directed at Georgiana, he ran down the vendor stalls in the opposite direction.

———❦❦———

Georgiana's head was pounding as Sallie led her into the front parlor. The freckled little woman poured her a brandy and told her to sip it slowly. She did as she was told and was thankful for the brandy and Sallie's clear head. She was still shaken up by the Haymarket scene and Elias's behavior. She thought Elias had made peace with his rejection but today proved that was not to be.

"My dear." Arabella came into the parlor, followed by her husband. "You're home early."

Georgiana didn't meet their eyes.

"We came home early," Georgiana began, trying to phrase it correctly. She didn't want to make a big deal or worry her family. She glanced over at her aunt and uncle and then back to Sallie again.

"We came home early because there was a scene at the market," Sallie finished simply.

"A scene?" Arabella wondered. "What sort of scene?"

Georgiana sighed heavily. "There was a scene with Elias," she told them bluntly, feeling her head ache more.

Arabella came to sit next to her niece and put her arms around her. "Tell us what happened."

She explained what happened at the market, and a stunned silence followed.

"The man must be mad." Arabella shrugged. "He hides it well but that must be it," she said, directing the words to her husband. "Surely."

"I don't know what to think," Richard said solemnly. "But I do know I don't like it. The man can't act as he does. Touching you and spouting such nonsense in public."

Arabella sighed. "And, darling Georgiana," she said softly, "you don't look well."

All three pairs of eyes turned to her. "I have a slight headache, Aunt Bella." Georgiana touched a palm to her forehead.

Her Uncle Richard said little, but she knew he was angry. He patted her on the arm, kissed her cheek, and left the room. Sallie left not long after. When she was alone with her aunt and tea was placed between them, she watched the older woman pour out the brown brew.

You've no business to come between a man and his property! None at all!

The words seem to ring in her ears. The look on his face had been so animalistic. He seemed truly convinced that she would be his. The fiasco in the house had been bad enough, and the scene outside the apothecary had been worrisome, but now? It was too much. It was escalating out of control.

"I think your uncle is worried about you," Arabella said slowly. "I think we all are, dearest."

Georgiana felt horrible. "I've brought you all into a difficult situation."

"No, no, my dear." Arabella shook her head. "Don't say that! That's not at all what I meant. This isn't your fault!"

"Isn't it?" she said, her eyes straying to her teacup. The brown tea swirled in the cup as her aunt added a bit of milk.

"It most certainly is not. The man is behaving very badly. I dare say when I was a young woman, I had numerous friends in London who would break proposals and get proposals sometimes in the same evening!" She smiled slightly. "Some women can be very careless with young men's hearts. But I dare say the young men were equally flighty."

"I don't think I was careless or Elias flighty," Georgiana said.

"My dear, you misinterpret me," Arabella said soothingly. "Of course, you weren't careless, quite the opposite. You gave the proposal some thought and gave him your answer. But you'll forgive me, my dear, I should have mentioned it sooner. I honestly had no thought that

Elias would propose. He never had before, and I thought he enjoyed your company but . . ." She hesitated.

"But?"

"He seemed very attached to you, very soon. And his attachment appeared to be rooted in an almost fascination of wanting you as a – a – " She tried to find the right word.

"Trophy?" Georgiana asked.

Alexander's words flooded back to her. *I think Hackett wants you as a trophy of sorts . . . He'll suck the life from you like a leech and leave you empty.*

"Exactly! An ornament of types. I saw him watching you at several parties, and he seemed fascinated by you. But it was a calculated stare, a hunter watching its prey." Arabella clutched at her throat. "Forgive me."

"Forgive you?" Georgiana shook her head.

"I had an uneasy sense about him and you, but as I said, I honestly never thought it would go beyond an acquaintance – "

The front door opened and closed, and Alexander walked into the room. He nodded in both their directions, but his eyes were fastened on Georgiana.

"Might I have a private word?" he asked Georgiana politely.

Arabella smiled at him. "Lord Lichfield. Of course." She excused herself, leaving the couple behind.

He turned to her, and when he came closer, his jaw was firmly set and there was little warmth in his eyes. "I assume you lied to me for a good reason."

"Lied about-"

He shook his head. "Don't. Everyone is talking about it, Georgiana. This isn't London. And even if it were, something like this would be fodder for the gossips."

"I see."

"The man put his hands on you," he said, watching her. "In public."

Georgiana said nothing.

"He grabbed you in front of a dozen vendors and called you his property," he reiterated.

"Yes."

"I won't stand for it."

"You can't call him out for this," she reminded him. "I've given some thought to the matter. I believe I might travel to New York. Give this all time to cool down."

"I have a better idea," he said, turning to her. "I will formally ask your uncle for your hand. Once I am a fiancé, a true fiancé that you have accepted, Elias will have to back down."

Georgiana's breath caught in her throat. "Fiancée? Your fiancée?"

Alexander looked about the room dramatically. "I see no one else here."

"I believe you offered to marry me in London and I turned you down then, did I not?" She placed her hands on her hips.

"You did. And you were quite cruel about it if memory serves. Something along the lines of trading one overbearing, uncaring man for another." His grin was lopsided.

"Exactly," Georgiana confirmed.

"Except that I'm not overbearing or uncaring, especially where you are concerned." The tone in his voice had changed to a deeper, warmer one.

"Alex – "

"Georgiana. It's simple. We announce our engagement. I came to Boston for work and came away with a bride. We can have a long engagement, which would not be questioned, and once enough time has passed, we can end it." He shrugged. "Simple."

Georgiana narrowed her eyes. "I can't believe you! You are more arrogant now than you ever were in London!"

He smiled at her with his lopsided grin, and it took everything in her not to smack it off his face.

"How is this for me? I'm trying to help you. To keep you safe from that madman that you almost chose! Under my protection, he wouldn't dare touch you," he insisted. "I'll see to it."

"I don't need you to keep me safe," she said, and her chin went up a notch.

"I disagree."

She shook her head. "There are other ways –"

"I threatened him with a duel, Georgiana," he reminded her. "That didn't sway him."

"Alexander – "

"The man has formed an unnatural attachment to you." His eyes were serious. "I told you already what I think of him. I don't think he's going to get better with time and only removing you from his grasp will do it. As my intended wife, you will be mine to protect," he said smoothly. "And I will."

Georgiana resisted the urge to close her eyes and sigh. He wanted to protect her. He wanted to keep her safe. If she was honest with herself, she knew she could no longer keep the madman at bay. He had grabbed her in public at a market with a dozen people there. He wouldn't stop until he did something much rasher. More violent. Might he harm her?

"Very well. I agree to this pretend engagement."

"You don't need to look quite so miserable," he murmured.

"I want to make sure we understand each other. I want to make sure we are both in agreement about the beginning and end of this," she told him.

"Very well." He crossed his arms over his chest.

"We can announce the engagement at the next supper party my aunt and uncle give." She watched his face but could not tell what he was thinking.

"Agreed." He nodded once.

"We don't let my aunt and uncle know it's false," she stated firmly.

"Why?" He frowned.

"Because they have no need to know. And when it ends, it will seem all that more real," she reasoned.

"Agreed."

"A six-month engagement, at the end of which we will break." She walked to the end of the room and turned to him.

"Agreed."

"Will you be able to be away from London for such a long time?" she wondered.

He shrugged. "I can make arrangements through the post, but I will need to return after that."

"Then it's settled." She nodded. "Shall we shake hands?"

"I prefer a kiss to seal the deal," he teased her.

She put her hand out. "To a not very long engagement."

Georgiana's head was pounding as she lay in bed fully clothed. She didn't know what was worse. The refusal of a proposal to a madman or a fake engagement to the arrogant, debonair Alexander. She did appreciate his concern. She hid it well from them all, but Elias's behavior had become more and more erratic.

She had known he would be angry at the refusal, but now? He seemed intent on having her as his own no matter what she said. After his last outburst at the market, she wasn't sure what he might do next. Alexander's suggestion would at least allow Elias to cool down and see reason. But pretending to be Alexander's fiancée? Having him always at her side with his handsome face and cool blue eyes?

Why did she suddenly feel warm? Why did she suddenly have a strange sensation that she liked the thought of being with Alexander?

She was a fool. Maybe her father had been right all along. She should have married when she had the chance long ago and never given it a moment's thought. What did it matter if the men had not loved her and only wanted an heir?

She thought of Alexander's blue eyes on her as she drifted off to sleep. What color were they? Azure?

Alexander stayed awake long after the house had settled. He had been surprised that evening, which didn't often happen. He had offered Georgiana protection through a false engagement, and she had accepted. She hadn't made some snippy comment and made a joke out of it, but she had agreed.

Her terms were not out of the ordinary, and when six months arrived, they would break the engagement. Except he had no intention of doing so. He wanted Georgiana just as much as he had in the hallway of the theater, as he had in the pagoda inside the pleasure garden, and his desire for her had only increased.

She seemed intent on keeping her distance, which only made him want her more. If the way to capture her hand and heart was through a false engagement, so be it. But there was another reason he wished this course of action, which was Elias Hackett. He had always thought the man a little odd, but now he sensed he was unhinged. He suspected he had set his cap on Georgiana and now even her refusal meant nothing.

He would do everything in his power to keep her safe from harm. But when it was all over, he fully intended Georgiana to be the next Viscountess Lichfield.

Two days later when the afternoon sun was low in the sky and there was a crispness in the air Georgiana entered the sitting room with Alexander. She had invited him over to speak to her uncle as it was the proper way to handle an engagement. She wasn't sure if her uncle would think her flighty going from one proposal to the next so quickly but she must risk it.

Elias's behavior had become too disconcerting, and if the solution was a fake engagement, so be it. Her uncle was reading alone before the fire, and he looked up in surprise to see Alexander standing beside her.

"Lord Lichfield," he stood and greeted him formally. "What brings you here this afternoon?"

"It's a matter of some importance," Alexander admitted to the older man.

"Would you like tea?" He asked Alexander and then Georgiana.

"I'll tell Cook," she said disappearing for a moment to tell Cook to prepare tea for three.

When she returned to the room, she saw the two men staring at each other.

Richard frowned at the man before him. "Did I hear you correctly? You wish to marry Georgiana?"

"You heard correctly. I want Georgiana as my wife," Alexander said decisively.

"This is very rushed. You've not been here long," Richard pointed out.

"I know what I want," Alexander said and thought that this conversation with Richard was more honest than any he'd had with him before.

"I see. And Georgiana?" Richard asked.

Alexander shrugged. "I would not have approached you had I not thought Georgiana wished to be my wife."

"We shall see."

Georgiana was asked to join the two men and she did so promptly.

"So, niece." He looked at her sternly. "You wish to be married this time?"

Georgiana looked at Alexander and then back at her uncle. "I do, yes."

Alexander came to stand by her side and picked up her hand to kiss the back of it. "My lovely bride-to-be," he said sweetly as she stared at him.

"I must say your choice has improved with Lord Lichfield," Richard said, amicable. "And as before, the choice is yours."

"Thank you, Uncle Richard," she said as he kissed her cheek and shook Alexander's hand.

Chapter 14

AN HOUR LATER, ARABELLA and Richard were toasting the happy couple. Alexander's eyes seemed to be on her most of the time.

"What a dark horse you are, Lord Lichfield," Arabella said, smiling up at him as her husband stood nearby, handing them glasses of champagne.

"Please call me Alexander," he urged them both.

Georgiana watched him that evening over champagne and a well-cooked meal, and he seemed at ease and affable. He charmed them both with his easy way and manner, and she remembered he could be so very charming she could almost forget herself. She remembered a night so long ago when she had moaned in his ear and arched into him.

She looked up to see them all staring at her. "Yes?"

Arabella smiled indulgently. "I had asked where you might like to go on your honeymoon."

Georgiana's cheeks warmed at the question. She looked once at Alexander and then away. "I'm not sure we've spoken of that."

"You make such a handsome couple," Arabella noted and Richard agreed. "You must go somewhere romantic."

"As long as I'm with Georgiana, I'll be happy." Alexander smiled at her.

Why was he laying it on so thick, she wondered.

"And we'll lose our dearest niece back to England," Arabella said in anguish.

"She was never going to stay forever, my dear," her husband chided her.

Arabella nodded. "But if we must lose her, at least it's to a viscount." She smiled suddenly. "Can you imagine, darling? You're going to be Lady Lichfield."

"I hadn't thought about it," she said honestly, knowing she never would be.

"Hadn't thought about it?" Arabella echoed.

"Her only thought was becoming my bride, isn't that right, sweetheart?" Alexander said, trying to smooth the way for her.

Georgiana jumped at the term of endearment he used and nodded. "Yes."

"What a day," Arabella said, shaking her head. "An engagement. So wonderful." Arabella kissed her niece on the cheek and embraced Alexander. "I'm quite overwhelmed."

Richard smiled at the couple. "Come, my dear. Let's go to bed and leave the couple alone for a time."

When the door was closed behind them, Georgiana moved away from Alexander. "That was all a bit much, wasn't it?"

He frowned. "What was?"

"Calling me your sweetheart and you'll be happy wherever I am." She rolled her eyes. "Good lord!"

"I was making it look realistic," he said, coming to stand before her. "Remember, I'm in love with you. We're to be married. It's not a public execution."

Georgina sighed. "I suppose so."

"And we must work hard to convince people," he noted. "So that Hackett will get the message. The sooner he does, the better for us both."

"That's true."

"So, pretend to be madly in love with me, Georgie." He caught her about the waist and kissed her forehead.

"Ridiculous," she said, pulling away from him, but she was smiling nonetheless.

When they did finally announce their engagement publicly, it was quietly done at the governor's house over a scrumptious dinner. Alexander made the announcement, and the governor clapped him on the back. Georgiana noticed several covetous looks directed at her never-to-be husband and then those same eyes returned to her with venom.

"Of course, he would choose her," an older woman said. "She's English and he wants an Englishwoman as his wife."

Another man muttered under his breath, "Can't say that I blame his choice. What a beauty!"

When it was time for a speech, Alexander looked over at Georgiana with a drink in his hand and raised it high. "To my sweetheart, my bride-to-be. May we be very happily wed."

Applause broke out. Someone from the back of the room called out, "Kiss! Kiss her!" and suddenly everyone was clamoring for a kiss.

Alexander held out his hand, and Georgiana stepped to him. In a quick movement, she was in his arms and his mouth was on hers. Her hand pressed against his chest, and she could feel the hard planes of muscle. His hand strayed to her hair before he broke the kiss. Cheers erupted around them, and when she looked up at his face, it was unreadable.

She was congratulated several times over, and when she finally found time alone in the garden, it wasn't long before Alexander joined her.

"I don't care for such a public spectacle," she said primly, pressing her lips together.

"What spectacle?" he asked, confused.

"The kiss? I think that was unnecessary." Her eyes strayed to his lips.

"Weddings are a festive occasion, Georgiana. People want others to be happy," he said. "They want to celebrate."

"I suppose." She nodded in agreement.

"Besides it's not the first time I've kissed you. I even recall *you* kissed me," he said in a shocked voice.

"I was drunk," she said, simply refusing to be drawn into his words

"Oh. Drunk. Is that the excuse you're going to use?" He smiled, coming towards her.

"It's not an excuse. I had far too much to drink that night," she said firmly.

"And Clyvedon Hall? Your excuse then?" he wondered, leaning in to whisper the words.

"I behaved badly," she allowed, stepping away from him.

Alexander grinned. "I thought you were quite extraordinary. And who knows? Had everything happened the same without being interrupted, we would be married already."

"How did you work that out?" she asked, confused.

"Had we not been interrupted that night, you might very well be with child." He shrugged.

Georgiana's breath caught in her throat. "What a thing to say!"

"You're irresistible," he said simply. "I lost control that night."

"Lost control." Georgiana rolled her eyes. "I don't think I've ever met a man more in control than you."

"Every man has a weakness."

Georgiana smiled lightly. "Is that what I am? Your weakness?"

He had said the words lightly, but they were too close to the truth. "Remember in the hallway, at Haymarket."

"Yes."

"I had been watching you move about the theater. I played a game with myself as I followed you," he recalled, and Georgiana felt mesmerized by his words. "I gave you an identity."

"You never said." Her eyes were full of wonder.

"Because it was nonsense," he told her.

"What was I?" she asked genuinely intrigued.

"A governess tortured by her charges." He growled playfully.

Georgiana laughed.

"A ladies' maid," he said in a horrified tone.

"Tortured by her lady?" She grinned.

Alexander nodded. "A member of the royal family."

"Ah." Georgiana nodded. "A member of the royal family."

"But instead of any of those made-up identities, you were simply a woman."

"An irresistible woman?" she asked coquettishly.

He was standing before her, looking down into her emerald-colored eyes. His hand came up to cup her face. He felt a strange emotion sweep into him, and he knew it was an intense desire but mixed with something else. "I hope this will keep you safe, Georgiana."

"I'm sure it will. And I'm sorry that all of this is such an inconvenience for you." She met his eyes and wanted badly to sway into him.

"It's not an inconvenience." He shook his head. "Don't think of it that way." The back of his hand caressed her face.

"Isn't it?" she whispered, and her voice sounded husky to her own ears.

"No. I'm helping you," he assured her.

"Why? Why are you helping me?" she wondered.

He brushed a tendril of hair back from her forehead, not noticing for the first time that she looked tired. She looked exhausted. The entire situation with Hackett had affected her more than she cared to admit, and she had been dealing with it mostly on her own.

"Have we been paraded about enough?" he said thoughtfully, looking down at her. "If so, I'll take you home."

A week passed by, and nothing happened. Lord Lichfield choosing a bride was on everyone's tongue, and Georgiana was congratulated at every shop she went to. She was fussed over and coddled, and several shops extended her credit. One glovemaker gifted her a pair of pale blue leather gloves with exquisite embroidery.

Georgiana tried to refuse the costly gift, but the glovemaker insisted. She looked longingly at the gloves as they were wrapped and placed in a glove box for her to take home. At the apothecary, she purchased several bars of lavender soap but was gifted several sachets of bergamot for her "bridal trousseau." The female clerk winked at her.

Georgiana enjoyed the attention and liked the good feelings that seemed directed at her. When they spoke of her intended, it was with respect. She realized that, for all her skepticism at Alexander's suggestion, it had worked.

She had not seen Elias at any event, and he seemed to have heard the news and understood that she was now beyond his reach.

A small weekly newspaper that circulated in Boston carried the news of their engagement, and it was widely discussed. Alexander had been right. His position and background would keep her safe. She felt a sense of relief and was able to relax finally. Spring would be coming soon, and she could look forward to the new growth in the city.

She was at the dress shop, ordering another cape trimmed with fox fur, when a young boy came into the shop and handed her a note.

"Who is it from?" she asked, looking at the note.

"From your intended," the boy said and disappeared as quickly as he had arrived.

"Lord Lichfield," several women whispered as they stared at her with envious glances.

The handwritten note read:

Georgiana,

There is a coach waiting outside. It has been hired to take you somewhere special.

Georgiana smiled despite herself. The man was incorrigible. What plans did he have for her now? A light rain had begun to fall outside so it wasn't likely to be a picnic or an outdoor event.

"What does the note say?" the dressmaker asked. "If I may inquire."

Georgiana shrugged. "A coach is waiting for me. It's a surprise."

Several women giggled, and one younger woman sighed. "So romantic."

Georgiana shook her head as all the women stared at her. Really! Alexander was too much. He was making such a fuss over their false engagement.

"I remember when Arthur took me on a winter coach ride," said an older woman, waxing nostalgic about her younger days.

"When was that, Bethany? When the Puritans landed?" said another older woman, obviously teasing her friend.

"Speak as you will, Dorcas, but my Arthur was very romantic in his younger years."

Georgiana finished her fitting and went outside to the awaiting coach. She identified herself. "I'm Georgiana Gainsford."

"Step inside, miss. It's but a short ride," the coachman directed.

Alexander was coming down the stairs, pulling on his wool coat, when he noticed the umbrellas lined up against the wall. He knew the lilac-colored one trimmed with lace was Georgiana's, as he had seen her use it. She would need it this afternoon since it was going to rain.

"What appointments did Miss Gainsford have this afternoon?" he asked her maid.

"She was to go to the dressmaker," she confirmed as Alexander picked up the umbrella to deliver to her.

No sooner had he entered the coach than a downpour of rain fell upon them. The coach slowed as they made several turns into the city and entered the lane filled with dressmakers and millineries. Georgiana should take better care of herself, as the rain could cause her to catch a chill.

He was nearing the dressmaker's shop when he saw her exiting from it through the window. He was about to call out to her when she stepped into a different coach not known to him. He looked at the shabbily dressed driver and the coach and made a quick decision.

"Follow that coach," he directed the driver.

Georgiana heard the rain falling outside as the rickety coach took several sharp turns and she was jostled about. When it finally slowed, she was glad the bumpy ride had come to an end. The driver came down and opened up the door.

"Take the steps up to that ship there." He pointed out one. "That's where the surprise is waiting."

Georgiana looked up to see a small ship before her. It was not as grand as the one that she had sailed into Boston on, but she didn't know what surprise Alexander had in store for her.

"Right up the steps," he told her again, and she nodded.

She remembered Alexander had been a privateer and knew it must be something connected to it. She walked onto the ship and was directed to a small cabin below deck. Glad to be out of the rain, she shook out her cape and wondered where he was. She heard voices out on the deck; one sailor told the other to cast anchor.

She frowned as she looked about the dark cabin. It was small with only a tiny bed for one person and a desk built into the ship. Something didn't feel right about it. She turned to the door, but as she placed her hand on the knob, it turned as well. Stepping into the small cabin was a man. He carried a lantern with him, and when he swung it before him, she saw the thin, angular face of Elias Hackett. Fear flooded into her.

"Hello, my dear."

Georgiana felt the floor sway beneath her, though it was not from the ship upon the sea. "Elias! What – what are you doing here? What is this?" She took a step away from him, but there was nowhere to go.

"What am I doing here?" He frowned in confusion. "I'm the one who summoned you here. It was my surprise."

"Surprise?" she said breathlessly, willing herself not to faint dead away.

"The note. The coach. That was me. Summoning my wife-to-be to my side," he explained to her, a small smile on his gaunt face.

Georgiana sighed heavily. "Elias, I'm not going to be your wife. You must stop this. I'm to marry Lord Lichfield. It's been announced – "

"No!" he cried. "They'll be none of that! I heard all about that in the gossip columns, and I knew it was exactly that, gossip. So, I have made my move. I have done today what I should have done long ago."

"What are –" She swallowed; her throat was so dry. "What are you going to do?"

"Do not worry, my dear. I will treat you as a respectful woman should be treated. I owe you no less. I am taking you to Martha's Vineyard," he explained.

"The island?" She shook her head. "Why there?"

"Because, my own darling, I have a dear friend who resides there. He is a man of the cloth. We are to be married," he said simply.

"Elias – no." She took another step from him. "You can't! You can't do this! I refuse to marry you."

He smiled at her, his cheeks looking hollower and his face taking on a skeletal appearance in the darkened cabin. "Resign yourself, Georgiana," he said coldly. "By tomorrow evening, we will be husband and wife in name and deed."

Elias left the cabin, and she could feel the ship move slightly in the water. She covered her mouth to keep from screaming. Dear God in heaven! Elias Hackett had kidnapped her, and nothing on earth was going to save her now. No one knew where she was; even the women at the dressmaker had thought the note from Alexander.

She sat down upon the small narrow bed and glanced out the tiny round window that looked out to the sea. The harbor was gradually moving away, and she cursed herself. What a stupid fool! This was all her fault. She was a stupid fool ten times over. And now, now she was going to pay the ultimate price. She would be married to the lunatic.

She dug through her small bag and already knew what she would find. A handkerchief, a small amount of coin, and a small brush for her hair. Nothing that would help her in this situation. She had no weapon, no money to try and bribe her way, and even if she did, the sailors might turn on her. Her best option was to get to the island and escape from there.

Georgiana searched the small cabin but found nothing useful. The more she thought about her captivity and her lunatic captive, the angrier she got. He had no right to do this! He had no right to hold her captive.

The ship swayed in the waves and flung her to the floor. Her knee was bruised, and she rubbed it as she sat back down upon the small bed. They would be at the island before nightfall and then she would have time to think and plan. Elias had told her that she would be his wife tomorrow evening. So tonight, she would have to act. She had no idea what she would do but once they landed, she must watch to see where they were and wait. She would make her escape soon enough.

The journey to the island from Boston was not long, and they soon arrived in the town of Edgartown.

Georgiana was not prone to seasickness, but she didn't feel well as the ship slowed and entered the dock of the small town. She could smell the sea in the air and heard the seagulls' call. Elias joined her inside the small cabin, looking pleased with himself.

"Come, my dear. I'm arranged for us to stay at a nearby inn," he said, taking her arm.

Georgiana had always thought he had a kind face, but seeing him now, she saw no kindness, only a hint of cruelty around the eyes. Had she turned him this way from one refusal? Or had he always been like this and his true nature was being revealed?

"I would advise you to act appropriately when we are in public," he said as they entered the deck. "I would very much hate to punish you in any way, but I will."

"No doubt," Georgiana mumbled under her breath.

Several sailors were cleaning the deck of the ship as they walked down the gangway. Elias's grip tightened on her arm, and she winced.

"I have been most indulgent with you, Georgiana, and I see that was a mistake." He nodded. "Women like you need a tight rein and I'm not against using corporal punishment on you."

Anger flared inside her, but the madman had the upper hand at this moment so she held her tongue.

"*Spare the rod, spoil the child* is an apt statement but it should be applied to women as well," he said, looking her over as they settled into the awaiting coach. "Women being little more than children anyways."

The sun was setting as the hired coach took them to the small inn where he had procured rooms. The harbor and its waterfront were picture-perfect with tall square-rigged ships that probably sailed all over the world. Georgiana admired the houses they passed, and at any other time, she would have probably enjoyed the trip to this little island.

Instead, she sat across from this demented man who was intent on marrying her against her will. While she had been so certain that everything was going well and Alexander had saved her from the unbalanced Elias, he had been planning as well.

"You'll be quite pleased, my dear, I have planned everything, *everything* to your taste," Elias said, grinning wildly opposite her.

"Is that so?" she said frostily, trying not to stare at his pale gaunt face that seemed like a stranger.

"I have secured our rooms so that everything is properly done. There will be no words spoken about my betrothed's reputation."

"Rooms?" Georgiana questioned.

"Rooms. We are not yet married. Our wedding night will be special. When we are joined together by God, only then will I make you my wife in body." His thin lips seemed to disappear completely as he licked them.

Georgiana felt sick to her stomach and light-headed. It was a nightmare come to life!

"I have also had a dress made. I think you'll approve." He looked over her frame.

"A dress?"

"And finally," his eyes were bright and wide, "the best news yet! My dearest friend Fortitude is to marry us! You'll remember him from the Commons?"

Jesus! Georgiana's heart clenched in anger. The misogynistic Puritan, who had looked at her with such disdain, was about to marry her to the brainsick Elias. She would receive no help from him. Her last hope to appeal to the preacher was dashed.

"Have I not planned everything just right, my dear?" He leaned across and covered her hand with his. His hands were cold, and she could feel the small bones in his fingers.

"You have planned it so well I'm speechless," she said sarcastically, but he paid her no mind.

"And tonight, we'll have a small supper, and tomorrow," he licked his lips as he stared at her, "you will be mine."

Georgiana's eyes darted about the sparsely decorated room. A small bed, a desk and chair, and a chest of drawers were all that decorated the barren room. The wood floors were cracked, and a hand-woven rug that might at one time have been vibrant and pretty was now worn and lacked luster.

She sat down upon the bed and stared for a long time at the rug. She traced the lines and colors with her eyes and then went to stand beside the one window in the upstairs room. The only redeeming quality about the room was the window and its view of a small patch of green lawn, a lane, and, beyond that, the sea.

She could jump out of the second-story window, run down the lane, and plunge into the sea! She smiled at the thought. No one would even know what had become of her, but if she drowned, she wouldn't marry the crazed Puritan.

A knock fell on the door, and she startled. Elias entered carrying a large box.

"For you, my dear," he said, setting the box on the small worn circular table. "Open it!"

"For me." The large rectangle box was before her, and she wanted nothing more than to shove it out the window.

When she didn't rush to join him in his excitement, he pulled out a dress and flung it out over his lap for her to see. The color was a bright orange-red with ruffles and bows on every inch of the dress. Lace lay at the neckline and hem of the dress, and it seemed altogether too much on one dress. The color was garish and bright, and she hated it immediately. He looked at her expectantly.

"That's quite a dress," she said woodenly.

"Your wedding dress!" he exclaimed brightly.

Georgiana wanted to smash the box over his head, but she calmed herself. "I'm sure you took time and effort to have it made."

"I did! My mother will wonder how I spent so much money on one garment." He giggled, and when he began to explain how he had designed it, she didn't listen.

Georgiana wondered idly if she could slice the dress up and use it to escape the room by the window.

"I'll allow you to freshen up and then we will go downstairs for our evening meal," he directed.

Left alone, Georgiana looked at the dress in the box, and in a moment of anger, she snatched off one of the ribbons. She hated the dress almost as much as she hated the man who had given it to her. But she must calm herself. She must bid her time and pretend that everything was fine.

Once night fell, she would run away from this place and leave Elias and his appalling dress far behind.

Georgiana looked down distastefully at the meal before her. Watery broth, followed by a roast that was chewy with fat and undercooked potatoes. Elias poured her a glass of ale, and though she sipped it, she didn't enjoy the bitter taste.

"Do you prefer something else?" Elias asked her solicitously.

Georgiana shook her head. She didn't want to ask him for anything. She didn't want him to be kind looking after her when he had kidnapped her against her will.

"How about the inn's sherry?" he asked and ordered that for her. "They make it themselves, so I was told."

The sherry arrived, and she decided the cinnamon- and clove-flavored drink was much better than the bitter ale. She drank a glass, and he ordered another for her.

"Is the meal to your liking, my dear?" he asked after he had consumed his entire meal and looked ready to consume hers as well.

"It's fine." Georgiana nodded, though the entire meal had barely been edible.

She looked around the sparsely furnished dining room with one couple and two middle-aged men drinking and wondered if any of them would mind if she threw the glass of sherry in his face.

They were served pudding as a dessert, but it tasted odd and soggy, with a dash of spice and a hint of dishwater.

"Are you tired, my dear?" A look of concern crossed his skeletal face.

"It has been a long day." She sighed.

Chapter 15

EXITING THE COMMUNAL DINING room, Georgiana and Elias took the stairs to the second floor. As Georgiana walked up the steps, she suddenly felt dizzy. She accidentally swayed into Elias, who steadied her by catching her shoulders and holding her tightly in his grip.

"My own darling," he said, nuzzling her ear as she pulled away from him.

"Stop that," she said, trying to shake the weakness she felt.

"We're to be man and wife very soon." He chuckled. "Sooner than you know."

"What?" She shook her head. "What are you saying?"

"It won't be long now." He led her into the drab little room as she felt the dizziness come over her again.

"Why am I so dizzy? I feel so drowsy." She shook her head as she made her way to the bed.

Elias giggled as he helped her to the bed, touching her bottom and then brushing the side of her breasts.

"Elias!" she said, irritated but so tired. "Don't."

She was sitting now on the narrow bed, and he was sitting beside her.

"Don't fight it," he told her calmly. "You won't be able to anyways."

"Don't fight what?" She frowned. "Don't fight what?" she repeated angrily.

He shrugged, looking almost superior. "Don't fight any of it. We're to be married tonight. Everything is arranged. Fortitude will marry us. He's pleased to do so. I've made all the arrangements with him, my dearest," he said, touching a lock of her hair.

"No." She swatted his hand away and then realized with terror.

She had been drugged!

That's why she was so dizzy. He had drugged her. Oh, God. No. He would not have done such a despicable thing. Surely not.

"Was there something in my food? What did you do?" she asked him, her eyes wide. "Tell me!"

He chuckled lightly. "Not in your food, my dear. The sherry. The cinnamon and clove mask the bitter taste of laudanum. It was a stroke of brilliance."

"Laudanum," she whispered.

Laudanum was used to soothe many ailments, including headaches and women's menstrual pain. She had never used it but had heard it spoken of. However, the side effects included fainting, drowsiness, dizziness, nausea, and generalized weakness. Damn him to hell! She swore angrily.

She felt his hand touch her cheek, and then boldly his hand moved down to her breast and he touched her lightly as if he was afraid to do so. His gaze was almost glassy as he caressed her. Her anger increased a hundredfold. The man had kidnapped her, drugged her, and now touched her against her will.

"Bastard!" she swore, firmly pushing his hand from her.

Elias gnashed his teeth. "This will be the last time you ever push me away! After tonight, I will know you intimately as a husband. Rest yourself, Georgiana. This will be the last night you ever sleep alone."

With that, Elias left the room, and Georgiana's hands curled into a fist.

"You monster!" She angrily tried to stem the dizziness that coupled with a wave of drowsiness, but she could not.

He would be coming for her tonight. She would be taken to the woman-hating vicar who would no doubt delight in marrying her to Elias and then she would be his by law. His property, as he had once so coarsely said. He would have his way with her. He would take her as he had every right to do, and she would not be able to stop him.

A sense of dread and terror washed over her. She wanted to cry out in frustration. She wanted to run out of the inn screaming vulgarities at him. She wanted to throw herself from the window to get away from the lunatic, but her eyes were so heavy. She had to get away from him, but the desire to sleep was overwhelming.

She looked longingly at the window once more. She could jump out of it. She would lie there with a broken ankle and be worse off, but even the thought of jumping out the window was too much.

She felt as weak as a newborn kitten. She lay back upon the bed and looked about the room. She could break the chair over his head, she thought suddenly and then almost let out a sob. She didn't even want to rise now. She looked up at the ceiling and noticed a spiderweb in the corner.

Poor little fly that would be caught in it. She knew exactly how it felt. She was in a web right now. A web that she had stupidly started by not telling Elias what she thought of him. Instead, her ego had been pleased with the attention, and she had let him think she would agree.

Georgiana closed her eyes. Soon she would be before Fortitude and her vows would be spoken. She would be wedded and bedded, most likely within the hour. She curled her hand into a fist. She would fight him. She must! She would curse him and fight him, and it was too much.

She couldn't fight it anymore.

Her eyelids were so heavy as she drifted off to sleep.

***

Georgiana woke with a start. A light rain pelted the window that looked out into the harbor, and everything was pitch black. She could not have been sleeping that long because Elias had not come for her. She tried to rise, but the dizziness returned. It was then that she heard a creak on the floorboards and realized someone was in her room.

Elias! He was here to take her to the pastor. She wanted to scream and yell for help, but who would hear her or want to help? He would say they were married, and in another hour, they would be.

She pledged to shout obscenities at the two men when they began to say the vows. She would repeat the words she had heard her father use when in a rage over some trivial matter at his company. She would rail the words at them with venom and shock and stun them! She would!

Her eyes focused on the door, and sure enough, he had entered her room. *Bastard*! She hated him with a passion that surprised her. How dare this man think to marry her against his will. He would never have her for long. Never.

His footsteps came closer. He was going to rape her. Her heart thudded wildly in her breast. Drugged. He had drugged her and now she was going to be taken against her will.

He was standing over her now. She squeezed her eyes closed. When he leaned over, she swung a small fist out, and it connected with his face but did no damage.

"No!" she cried out.

A wave of nausea overcame her as he sat beside her, holding her hands above her head to stop any further violence.

"Georgiana!" His voice was so familiar, and she hated that it should be so.

"I'll kill you for raping me," she sobbed, and the words sounded slurred to her ears. "I swear I will!"

"Georgiana! Look at me! For God's sake!"

Georgiana opened her eyes to see the face above hers was that of Alexander. Handsome Alexander with that sarcastic smile always on his face. Only he wasn't smiling now.

"Oh, my God!" She shut her eyes tightly, shaking her head from side to side. "Why do you look like that? Why do you look like *him*?"

"Georgiana! It is me! Alexander!" He took her by the shoulders. "Look at me!"

She opened her eyes, and Alexander's face swam before hers. "Alexander," she whispered.

"Yes. It's me. Jesus! What did he do to you? I swear I'll kill him!" He swore under his breath.

"He's coming back." She closed her eyes again. "He's going to marry me tonight. He kidnapped me, Alex." Her head bobbed to the side. "He put something – in my – drink. Lauda –" She didn't finish the rest.

Alexander was filled with such a penetrating moment of rage that it frightened him. Had the man been standing in front of him at that moment, he would have easily slit his throat.

He looked down at the sleeping Georgiana and then turned his attention to the small sparse room on the second floor. He didn't want to risk carrying her down the stairs. There would be too many questions, but the window wasn't much help either.

He could easily use the bedsheets to climb out, but he couldn't take her with him. She was barely awake at the moment and was not capable of scrambling down the side of the building.

When he was a privateer, he had taken to carrying a long knife with him that could be strapped to his ankle. He had brought it with him, and he pulled it out of his sheath now, holding it in his hand. He looked at the blade in the darkness and grimaced. He would gut that bloody vicar from stem to stern the next time he laid eyes on him.

He looked down at Georgiana, and his emotions crashed into one another. She was so vulnerable lying in this dark room, so far away from anyone who could help her. But luckily, a discarded umbrella had brought him here. And she was no longer alone.

He knew what he would do. There were not many places to hide in the room, but behind the door would work and give him the element of surprise. He didn't know what would happen once Elias was inside the room, but he knew one thing with certainty.

The madman would never touch or bother Georgiana again.

He glanced out the dark window several times. It wasn't long before he heard voices below, but they seemed to be men greeting each other and moving along. Several minutes later, there came a creak in the hallway, and his body tensed. Footsteps sounded outside and then stopped. When the door opened, every muscle in Alexander's body was ready and alert.

The vicar entered the room and closed the door behind him, not seeing Alexander as he walked past him. He took several steps towards the bed and seemed mesmerized by the sleeping Georgiana. He was waiting to see if the man was going to touch her to give him the excuse to knock him out.

"You'll be mine soon enough," Elias whispered in the dark. He sat at the edge of the bed and brushed the hair back from her forehead.

"Touch her once more," Alexander said lowly, his knife pointed at Elias's slender throat. "Give me a reason – *any reason* – to shove this knife into you."

Elias squeaked loudly and flung himself off the bed. "What are you doing here?" he asked, his eyes wide and fearful in the dark room

"It seems you take things that don't belong to you," Alexander said coldly, gripping the knife tighter.

"She's mine!" Elias hissed. "Long before you even arrived."

Alexander smiled with a cool, lopsided grin. "Oh, but that's where you're wrong, Hackett. Georgiana and I knew each other in London long before she came here. She was mine the moment I kissed her months ago. I just didn't realize it then."

Elias narrowed his eyes. "I had the best of intentions! I did! I am taking her to be married. I haven't touched her!"

"Were you?" Alexander asked, playing innocent. "You were taking her to be married?"

"Yes." Elias nodded vigorously. "My dear friend Fortitude performs ceremonies. He lives on the island, and he agreed to it already."

"So, you had it all set up? Everything is arranged?" Alexander asked, his tone cool, his eyes watching Elias's every movement.

"I did. My intentions were honorable." His chin darted up.

Alexander took a step towards him, his grip tightening around the knife's handle. "You kidnapped a woman against her will and drugged her. You are anything but honorable."

"She needed coaxing." Elias swallowed visibly. "She was capricious!"

"Where is this friend? Fortitude?" Alexander asked suddenly.

"A ten-minute walk from here."

Alexander nodded. "Then let's take a walk."

"What? Why?" Elias asked, his eyes wavering between Alexander's face and the knife he held in his hand. "What do you intend to do?"

"I'm going to help Georgiana stand and you are going to lead the way to Fortitude's," he directed. "I would advise you very strongly not to pull any tricks. If you do exactly as I say, you won't get hurt." Alexander pulled Georgiana into his arms and placed her on her feet.

He pointed the knife at Elias. "Lead the way."

Alexander supported Georgiana, who was able to walk on her own, but she was very drowsy and he had to support her about the waist. Elias walked in front of them, sullen and sulky. Less than ten minutes later, Fortitude opened the door, smiling at his friend until he saw the stranger holding Georgiana.

"Elias?" Fortitude said, frowning as Alexander carried Georgiana inside. "Who is this?"

Elias seethed but said nothing.

"I don't think I know you, sir," Fortitude said, his gaze cool upon Alexander and the prone woman in his arms.

"No, you don't. But you know Hackett here, and what you were going to do for him, you'll do for us," he said simply.

Fortitude looked at the tall muscled man standing before him and noticed the knife in his hand.

"I can't marry you – she's not," he stumbled over his words. "That is to say – I'm not – "

Alexander said nothing as he waited for the man to finish his words. As Fortitude was babbling, Elias made a dash to pull Georgiana from him. He slammed his elbow into the man's nose, and Elias sobbed loudly, grabbing at his bleeding nose.

Alexander turned back to the vicar. "You were saying?"

Fortitude's beady eyes took in his friend bleeding and then Georgiana. "Does this woman even want to marry you?"

"Did she want to marry your friend here?" Alexander countered.

"He's a man of God. What are you, sir?" Fortitude said, sneering.

"A man who doesn't kidnap and drug a woman who doesn't want to be his," Alexander said coolly. "You were to marry a couple tonight. And so, you shall."

Fortitude licked his lips and pulled out his worn Bible. Alexander knew she might very well hate him when tomorrow came, but he saw no other way to keep her safe. This would be the final act that would drive Elias away forever. He would respect marriage. Fortitude spoke the words sourly as Elias held a handkerchief to his bleeding nose.

"I, Alexander Mayson, take thee, Georgiana Gainsford, to be my wedded wife." His eyes were warm as he looked at Georgiana. She stared back at him, so drowsy and sleepy, yet frowning. "To have and told from this day forward, for better for worse, for richer or poorer, in sickness and in health, to love and to cherish, till death do us part." He spoke the words quietly and solemnly and meant every syllable.

When the time came for Georgiana to speak her vows, Fortitude asked her to say "I do," which she repeated after him dutifully. Alexander's blood ran cold. How easy it would have been for Elias to have made her his wife.

He removed a small gold band from his finger, placed it on her ring finger, and kissed her once on the lips to seal the bargain. Fortitude begrudgingly wrote out the marriage certificate and handed it to Alexander. He placed the precious document in his coat pocket and took a step towards Elias.

"She's my wife now, Hackett," he said in an even tone. "She's the Viscountess of Lichfield. Don't ever come near her again. If you stay away, I won't have you arrested for kidnapping. Do we understand each other?"

Elias nodded, though his eyes were filled with resentment.

"Good."

Pulling Georgiana into his arms once more, he left the little cottage and the two men behind. Walking the short distance to another inn, he took a pleasant room that overlooked the ocean. After placing Georgiana on the bed, he removed his jacket and stretched out beside her. There was a chill in the air, but the fireplace was burning brightly. He turned to look at her beautiful face, and a sense of peace filled him. He had saved her from Elias and that thought satisfied him.

But more importantly, she was his. The green-eyed temptress was now his wife.

Georgiana woke the next morning with a feeling of disorientation. She looked up at the ceiling, and it didn't look the same as the one last night. The night before was hazy, and she remembered parts of it but only in small increments. She knew she had dreamed much of it. The last clear memory she had was eating supper with Elias, and the food had been barely edible and the drink worse. He had offered her a sherry and then – the sherry!

Her heart raced. The sherry had been drugged. He had taken her upstairs then . . . *Not in your food, my dear. The sherry. The cinnamon and clove mask the bitter taste of laudanum.* The bastard! The rotten, lying bastard! But then everything became hazy.

Oh, my God! Why do you look like that? Why do you look like him? she had said to him. He had looked exactly like Alexander. Handsome Alexander. Sarcastic Alexander. What witchcraft had Elias performed to transform him from the skeletal face of his own to Alexander's? She closed her eyes.

And then Fortitude had been in the dream. The crazed, woman-hating Puritan from the park who had been so nasty in his sermon. Why had he been in the dream? To marry them! Then she remembered. Oh, Jesus! She remembered.

"To have and told from this day forward, for better for worse, for richer or poorer, in sickness and in health, to love and to cherish, till death do us part." He had said the words so solemnly and she had said, "I do," as well.

Dear God! Please make it not so. *Please.* She wasn't married to Elias Hackett. She couldn't be. Suddenly she realized for the first time that something heavy was lying over her waist, and when she turned to look, she saw Alexander sleeping beside her.

"Oh, my God!" she said aloud and looked about the room. "Where are we? What have you done?" She tried to push his arm off her.

Alexander was slow to wake, and as he looked over at Georgiana, instead of the sleepy-headed darling he expected to find, she was sitting up, staring at him.

"Good morning." His grin was lopsided.

This time she punched his chest with one small fist. "What did you do? What happened last night?" she said, agitated.

"What do you mean?" He frowned.

"Did you take advantage of me? What did you do?" She looked down at her clothes, but she was completely dressed minus her shoes.

"Take advantage?" Alexander sat up.

"Yes. Take advantage of me. While I slept."

Alexander tried to bite back a smile. What man had ever wanted to make love to a woman asleep? Absurd. And it proved her innocence.

"Of course, I didn't," he said, standing and stretching.

"Oh." She breathed out a sigh of relief.

"But you are my wife."

"Your wife?" She was stunned. "What do you mean I'm your wife?" Her heart pounded inside her chest.

"Just what I said. Elias's plan was to have his friend marry the two of you while you were semi-conscious. I thwarted his plan and had his friend marry us instead." He shrugged.

She looked down at her hand and saw the plain band of gold. Then she remembered. "Fortitude."

"Yes." His tone was serious.

"So, it wasn't a dream." She let out a shaky breath.

"A dream?" He came towards her.

"I thought the whole thing was a dream. I remember seeing your face last night and being taken somewhere –" She shook her head.

"It all happened." He stood before her.

"And Elias?" She glanced up to meet his eyes.

"As my wife, he will never touch you or contact you again. You can be sure of that." A muscle clenched in his jaw.

"Did you do this for me?" she wondered.

"To protect you." His face was devoid of emotion but his words said so much.

Georgiana swung her legs over the bed and stood to face him. "I didn't want to marry Elias, and I didn't want to marry you."

"Too late," he said nonchalantly.

"I want it annulled." She clenched her fists.

"Why?"

"Why?" she repeated. "Because you took it upon yourself to marry me. You gave me little choice." She almost had the urge to stamp her foot like a wayward child.

"I suppose I shouldn't have given a damn then, huh?" he said, walking the length of the small room and then returning to stand before her. "Never mind that I was outside the dressmaker's when I saw you get into the coach. I followed you and was able to ready a ship immediately to come to Martha's Vineyard. I was protecting you!" he said heatedly, his voice rising as he spoke.

"Well, I don't want your protection!" she said hotly. "I don't want to be your wife."

He shook his head. "Georgiana – "

"Don't tell me it's too late." She warned him, her eyes flashing the famous green fire.

"But it is," he said simply.

"So, *you* want to be married? You, who never seemed to care for the institution, want to be married now?" She scoffed, wanting to smile though there was nothing funny here.

"Yes." He nodded.

"Well, I don't. I want an annulment," she declared angrily and turned from him.

He walked to her and turned her to face him. "On what grounds?"

"On what grounds? Take your pick. I was deceived!" She shrugged out of his grip.

"Deceived?" He raised an eyebrow.

"I'm not going to stand here and explain the reasons why we must annul the marriage," Georgiana said sharply.

Alexander looked over carefully. "Very well. We can annul the marriage."

"Thank you." Georgiana nodded.

"But if that is the case, I think we should explain to your aunt and uncle why we eloped and then return to England. There will be fewer questions and it can be quietly done," he explained.

Georgiana thought about it and nodded. "I agree. We can explain that we took a short trip here and were married on the spot and that you must return to England on business."

"But, my darling!" Arabella said, embracing her niece and then Alexander when they returned. "We hoped to throw you such a grand wedding and then a feast afterwards!"

"I, for one, am thrilled you are married," Richard said firmly. "You were gone an entire night, Georgiana." He eyed Alexander as if he were to blame.

Alexander nodded. "Yes, and I apologize for that. We took an innocent outing and ended up staying too long. Luckily the pastor was on the island, and I have the certificate to prove it. So, the gossip can be avoided."

"Quite." Richard nodded, shaking the young man's hand. "Congratulations."

"But to leave and return to England?" Arabella sighed. "It's just too much. We've so enjoyed having you, my dear," she told Georgiana.

"Alexander has business to return to," she explained. "So, I'm afraid we must."

"Never mind all that," Arabella said. "I'll have Cook prepare a splendid supper tonight, and we'll have your things moved to Alexander's room, which is so grand."

Georgiana started, and Alexander looked back at her, hiding his grin.

Georgiana swept into his room as he was dressing for the evening meal. "You're enjoying this."

Alexander smiled then. "Tell her the truth. Tell her this marriage is a sham and that it will be annulled once we reach England."

"I can't do that." She shook her head. "You know I can't! We'd look ridiculous. And we spent the night together."

"I would have never been so improper and so obvious, but Hackett was too rash," he commented.

Georgiana looked about the room. "I'll bring my clothes and change behind the screen." She nodded at the screen in the room. "And then . . ." She assessed the situation.

"Then?" Alexander was fascinated to see what she would decide next.

"We can place several of the larger pillows between us."

"That sounds like a fine plan, Lady Lichfield."

Georgiana looked up at him quickly. "Lady Lichfield," she murmured.

"What? Don't you like it?"

"No. It wasn't that. I actually thought it sounded quite nice," she said slowly.

"It does," he agreed.

After the delicious supper in which her aunt and uncle toasted them several times over with champagne, Alexander and Georgiana lay side by side in bed. As agreed, there were pillows piled between them, but the champagne she had drunk made her reckless.

"We don't need quite so many pillows," she said, throwing one onto the floor.

"Is that wise?" Alexander asked.

"Wise? Am I worried you'll ravage me in the night?" She scoffed, kicking off the top blanket and exposing a leg.

"Ravage you?" Alexander turned to face her. "I've had other chances to ravage you as you say and never done it. Tonight will be no different. You'll come through this night intact."

"Intact?" She frowned. "What does that mean?"

"Intact," he repeated. "Unharmed."

Georgiana threw another pillow onto the ground as she faced him on her side. "Unharmed? Intact? The words you use I don't understand at all. What harm?"

Alexander waved her away. "Go to sleep, Georgiana. You drank too much champagne."

"Little wonder." She sighed. "I was chased by a madman and am now married to a viscount. It's too much, really." She shook her head and was quiet for several seconds before speaking. "And when did you have a chance to ravage me? As if I would let you." She mumbled the last words.

Alexander sighed. "Haymarket Theater."

"The theater?" She scoffed.

"Yes." He turned away from her.

"Impossible." She gave his shoulder a little push.

"Not at all." He moved onto his back.

"Really?" She touched his shoulder.

"I could have taken you to one of the empty boxes," he said with an even tone.

"Hmph." Georgiana rolled her eyes. "Empty box."

"And the pleasure garden?" Alexander grinned. "Any little nook or cranny would have been perfect. But I remain then and now a perfect gentleman."

"No doubt you've had much experience in these matters," she grumbled, punching her pillow.

"No doubt. Now why don't you go to sleep, wife," he said good-naturedly.

"I'm not your wife, Alexander," she said crossly, flinging herself on her back.

"I have a marriage certificate that disagrees." He shifted onto his side to face her.

"You know what I mean." She refused to meet his eyes.

"In name only. Well, if you don't stop irritating me and not letting me sleep, I might change my mind about leaving you intact." He closed his eyes.

Georgiana glared at him in the dark. What an arrogant ass! Just because he was handsome and educated, he thought so highly of himself. She was looking forward to being back in England. She wanted to see her old friends again.

As she drifted off to sleep, she wondered what life would be like if she was truly Lady Lichfield in all aspects.

Chapter 16

THE SUN HAD NOT yet risen, but the room was filled with a grey haze. Georgiana was lying on her side, and a feeling of warmth surrounded her. She sighed with pleasure. It was a wonderful feeling. Something firm, yet warm was behind her, and something strong and sturdy held her tightly.

She felt something lower, something hard pressing into her, and her eyes opened. Sometime in the night, she had nestled against Alexander, and he was the warmth and the strength that she felt behind her. He was holding her possessively, with his arm draped about her waist. She was caught between a feeling of belonging and fear.

She realized she liked being held by him. She liked it very much, but she shouldn't. His one leg was wedged between hers, and it was intimate and not anything they should be doing. How could she ask for an annulment when all she wanted was for him to kiss her and claim her as his own? What a ridiculous thought. He had only married to keep her safe.

The entire marriage was a fiasco and a sham. The sooner it was annulled, the better for them both. She edged away from him and sat up. She immediately missed his warmth and possessive arm, but she shook her head with firm resolve.

When she turned to look back at him, he was still sleeping. She resolved to make certain that once they were on the ship, they would occupy separate cabins.

It took everything in Alexander to remain cool and calm. He had woken up to a reality better than any dream he had ever had. In his arms was Georgiana. Feminine and lovely Georgiana nestled against him in sleep. He had such an intense desire to grip her hips and— But he stopped himself. That way of thinking only tortured him. The desire to have her was forbidden.

It was ridiculous. She was his wife. But not truly. She wanted the annulment, and he wanted her as badly as he had ever wanted her. Even more so than before. But there was not much he could do. How did a man go about seducing his own wife? Most men did that before the ceremony. He had everything backwards.

She pulled away from him and stood looking down at him. He remained with his eyes closed. He didn't want her to feel awkward. When she pulled on her wrapper, he opened his eyes.

"Good morning," he said, yawning.

"Good morning," she greeted him, sitting on the edge of the bed. "Alexander. I was thinking for the trip back, perhaps we should occupy separate cabins."

"Separate cabins? Do I snore?"

Georgiana shook her head. "I don't know. I'm not sure. I just thought – "

"Separate cabins. I'll arrange for it."

But when Alexander went to the shipping office to procure their passage home, he did the opposite. He made sure their room was large and spacious. Separate rooms be damned. When he returned, he informed her that they only had one cabin, and she looked at him with skepticism.

When their departure date arrived, Richard and Arabella saw them off with a large number of embraces and kisses. Georgiana told her aunt and uncle that they should visit them anytime, and they promised faithfully they would. Suddenly, Georgiana was back at sea, traveling once more for England.

"Will you miss it?" Alexander asked as they watched the shoreline retreat.

"I'll miss my aunt and uncle but not much else. I've missed England more than I cared to admit." She looked across at him. "And my father got his wish in the end. So, what was the point of being exiled?"

"Got his wish?"

"He wanted me married and out of his hair a long time ago," she revealed, though Alexander remembered the desire of Jonathan to have his daughter married and off his hands.

"Yes, but the marriage is at your choosing now and the power with you," he reminded her.

"Power? In marriage?" She almost laughed.

Alexander smiled lightly. "Well, yes. You didn't want to be married. But as a viscountess, as Lady Lichfield, you and I have a position in society. And the land and the tenants need to be looked after."

"Alexander-"

"The marriage was the spur of the moment. You wish it to be annulled. But why not spend the first six months enjoying ourselves? We can spend a few weeks in London and then travel to the country estate so you can see for yourself. I'll make no demands on you. I'll behave appropriately."

"Make no demands?" Georgiana wondered at his words. "Hardly seems fair to you."

"I'll have a lovely new bride on my arm to show off, and the men will be extremely jealous." He shrugged. "That's enough for now."

Georgiana nodded. "Then I agree."

But though Alexander appeared to be blasé about the entire situation, he wasn't. He had known it was happening for some time, but he had not wanted to admit it to himself. The last straw had been the ridiculous Puritan and his obsession with Georgiana. When he followed them to Martha's Vineyard, he had been frantic.

Had the mad parson harmed a hair on her head, he would have killed him on the spot. As it was, the moment had presented itself, and they had been married. But Alexander was falling fast into a spiral that he was unable to extract himself from and didn't want to. He was in love with Georgiana. He had realized it the moment he waited for Hackett to arrive in the room and wanted to drive the knife straight into his heart.

He had held himself back, but the white-hot anger was there. And when he looked down at Georgiana sleeping so peacefully and so innocently, completely unaware of someone set on doing her harm, he'd known he must protect her at all costs. He must because he loved her.

That knowledge was not as painful as the fact that she seemed unaware of it. He knew she was attracted to him. It was not a boast. His face and form were pleasing to the female eye, and that had always been used to his advantage. But beyond the kisses and time spent together, she displayed nothing out of the ordinary.

She was innocent so he assumed she liked the attention and adoring eyes of male admirers, but she had said nothing to him beyond enjoying his attention. It was a strange place to be in. He was in love with her, and she tolerated him. The marriage had occurred, and now she wanted it annulled. But now every moment with her was torture.

Never mind that first night spent together in his arms and in his bed when nothing had happened. Who would believe it? He never would have if it had been someone else. But he had experienced it. The desire of sliding his legs between hers and holding her tightly against him. He groaned.

Now, onboard the ship for several weeks, possibly two months, was nothing short of impossible. He should have listened to her and secured the two cabins. But the ship they traveled on was mostly cargo, and there were only four cabins available.

The first night they slept in the same bed, and she stacked several blankets between them. In the night, she shifted and turned to face him in sleep. He spent an hour tracing the delicate lines of her face, wishing he had never kissed her oh so long ago at the theater.

Another night the sea tossed them about, and they got no sleep. She lay on the bed, feeling slightly queasy as he sat on the floor, telling her stories of his time as a privateer.

"Was it very adventurous?" The swaying of the ship made her slightly dizzy.

"It was." He placed his legs out before him.

"You said you had been most places on earth?" She turned to him.

"Most," he agreed.

"I should like to see them." She smiled lightly.

"If we were truly married, I would take you to see them on our honeymoon. However – " He stopped speaking.

"However," she repeated softly. "I never thanked you." She suddenly looked at him from the bed. Her hair was falling down her back, and she looked lovely. It took everything in him not to pull her into his arms and kiss her senseless.

"Thanked me?" He frowned.

"For saving me that night," she acknowledged. "For saving me from Elias."

"I don't want your gratitude, Georgiana," he said solemnly. "I wanted to keep you safe."

"Keep me safe?" She said the words again. "I never thought Elias would go to such lengths. I was quite shocked, and it happened so quickly. I actually thought it was you summoning me."

"Me? Why would you think that?"

"He had a boy deliver a note to the dressmaker. It was very cryptic now that I think on it. It said: *There is a coach waiting outside. It has been hired to take you somewhere special*," she repeated the note to him. "When I asked the boy who had sent it, he said my intended. So, I naturally thought it was you, as we had announced our engagement."

"I see." He nodded.

"Little did I know. I arrived at the dock, and once inside the cabin, Elias was there. I was so stupid." She shook her head.

"Forget all of that now. It's the past, and we're headed home."

"It's in the past," she whispered.

He looked up and cocked his head. "The storm is passing."

The journey passed by smoothly, but Alexander found that a side effect of being in such proximity to Georgiana and not being able to touch her was that he was insanely jealous. When the young sailors were friendly and paid a bit of attention to her on deck, he seethed.

At dinner, the captain made a particular comment about her dress and how the color suited her, and he became irritated. He knew it wasn't Georgiana's fault, and the captain had even made a comment to Alexander, saying she was "a very fine-looking woman." But the compliment did nothing to soothe his nerves.

He found that he began to fixate on her bow-shaped mouth, her breasts that pressed against the fabric, and her eyes that were so expressive and lovely. She was kind and courteous to everyone, which only irked him more. There was a young sailor on the ship who had taken to following her about. It was a true puppy love sort of worship, and in return, Georgiana taught him basic French to pass the time.

"How do you say, you are beautiful?" he asked her one afternoon as they sat on the desk while Alexander looked on.

"Are you complimenting a woman," she asked.

"Yes."

"Then *tu es belle*," she said and repeated it.

Later in their cabin, Alexander was irritated, more at himself, not the young lad who couldn't even shave.

"You shouldn't encourage him," he told her.

"Encourage who?" she said, bewildered.

"You know who. The young lad."

"You're being ridiculous, Alexander. I'm not encouraging him. But it does pass the time teaching him French. Years from now, he might use it to attract his would-be wife," she reasoned.

"There are other ways to pass the time," he said mysteriously.

"Such as?"

He pulled her into his arms. "Such as."

She smiled lightly and pulled away from him. "I enjoy teaching him French. I rarely use it, and it's such a beautiful language."

"Practice with me."

"You never said you spoke French?" She turned to him. "How have I never known that?"

"It never came up I suppose," he said lightly.

"Another thing about Lord Lichfield that I never knew, hmm," she said lightly as she turned from him. She pulled the hooks from her dress that fastened in the front, and as she looked down, a curl got stuck in the dress. "Ow!" she cried out.

Alexander came to stand before her. "Hold still," he said as he carefully took out the curl that was lodged in the hook and, in doing so, popped the hook and several with it.

"I can manage," she assured him.

But as Alexander stood still, watching her carefully, he had the powerful urge to throw her onto the bed and the devil care what happened. She might hate him afterwards, but at least he would be able to stem this insane desire that swept through him every time he looked at her.

"I'll leave you for now then," he said, allowing her to undress as he did each night.

Reaching the deck, he took several deep breaths of the salty sea air, looking up at the dark sky. He had enjoyed his time at sea and was glad he spent his youth as he had. His family had never been entirely positive with the choice, but it had been his choice. And now, he was saddled with the Lichfield wealth, all its entails, and a grand country estate to run.

He was deep in thought when the captain came to stand beside him with a pipe between his lips.

"Lichfield." Said with a nod.

"Captain," he acknowledged the older man.

"We're halfway to England, but then I expect you know that." He took several puffs on his pipe.

Alexander nodded. "Yes. I've taken this journey many times, though not as many as you."

"Your wife has attracted much attention. You are a fortunate man. She's quite beautiful," he admitted and blew out the smoke.

"She is. Thank you."

"I was married many years ago. She's been dead ten years now, but I still think of her." He reminisced of his past.

"You never remarried?" Alexander asked as he looked out over the water.

The captain shook his head. "I was very much in love with my wife. When she died, I never thought such a strong emotion could be duplicated. So no, I never did."

"I understand."

"But sometimes, especially when I look at a particularly lovely sunset, I wish I had someone to share it with me." He passed by Alexander, pipe firmly clenched in his teeth.

When Alexander returned to their cabin, Georgiana was under the bedsheets. He took off his shirt and jacket but left his breeches on as agreed. Settling into bed, he saw the pillows piled between them. What wouldn't he give to pull Georgiana into his arms and kiss the back of her neck? Torture.

"Georgiana," he said softly.

"Yes?"

"We're halfway home."

"That's good."

"We'll stay at the Lichfield townhouse in St. James Square," he remarked. "You'll be very comfortable there."

"Hmmm," she said sleepily. "Glad to be going home."

As he often did, he turned ever so slightly to watch her sleep. His eyes caressed her face the way his fingers could not, and when he closed his eyes, his dreams were chaotic and filled with Georgiana. The London fog was thick, and she was always disappearing just out of reach.

Georgiana was pleased to be back in London and smiled brightly at the familiar sights of the city as the ship pulled into the dock. Their trunks were loaded onto the waiting coach, and when they arrived at the townhouse, Alexander introduced her formally.

"This way please, Lady Lichfield," the housekeeper directed Georgiana, and the maids eyed her as she took the staircase up one floor.

"This was the late Lady Lichfield's room. It has been redecorated in the last year. You will let me know if the colors do not suit your tastes," the older woman informed her.

Georgiana looked about the room decorated in warm earth tones, and a pale peach color dominated the room. A large tapestry hung on the wall, with two chairs and a table beneath it. A large four-poster bed sat at one edge of the room with an armoire and fireplace facing it. The room overlooked the street down below.

Georgiana smiled at it. "Not at all. It seems very comfortable."

Alexander joined them and, playing the bridegroom part for his servant, spoke to Georgiana. "Well, sweetheart, is it to your liking?"

"Very much so." She nodded as he kissed her hand.

***As they dined alone, Alexander warned her, "Once word gets out that we have married, the poor footman will be serving us invitations all day long." He shook his head.

"Will you mind terribly? I haven't been to a proper dance since I left," she said.

Alexander looked over at her. "Wherever you want to go or do, you'll let me know. I'll take you. But as I mentioned, one month, give or take, and then we need to travel to the country."

Georgiana came over to him and hugged him briefly about the shoulders. "Thank you."

When she had gone up to bed, he thought briefly of visiting Madame Auclair's establishment. He hadn't been in over a year, and he wondered if a brief liaison with another woman would cure him of his desire for Georgiana. He already knew the answer to that. It wouldn't. His desire was entirely wrapped up in the slim package of Georgiana and her emerald-colored eyes.

The next evening, they attended Haymarket Theater, and word began buzzing about them almost instantly. Peregrine Thornhill was the first to shake Alexander's hand when he entered their box. He bowed slightly to Georgiana and then turned to his friend.

"My God, Lex!" he said, using his old nickname. "I can't believe you're married! I thought it was the gossip mill!"

"No indeed. We were married in Boston," he said, looking possessively at Georgiana.

"Good Lord, Boston! Is it even a legal marriage if you're married by a savage?"

Alexander gave him a smile. "The marriage was very much legal."

"Not that I blame you," Perry said, lowering his voice. "I think I might sell my soul for one night with her."

"Careful," Alexander warned. "That is my wife you are lusting after."

"Well, admit it, old man! She's a dream!" Perry said.

"She's very lovely."

"Should we take bets on when the next Lord Lichfield is to be born?" Perry winked. "I doubt you waited until your wedding night."

Alexander groaned inwardly. *If you only knew*, he thought.

"By the by, I was sorry to hear about your father and brother. All sorts of nasty stuff in the Continent," he complained. "Most unfortunate."

"It was a shock," Alexander acknowledged.

"Well, I'll leave you to the show," Perry said to them both before leaving.

Alexander settled next to Georgiana in their box, smiling. "Now that Perry knows, the whole theater should know by the time the show ends."

As Alexander predicted, they began to receive cards and invitations for card parties, supper parties, balls, and picnics almost immediately. Georgiana was thrilled to receive the invites and immerse herself back into London society, while Alexander had no opinion on the matter. If he was bringing Georgiana home each night and taking her to one of the bedrooms to make love to her, he would have been content. Instead, each night they went to separate bedrooms, and she slept alone while he tossed and turned.

One morning over coffee and breakfast, he made the offer to have a new wardrobe made for her, but she declined almost immediately.

"Why decline?" he asked. "You've been away for some time, and your wardrobe needs to be renewed."

"I can't." She shook her head. "Not at your expense."

Alexander dismissed this. "I've paid for many things since you have become my wife, Georgiana. I'm not keeping books."

"Maybe one dress," she allowed.

"Spend what you like and send me the bill," he told her and gave her the name of a very well-known and expensive dressmaker before he left that morning.

When Georgiana went to the dressmaker in a fashionable part of town, she looked about the shop and secretively eyed the expensive fabrics and patterns that were displayed.

"Can I help you?" the woman asked, looking her over.

Georgiana nodded. "I would like to order some dresses. Something for the evening and a riding dress perhaps."

The older woman nodded, looking at her frame. "You have an excellent figure, mademoiselle."

"It's madame, actually," she said, correcting her.

"Madame . . . ?" she said, drawing out the word as she asked for her name.

"Madame – well, Lady Lichfield," Georgiana said.

"Lady Lichfield?" the woman asked, and several women in the large shop turned to stare at her.

"The viscountess," she heard someone whisper.

Someone else said, "Alexander's wife," and she turned and smiled at them.

"Lady Lichfield! Please, have a seat. Your husband is so generous. He wrote me but yesterday saying that the shop is at your disposal. You mentioned two dresses? But no." The woman scoffed lightly. "That won't do. Two dresses? You must have what you like. Petticoats, stays, gloves, hats."

"Please!" Georgiana almost giggled. "I don't need all that."

"But no! Your husband disagrees." She shook her head. "And with such a figure, he will want you properly clothed. Who can blame him?"

The woman snapped her fingers and asked for tea to be brewed for the viscountess. Georgiana looked at the fabrics and relished the feel of them. She had been treated well by her past dressmaker, and her father had never denied her anything. But Alexander seemed to want to make her happy. He wanted her to have the finer things for her sake. He wanted her to be adorned. It made her feel warm and comforted.

"And, my dear," the French dressmaker said, lowering her voice, "I have some very fine lingerie that can be handmade for you. Your husband will not mind paying that bill, I assure you."

Georgiana warmed and stammered, "I don't think he would –"

"*Mon dieu*! You blush like a virgin, not a married woman at all," the dressmaker teased her. "Come now! Lingerie made for such nighttime pleasures." She smiled. "He will enjoy them very much."

"Very well," she said, just to make the woman stop talking about lingerie and nighttime pleasures.

Eh, God! If the woman only knew that even with all this time spent in close confined quarters with Alexander, she remained a blushing virgin.

She was running her hand over a very fine pink satin when the bell over the door tinkled and laughter rang out as a new patroness joined the shop.

"Hello, madame! How are you this fine morning? I'm here to try on my evening gown – " The woman stopped speaking and stared at Georgiana. "Georgiana? Is that you?"

Georgiana frowned. The woman's hair was heavily powdered, and she looked to be very pregnant as well. Then she saw her face.

"Madeleine!" she cried out. "Madeleine, how are you?"

The two friends hugged each other as the dressmaker looked on.

"I'm well. Very well as you can see," she said, touching her belly.

"Madeline! I'm so angry at you! You never wrote to me once - not once - in the whole time I was in Boston!" Georgiana scolded her as they sat down together.

"I have a very good excuse!" she said, smiling. "I met the most handsome man. French, of course. And he swept me off my feet. We ended up spending a glorious month in France, and one thing led to another. I'm pregnant and married." She laughed.

"Darling Madeleine, congratulations!" Georgiana exclaimed, remembering her friend saying something about never being intimate with a Frenchman, but brushed it aside.

"And you?" Madeleine asked. "What have you been up to? You're back from being exiled!"

Georgiana thought about telling her friend the truth but then decided against it. "I'm also married. I married Alexander Mayson."

"Here you are, Lady Lichfield," the dressmaker said, placing the tea tray between them.

"Lady Lichfield?" Madeleine frowned. "Alexander Mayson! That handsome devil! You sly thing!"

"He's the Viscount of Lichfield."

"Oh, my God!" Madeleine squealed. "He's handsome and with a title. You are so lucky! Imagine that stallion between your legs each night."

"Maddie!" Georgiana said, trying to sound shocked but remembering her friend spoke her mind.

"We're hosting a dinner party at the end of the week," Madeleine explained. "You both must come. It will be such fun. We'll play parlor games and eat and drink. And you can see the darling dear I married. Say yes!"

"Of course, yes!"

Madeleine promised to send her the invite, and then after her dress had been fitted, she kissed Georgiana on the cheek and was gone.

Chapter 17

GEORGIANA PICKED AN ESPECIALLY daring gown for the night of Madeleine's party. The neckline was exceedingly low, and the purple taffeta looked well against her dark hair and pale skin. When she stepped onto the landing, Alexander was waiting for her below, his eyes hotly moving over her.

"Do you like the dress? I did as you asked and visited the dressmaker." She made a little turn.

His mouth seemed to water as he looked at her luscious breasts and then her sweet face. "You look good enough to eat," he said, entirely serious.

"Did I tell you what happened to Madeleine? She met some Frenchman and took off to France," she said as they entered the coach.

"Presumably France is where Frenchmen live," he said dryly.

She smacked his arm with her fan. "They were apparently having an affair when she came up pregnant. So now they're married."

"Your Madeleine is quite wild," he recalled.

"She is but she's also quite sweet," Georgiana defended her. "Don't set yourself against her."

"I've done nothing of the sort. I don't know her at all."

"Good."

When the coach deposited them in front of the townhouse, the lanterns and music inside guided them in. Madeleine greeted them warmly and offered them both a glass of champagne. When she disappeared, Georgiana moved about the rooms, seeing a buffet table set up, six musicians playing in one room, and a large punch bowl set up in the corner.

Helping herself to a glass, she drank it down quickly, not realizing how thirsty she was. She took a second glass when she felt eyes upon her and she turned to see a young man watching her. His hair was inky black, and his brown eyes moved over her. He was handsome but seemed infinitely sure of himself.

"*Ma chere*," the man said warmly. "You are absolutely the most beautiful woman I have seen in England in some time."

"*Merci*," she replied.

"I think we should find a way to leave this place behind and spend the night in each other's arms," he told her boldly.

Georgiana choked on her punch. "Is that how you greet all women?"

"Only the beautiful ones." He shrugged. "The ugly ones I leave to fend for themselves."

Georgiana laughed. "Monsieur, you should behave. Someone might take you seriously one day."

"But I wish you would." He leaned into her. "I would like nothing more than to show you how a man can love a woman with only his tongue."

Georgiana had the good grace to blush and stepped away from him. "Sir. Refrain from such intimate conversation. I am married, and it's unseemly that you should speak to me so."

"But why do you blush? You aren't a maiden. You just said you are married. So, what could be more agreeable?" the man said flippantly.

Georgiana was trying to think of a way to put the wayward Frenchman in his place when Madeleine joined them.

"Ah-ha! I see you two have found each other!" she said happily. "Now you two must be the best of friends and get along very well. Darling Georgiana, this is my husband, Jean Michel Sartin, and Jean, this is Georgiana," she said proudly.

"Of course, we shall." Jean Michel took her hand in his. Leaning over it, he kissed the back of her hand innocently but fingered the palm of it intimately. "I hope it will be my pleasure," he said lowly before he and Madeleine moved together to greet another one of their guests.

Georgiana was flushed over the interaction with Jean Michel. He was a flirt and a rake and had obviously hooked Madeleine the same way, and now he was openly flirting with her. She wasn't flattered or happy about the attention. He was married to her friend. He seemed to be playing a personal game with her, and she would have none of it.

"Here you are," Alexander said, coming to her side.

"Don't leave me alone again," she hissed.

"Why? What's happened?" he asked, his tone serious.

"I just met Madeleine's husband."

"Jean Michel."

"Exactly. And the man is – the man is not a gentleman."

"What did he do?" he asked. She told him that he was flirting with her, though she tamed down the words. "I understand." Alexander nodded.

"Don't hurt him!" Georgiana pulled at his sleeve.

"Jesus, Georgiana!" He shook his head. "I won't hurt him. At least not in the way you think."

When next Jean Michel came near her, Alexander was standing nearby. Not giving her a chance to respond, he pulled her into his arms and kissed her passionately, lightly touching her on the bottom.

"I can't wait to take you to bed tonight," he whispered in her ear when he released her. He looked over at Jean Michel and shrugged. "Newlyweds."

Jean Michel looked displeased as Georgiana licked her lips and looked over at Alexander. He looked back and his expression seemed to say, *See? Done.*

Georgiana nodded, but her knees were weak from the kiss, and she felt a warmth and wetness between her legs. She shook herself mentally and moved away from both men. Scanning the crowd, she saw a very attractive woman standing in the back of the room with a drink in her hand. Georgiana recognized her immediately.

"Madame de Froissy," she said, coming to stand beside her.

"Madame Gainsford," she said in greeting. "No, It's Lady Lichfield now." She simpered. "I must say, I never thought I would see the day Alexander married. But then I guess when his father and brother died, duty called." She looked her over.

"Yes, duty called."

"But you have the better bargain, don't you, my dear." Philippine sipped her champagne. "Such a handsome husband and so demanding in bed. Aren't you a little sore? I know I always was afterwards."

Georgiana looked away from her.

"I'm sure I'll only have to wait six months and he'll be bored silly of you." She smirked. "Then he'll back in my bed where he belongs."

"Why wait six months?" Georgiana turned to her. "Why not take him now? Or are you worried he doesn't want you?"

"Oh! The little kitten has claws, how cute," Philippine said, moving away from her.

Georgiana's interaction with Alexander's mistress irritated her, and against her better judgement, she took a champagne glass from a footman and drank it down, followed by a second. By the time she realized it was her third, she felt light-headed and knew that had been a mistake.

She heard the small orchestra begin to play and saw Jean Michel watching her from across the room. When he came towards her, she didn't run from him.

"Let's go upstairs, madame. I'll be quick," he said in her ear. "No one will know."

Georgiana looked him over. "Go to your wife. It's disgusting that she's pregnant and you're here talking to me like this."

"You're drunk." He smiled. "I like that."

He pulled on her arm and began to lead her up the stairs, even as she tried to evade his grip.

"Monsieur, let go of me before I make you very sorry," she said, pulling on his grip.

As they were on the landing, a door opened up and there was Alexander, leaving the bedroom with his waistcoat unbuttoned and Philippine behind him.

Georgiana's eyes went wide with disbelief and then anger, but Alexander reacted much quicker. Bridging the distance in a few steps, he smashed his fist into Jean Michel's face. While the Frenchman held his nose and cried, Alexander grabbed Georgiana by the arm and dragged her down the stairs.

"I can't believe you!" she said the minute they were in the coach. "You disgust me!"

Alexander scoffed at her. "Me?" He almost laughed. "What about you, madame? Letting that French dandy toss up your knickers? Have you no self-respect?"

"No self-respect? At least he's not a prostitute that all of London has been with!" She flung herself back into the coach. "I'm not surprised. The things she said to me. She's just your sort."

"And what is my sort?" he asked as the coach slowed to a stop.

She flung open the door and marched into the house, with Alexander following her. "Your sort," she said, moving into the parlor and pouring herself a drink.

"You've had enough," he said, taking the glass from her. "Go sleep it off."

She looked at him angrily and then picked up the bottle and drank from it.

"Very elegant," he said wryly.

"You know what your little slut told me? Hmmm? She said I had the better bargain. That my husband was so handsome and so demanding in bed. Well, she should know," Georgiana said bitterly.

"You already know Philippine was my mistress," he pointed out.

"Was?" Georgiana took the bottle with her into the foyer. "Is. I mean, how disgusting. You two couldn't wait until the party was over? You had to have her at my friend's house?" She flounced up the stairs.

He didn't deny the allegation but instead smirked. "What about you?" He followed her up the stairs. "Your friend's husband? And she's pregnant!"

"That's not what happened! You don't know anything!" She opened the door to her room and tried to slam the door in his face, but he stuck his foot in the door.

He walked into her room and closed the door behind him. "So, tell me. Or is this Elias Hackett over again?"

"Elias Hackett? You are an ass! Elias drugged me and dragged me to that island to marry me against my will!"

She put her hands on her hips. "How can you even compare the two?"

"And Jean Michel? So taken with your charms, he had to have you in his own house?" He ran a hand through his hair. "In his own bed?"

"I don't have to tell you anything, and your little whore was wrong," she recalled. "She didn't have to wait six months - she only had to wait six hours."

Alexander wretched the bottle from her and placed it under the bed, out of her reach. "Go to sleep, Georgiana," he said coldly.

"Do you know what she said?" Georgiana said, standing in front of him. "She said I would only have to wait six months and you'd be bored silly of me," she said, narrowing her eyes at him. "She said you would be back in her bed where you belong. Well, I guess that's right. Two pigs in the trough."

Alexander felt something tenuous inside him snap. "And what of you, my darling bride? How many times did you say no before the Frenchman led you upstairs?" He placed a tendril of hair behind her ear.

"I didn't say no," she lied, looking up at him and smiling.

"You didn't say no?" he asked her suddenly, grabbing her arm. "I'm sure no is only a word you use with me."

"That's right!" She nodded. "I only tell you no. Every other man is a yes."

"I'm sure." He nodded. "Which is funny. Because you put down Philippine for being exactly what you are. Aren't you both just whores in pretty clothes?"

"Bastard!" Georgiana reached out to slap him, but he stopped her.

"Is that what's wrong, Georgiana?" He released her arm and suddenly pulled her against him. "Did I not kiss you enough? Did I not give you what you need? Is that why you seek other men's attentions?"

"I want nothing from you, Alexander," Georgiana said, trying to jerk out of his embrace. "Nothing."

"It's my fault." He moved close to whisper in her ear. "I haven't treated you as a proper wife. I haven't given you what you need."

Georgiana jerked back. "What is it that you think I need? What do you have that I could possibly need?"

"Besides my money, my position, and my title –"

"None of which I asked for," she told him hotly.

"I think you need a good fucking."

Georgiana gasped. She wasn't frightened or bewildered but absolutely thrilled. She wanted him too.

"You're exactly base enough to think something like that. Especially since you've already had one woman tonight." She narrowed her eyes. "Don't you think that's enough?"

"Nothing happened," he said lowly, eyeing her intently.

"Of course, I'm stupid now." She rolled her eyes. "You both come out of the bedroom with your jacket unbuttoned, but nothing happened."

Alexander nodded and began unbuttoning the same jacket. "She wanted me. That's true. I refused her. She was quite angry actually, now that I come to think of it."

"I wonder why. Since you are so handsome and so demanding in bed," she said sarcastically, quoting Philippine.

"Handsome and demanding in bed?" Alexander smiled, throwing his jacket and waistcoat onto the chair nearby. He stood before her in his breeches, hose, and shirt.

She frowned. "What are you doing?"

"Making myself more comfortable."

"Why?"

Putting his hands on her hips, he spun her around and deftly undid the hooks of her gown that the ladies' maid he had procured for her had done so only a few hours ago.

"What are you doing?" she asked, breathless at his hands on her.

"That should be quite obvious."

Georgiana looked over her shoulder at him. When the task was done, the garment fell about her ankles. Her hoop followed the gown, and then his hands were undoing the ties of the corset that held her waist tightly nipped in. He deftly undid the laces, and she caught it to her chest for a moment before letting it fall.

The petticoat was the last to go and then she stood before him in her thin chemise and small heeled shoes.

"What's the point of this?" she asked when she turned to face him. "What do you want?"

"What I've wanted since that night at Haymarket Theater," he said honestly.

"I'm not prepared to be your wife in deed," she said coolly. "I want an annulment. That hasn't changed."

"No," he said softly. "I imagine that hasn't changed." He drew a finger under her chin, tipping it up to meet her eyes. "But so much has changed with me, Georgiana. I can hardly fathom it."

"Such as?" she asked him. "What has changed, Alexander? That you need to have two women in one night now?"

He shook his head. "There's no need to be jealous. Philippine is my past, that's true. And there she will remain. But there's only one woman in my future. There's only one woman in my heart."

"You don't need to tell me lies," she responded.

His arms encircled her waist. "It's true. There's a reason I've been so jealous. It's the reason I couldn't stand that Frenchman touching you."

"No one touched me," she said. "Jean Michel is a pig. He was behaving monstrously. I called him disgusting to his face."

"Stop fighting me," he said lowly. "I only want you. As my wife, as my lover. This was meant to be. Since that night so long ago when I kissed you for the first time."

"Why are you saying these things now?" she asked but was warmed by his words and his touch.

"It's taken me some time to build up my courage, and I've been a coward, but when I married you, it was entirely selfish," he said, his eyes meeting hers.

"Selfish?" She looked up at him.

"I love you, Georgiana." He said the simple words but his heart was racing. "I have for some time. And when Hackett took you away, I was crazed. When I knew his intentions, I took the opportunity to keep you safe. But I wanted to marry you. I wanted you by my side."

He pulled out the two combs holding her hair in place, and the curtain of brown hair fell down her back. She was drunk, but it was the floating sort of tipsy that made her feel free and light.

"Let me love you tonight," he whispered.

Georgiana remembered the times they had spent alone and all of the emotions she had felt. She did desire him. She knew that was not a false feeling, but something she had felt with him often. It was not difficult, as he was handsome and self-assured.

"Don't run," he whispered to her. "Not tonight."

She shook her head. "I won't."

When he pulled her into his arms, the kiss was unlike anything she had experienced. It was so possessive and powerful, and her knees were weak. His fingers threaded into her hair even as she clung to him. When he backed her up against the bed, he picked her up lightly and laid her down before him. Quickly, he rid himself of his clothes, and the thrill of lying naked with her was intoxicating.

She shivered as she pulled the chemise over her head and was only clad in her stockings that were held up by delicate-looking garters. When she reached down to remove them, he stopped her.

"No, don't. You look so lovely." Spreading her legs ever so slightly, he settled his weight above her. "I think I've dreamed about this moment since first I met you. I've wanted you for so long I can't remember a time before then."

He kissed her once, then twice, and moving his hand up her leg, he touched her as he had done so long ago. Once more, his fingers delved past the delicate curls and into her warm core. She moaned, and her nails gripped his shoulders.

"Alexander," she said breathlessly, even as he kissed her again, and his fingers delved in and out of her. She felt everything at once as the feeling of his mouth and fingers consumed her.

"It might be a little uncomfortable at first," he warned her.

"What might be?" she asked, confused.

He sighed in her ear. "You're so wet."

Georgiana frowned. "Is that bad?"

"No, you're perfect."

Kissing her deeply, he moved between her legs, but this time, he separated them wider and settled between her thighs, trying not to move too quickly but wanting her so badly. He had his cock in his hand and ever so slightly eased inside her, trying not to harm or frighten her.

"God, Georgiana." He groaned. "You are so tight."

Georgiana could feel the weight of Alexander above her even though he was using his forearm to support him as he guided his cock ever so slightly into her. As the tip entered her, she felt a sharp twinge, followed by the feeling of being filled completely. It was such a new sensation that she gasped at the welcome intrusion. She rocked her hips once, and he groaned.

"Don't do that," he almost cried out. "I'll come too soon. I'm not going to last long."

He kissed her once, then twice. Pressing into her, he moved back and forward, causing her to moan at the thrusts and close her eyes.

"That's it." He watched her carefully. "Come with me."

Georgiana felt amazing. The feeling of him inside her, stretching her, was so blissful, and she knew instinctively that there was a place she was supposed to reach if she only could. She rocked her hips, even though he told her not to, but she wanted to reach the end.

The climax was small but still there. She let out a small cry as Alexander gripped her hips harder and, without words, spilled his seed inside her.

Lying side by side in the dark, Georgiana turned to see that he was breathing lightly and his eyes were closed. She stood up, and wetness slid down her leg. She cleaned herself off and pulled on a wrapper. As she looked down at Alexander, he appeared so young and innocent.

She went downstairs to the kitchen for a glass of water and thought about what had just occurred. She was not sorry. She had wanted Alexander. She might be married for convenience, but she liked the attention, and the act itself was most enjoyable.

No wonder Madeleine had always lost her wits over some man in the time she had known her. But now, now what was she to do? Alexander had said he loved her. Had he really meant the words? Or only said them to bed her? That seemed unlikely. They had spent so many weeks at sea, and nothing like this had happened. But she wasn't sure how she felt.

She drank the last of the water and set the glass aside. It must be early in the morning. The sun had not yet risen, but the sky was grey and cloudy. Was it going to rain? She looked out the window as she left the kitchen. She felt torn and so unsure of herself.

She had wanted Alexander. It was hard to deny such a man. He was so certain of himself, and he always seemed to know his own mind. He took what he wanted, and that was an admirable quality. But sadly, she did not know her own mind. She had remained married for her own reasons, but once the marriage was annulled, what then? Return to her father's home? Absolutely not.

Did it even make sense that she should have remained married one day more if she did not wish it? It didn't have anything to do with the position, though she liked being Lady Lichfield, and the money was also desirable, but she had to admit it was the man behind it all. Alexander Mayson, Lord Lichfield.

I think I've dreamed about this moment since first I met you. . . I've wanted you for so long I can't remember a time before then . . .

Those words he had said and she knew he meant them.

I love you, Georgiana . . . I have for some time . . .

He loved her. Those words had shocked her, but in the moment, she had been too caught up in it all. Now in the cold grey light of day, she could reflect on them. He loved her. It made her feel warm and comfortable being loved by such a man. But what did she feel for him? Did she love him? She admired him. She thought highly of him. But she didn't think she loved him.

Georgiana sighed as she moved up the staircase and opened the door to her room. He was still sleeping where she had left him, lying on his back with the sheets covering his lower body, and even in sleep, he was handsome. She was attracted to him, but she didn't love him. And knowing herself, she didn't want to stay married for convenience.

Her father had wanted her to marry for convenience, and she had fought him so hard she'd ended up in Boston and in the arms of this rascal. But thinking about the situation, she had a solution. She would tell Alexander and see if he agreed.

Chapter 18

ALEXANDER OPENED HIS EYES and frowned at the surroundings. Nothing looked as it should, and the room was cool and decorated strangely. Then he saw a figure seated below the window seat, looking out over the street. Her chestnut brown hair fell down her back.

Georgiana.

He smiled lightly as he remembered the night before. Finally. After so much time apart and then being forced to be together on the voyage back to England, finally Georgiana was his. She was his wife in name, and now she was his wife in deed.

He didn't want to appear too brash, but he was delighted. There could be no more denying what had occurred between them. She had wanted him, and God knew he had lusted after her for far too long. His only irritant was that she wasn't naked in bed with him. He wanted nothing more than to roll her underneath him and press his cock inside her once more.

"You're up," she said, looking at him from the window.

He looked down at his member and then back at her sweet face. "I am."

"Did you sleep well?" she asked.

"I did. Did you?" He sat up into a sitting position, pulling the sheets about him as she came to sit on the edge of the bed.

"Reasonably well."

"I had hoped to wake with you beside me," he said softly, touching her hand.

"Alexander," she said, taking her hand back. "I want to talk with you."

Jesus! That sounded awful. "Talk."

"I wanted to – " she said. Looking at his naked body was disturbing.

"Yes? What did you want?"

"About what happened last night – " she began awkwardly as he watched her.

"Last night," he prompted her.

"I think perhaps we rushed things –"

"That's entirely my fault. Next time I'll go slower," he told her.

"No! That's not at all what I'm saying."

"I was teasing you, Georgiana."

She frowned. "Well, don't. This is serious. I'm not saying last night was a mistake. I enjoyed it. But I don't want it to mean too much."

He tensed. "Not mean too much? Don't you think it means everything?"

Georgiana shook her head. "How can it mean everything? Don't men keep mistresses? Isn't that a large part of what you do with them?"

"Are you comparing yourself to a mistress?" he asked.

"Of course not! I'm merely saying that it doesn't have to mean so much. What happened between us," she finished.

He shook his head. "So, the morning after, you regret what happened."

"No. I don't. It's just, after what you said to me – "

He frowned. "What did I say?"

"You said you – you said you loved me." When he met her eyes but said nothing, she continued. "Did you mean it?" Her face was full of innocence.

"What do you think?" He was worried she regretted what had happened between them.

"Did you say it just to – " she began.

"Just to what?" His words were curt.

"Just to bed me?" She said the words quickly, unsure of him.

He smiled and shook his head. Pulling the sheet about his waist, he stood up and went to her. "I have had more than enough opportunities to bed you, Georgiana. I didn't need to say sweet words to get you to lie with me last night."

"So, it was true?" She held her breath for his response.

"Does it matter?" he asked.

"It matters," she said, her eyes full of sincerity.

"If you want to say what happened doesn't mean anything, I can't do that. It meant something to me. If you regret it, I can't help that," he admitted to her.

He stood before her swathed in a sheet like a dark Greek god, and she felt a strange desire to kiss him and pull him to her. She stopped herself. "I would like to go to your country estate," she said suddenly.

He frowned. "Lichfield?"

She nodded. Georgiana thought of her reasons. She wanted time to think about her situation and assess her feelings. Away from London and the peace of Lichfield was her solution.

"Why do you want to see Lichfield when you don't even want the man attached to it?" he wondered.

"I never said I don't want you, Alexander. That's never been the problem."

He studied her. "I see. Very well. I'll take you to Lichfield."

"Thank you." She pulled on the ties to her dressing gown.

"When do you want to travel there? It's a several-hour coach ride from London to Derbyshire," he explained, holding onto the sheet about his waist.

"Derbyshire?" Her voice rose in a question at the name.

"There are many grand homes in the area," he said, looking away from her. "You mustn't be disappointed with Lichfield Abbey."

"I'm sure I won't be." She tried not to stare at his mostly naked form.

"We can leave at the end of the month."

Without saying another word, Alexander left the room, leaving Georgiana sitting on the bed.

Alexander dressed for the morning and replayed the conversation with Georgiana in his head. She regretted the night they spent together. How could it be that two people could share a similar experience and one recalled the memory with such bliss, while the other with regret? It was unimaginable that it should be so, but it was.

He could see the emotions play across her face when she'd spoken of love, and she seemed shy and almost embarrassed by it. How could such a lovely woman be afraid of the emotion? He realized that he must do what he had not done until now. He must spend his time wooing and courting Georgiana. She may be his wife, but it was only in name.

Suddenly, he stopped dressing for a moment. It had not occurred to either of them, and certainly he had not thought of it in the moment of passion, but Georgiana may be tied to him already in this lifetime. She might very well be carrying the next earl in her belly this very morning.

The thought stunned him. That they might already be joined together with a child thrilled him beyond comprehension. He must do as he set out to do. He must woo and court her so that their time together in Lichfield would be well spent. He would send a footman to have the house ready and make certain everything was to her liking.

As Georgiana dressed for the morning, she thought she had handled the conversation with Alexander awkwardly. She did not want him to think she was ungrateful or that he was not desirable to her, but love was the question that she could not answer.

She had an appointment to visit the shoemaker who had been recommended to her. She stepped into the store, looking at the exquisite shoes on display. The first small room was filled with different shoes, each on a pedestal. One pair was made of bright yellow silk with delicate pink flowers embroidered on them. Another shoe in purple and another made of light blue silk with a darker blue embroidery all about it caught her eye.

A woman greeted her and motioned for her to follow her. The next room was much larger with several women seated in pairs, with women kneeling at their feet as they tried on the shoes. She was shown to her own plump settee and told someone would be with her shortly.

The curtains in the windows were silk, and the wood floors were polished and shone brightly. The other women were well-dressed and talked amongst themselves, though several stared at Georgiana. Her father had preferred another shoemaker who was not nearly as fashionable as this one.

An older woman approached her and smiled lightly. "Lady Lichfield, is it?"

"Yes I am," Georgiana said to the stranger.

"I'm Lady Durham." She looked at the seat beside Georgiana. "May I?"

"Please." Georgiana nodded.

The woman sat next to Georgiana. "I was surprised to see you here. We've heard of Alexander's marriage but few have met you."

"It happened very suddenly, the marriage," Georgiana told the woman. "We were married in the colonies. In Boston."

"Boston?" Lady Durham raised an eyebrow. "So far removed."

"It is." Georgiana nodded.

"I dare say," she said. "It was such a shock to learn of the old earl and his son. A tragedy."

"I imagine it was." Georgiana brushed at her skirts as she eyed the older woman.

"I knew the old earl well. Though not so well Alexander as he made his own way, as I'm sure you know," she said.

"I do," Georgiana said politely.

"Though I can quite see what he saw in you, my dear, such a beauty," she said complimentary. "What was your family name?" she asked pleasantly.

"Gainsford," Georgiana supplied.

"Gainsford?" The woman repeated the name. "Any relation to Jonathan Gainsford?"

"My father," she admitted.

"Such a shame about him, but I'm sure we all saw it coming." She shook her head. "The woman is disgraceful. All that one cares for is shillings and pence," she whispered.

"Mariah Gower?" Georgiana guessed, though uneasy at the woman's words.

"Hmmm. I was surprised your father didn't see right through her, but he didn't. And I fear it will be his ruin." She shook her head.

"In what way?" Georgiana asked, peering intensely at the woman.

She hadn't spoken to her father since she left for Boston and was unaware of his circumstances.

"You've not heard?" the older woman asked, surprise on her face.

"As I've said, I've been away some time," Georgiana explained.

"I see. Your father purchased a very expensive house for himself. I think it was more for Mariah. And the house is quite extravagant. I've heard through different sources that he can't afford it but refuses to give it up," Lady Durham shrugged her thin shoulders.

"What house did he buy?" Georgiana leaned forward.

"Clyvedon Hall."

"Clyvedon Hall?" Georgiana repeated incredulously. "That's an enormous mansion for two people."

The older woman searched in her small bag for an item, and extracting it, she handed it to Georgiana. "My card," she said simply. "You must come and have tea with me one day when you are free."

When she had gone, a sense of sadness swept over Georgiana. Her father had purchased the extravagant Clyvedon Hall for Mariah and was now in dire straits. She felt sorry for him. She had known all along that Mariah Gower was not a woman to be trusted, but her father had not seen the woman and her true face.

There was nothing she could do. If she called on her father, he might be embarrassed that she knew his circumstances, and there was no way she would ask

Alexander for any money. Her father should have known better.

The proprietress came to her, and Georgiana asked to see the blue silk shoes. Georgiana already knew that she wanted them, as well as the purple ones, which had caught her eye. She was waiting for the proprietress to return to her when a new woman entered the store.

She was dressed in a low-cut frock in light pink silk, with a hat and small veil over her face. She was staring at Georgiana and made her way to sit beside her without invitation. "Lady Lichfield," she said in greeting.

Georgiana tried to stem her irritation. "Madame de Froissy," she acknowledged the woman.

"You and your husband left so suddenly the other night," she recalled. "And Alexander? In such a state! Did he actually attack our host?"

Georgiana refused to be pulled into the discussion with the vulgar woman. Philippine knew very well what had happened. She had been standing right there.

"One might think Alexander was wound up because his home life is unsatisfying," she simpered. "Though I'm not sure why that should be? I was able to satisfy his needs quite well last night."

Georgiana narrowed her eyes. "Is that so?" She said the words coolly, but her heart was beating heavy in her chest.

"But *oui*." She shrugged. "Old habits die hard. And unlike you, *ma petite*, I know well how to satisfy Alexander."

Georgiana hated the woman calling her husband by name and speaking about his wants and desires as if she knew them so well. But she did, she thought sickeningly.

"I'm sure you do." Georgiana nodded, speaking lowly. "That's what whores are paid for."

"Oh, now." Philippine smiled lightly. "Don't use such rude terms, or I'll think I've struck the quick."

Georgiana did swear inwardly. She mustn't appear to be such a jealous cat. "You don't need to seek me out every time we meet in public, Madame de Froissy, to speak about your past with my husband. I know it well."

Philippine nodded. "The past, yes, but the present too."

"Alexander told me all about last night," Georgiana said, feeling certain of herself. "Nothing happened. So don't pretend otherwise."

"Well, he would have to say that, wouldn't he? After all, some men don't believe oral play is truly the complete act."

Georgiana looked about the room, but the other patrons were not paying attention to their conversation, and Philippine was speaking quietly. "I don't believe anything you say," Georgiana said coolly. "If anything had happened between the two of you, why would you tell me now? It's not as if we were to be married and I could break off an engagement. We are married."

Philippine smiled lightly. "You're a smart woman. And beautiful, I'll give you that much. But whatever reason Alexander married you, you really aren't his type. I'm telling you this from experience. And to save you some heartache."

"So, this is for my benefit?" Georgiana said, her eyebrow raising.

"You'll see." Philippine nodded. "He'll be bored to death of you soon enough. And then he'll be back to me." She stood.

"I'm curious," Georgiana asked the woman standing above her. "If you were such a good match, why did it end?"

"I wouldn't say it ended." Philippine shrugged. "Maybe it's a brief reprieve."

When Philippine left, Georgiana ordered the pairs she liked, but the afternoon was soured. She had no doubt that much of what his past mistress had said was true. A handsome man such as Alexander would have his pick of women, and they were probably very accomplished.

Philippine was accomplished in ways that a mistress would be and no doubt did things in the bedroom no self-respecting wife would do. She didn't think anything had happened that night, not because she believed Alexander so much as she didn't believe Philippine. She seemed to go out of her way to insist on something, which made Georgiana distrust it.

Then the words she used were absolutely baffling. *Some men don't believe oral play is truly the complete act.* What on earth did that mean?

They would be leaving at the end of the week for the country, and she was looking forward to it. The morning, which was meant to be a nice excursion to buy some lovely shoes, had turned into a trial.

First Lady Durham and the news of her father and then the jealous mistress who wanted nothing more than to make Georgiana second-guess her new husband. Well, Georgiana didn't need Philippine for that. She already distrusted Alexander immensely, and her time in the country was needed now more than ever.

When she returned home, she changed into a simpler gown for dinner and went downstairs. Alexander was in the parlor pouring himself a drink.

"Good evening, Georgina," he greeted her. "How was the shoemaker's? Enjoyable?"

Georgiana took the sherry he offered her. "I met a woman there. Her name was Lady Durham. Do you know her?"

"Lady D?" he asked, surprised. "She was good friends with my father. I knew her but briefly."

"She gave me her card. Asked me to tea when I had the time."

"Excellent."

"She mentioned my father as well," she noted. "Have you had any news of him?"

Alexander was silent and then nodded. "I didn't want to burden you. But yes. I have news of him."

"What news?" she pressed.

"Sometime back after you left, he purchased Clyvedon Hall. It was quite the news for many reasons. No one thought old Clyvedon would sell, and the property is quite vast."

"It is."

"It was around the same time he married Mariah Gower. Some think he purchased the property to impress her," he said.

"I know that's the exact reason he purchased the property," she replied.

"Apparently once married, Mariah began to rack up gambling debts and spent a fortune on gowns and jewels, none of which your father could afford," he said simply. "She was also known to – " He looked awkwardly at her.

"Known to . . . ?" she asked.

"She had lovers. Several. Which in itself is not scandalous, but she was quite open about it, and your father was shamed when she attended a concert on one of her lover's arm," he recalled.

"I knew she was only marrying him for his money and position, but he would hear no ill spoken of her," she said softly.

"I've seen it happen before." He exhaled. "Once an infatuation happens, you cannot sway the one infatuated."

She remembered well her father and Mariah. Her father full of desire for the younger woman, and Mariah with only shillings in her mind.

"And Clyvedon Hall? What will become of that place?" She shook her head. "To buy that enormous building seems so unlike my father. He was usually so prudent with money."

"Love makes fools of us all."

She toyed with the sleeve of her dress. "I also saw your – your – " She struggled for the right word and then settled with "Philippine."

"She's not mine," he said swiftly.

"It seems she wants to be. I didn't bring it up to quarrel, just to let you know I saw her."

"She distressed you?" he wondered.

"No. She said much the same as before. That you'll be back with her soon enough." She shrugged.

"Impossible."

"Even if your wife is not your wife?" Georgina asked him in a whisper.

He wanted to go to her then and take her in his arms but he held himself in check. "I can be very patient when it's important," he said quietly.

"Can you?" Their eyes met.

"Yes." His word was a simple affirmation.

Georgiana said nothing more to him.

Later in the night, Georgiana lay in her bed, staring at the ceiling, not tired at all. She had not wanted to mention the encounter with Philippine, but she didn't want to keep it a secret either. If Philippine found out somehow that she had not told Alexander about seeing her, the woman would think she had power over her. Georgiana was wise enough to know that their past relationship would always be there but instinctively knew that Philippine wanted to make her jealous and cause trouble.

Love makes fools of us all.

He had said the words with a slight smile in reference to her father and Mariah, but perhaps he was speaking of her. She had a nagging feeling that Philippine was right about certain things, and though Alexander had married her in a moment of craziness, he regretted it now. He wanted an annulment as well but didn't want to ask for it. He also viewed her as a nuisance and was ready to be rid of her.

Her head ached at the mess of emotions she felt. What was she to do now? Once she annulled the marriage, she couldn't go back to her father, and she had very little of her own money. She might consider returning to Boston, but she dismissed that idea.

She had enjoyed spending time with her aunt and uncle, but she belonged in England. She might approach Alexander for a settlement, though she would hate to be beholden to him in that regard. She was not a true wife, and to ask for a settlement once their union was dissolved seemed disingenuous.

She had thought being back in England would make everything seem clear; instead she felt more confused than ever. When sleep finally came, she was restless much of the night.

Chapter 19

SEVERAL WEEKS LATER, AS Alexander had promised, he and Georgiana were cozily ensconced inside the coach on their way to the Devonshire home. She was looking forward to her first glimpse of Alexander's home and wanted very much to like it.

When Lichfield Abbey came into view from the coach, it took Georgiana's breath away.

"It was an Augustinian priory from the 12th century until its dissolution by Henry the Eighth," Alexander explained to her as the coach road past the entrance of ten-foot-high wrought iron fence.

Looking out from the coach at the magnificent building, she saw the three-story structure decorated in a cream-colored brick with large sash windows on each floor.

"The estate is quite vast," Alexander explained to her. "There is a stable, a farm, a brewhouse linked to the main house by a tunnel."

"A tunnel? How unusual!" Georgiana said brightly.

"There is a walled garden and a flower garden that my mother particularly enjoyed," he told her, "and an ancient deer park. You will see them quite often on the estate."

"Deer?" Georgiana smiled. "How charming!"

When the coach pulled up in front of the main entrance of the house, several maids, a footman, a butler, and a housekeeper greeted them. Alexander placed his hand on her lower back as she was introduced to the servants as the Viscountess of Lichfield. Georgiana glanced sharply at Alexander and then smiled lightly in greeting to the servants. As they entered the vast mansion, she looked up at the vaulted ceilings and passed by the paintings of several Lichfields from the past. She was impressed by it all.

"Did you grow up here?" Georgiana wondered as she looked up at his ancestors' portraits that decorated the walls.

"Yes. Until I went off to university. Let Mrs. Trevor take you to your room, Georgiana. You must be tired," he said before handing her over to the housekeeper.

Mrs. Trevor nodded deferentially to Georgiana, and they took the grand oak staircase to the second floor.

"I've given you the room overlooking the garden, Lady Lichfield," Mrs. Trevor spoke quietly. "It's a grand room. I hope you'll be pleased. If it doesn't suit, you must let me know immediately."

But as she looked about the large room, Georgiana was enraptured. The room was magnificent, spanning twice the size of her old room when she lived with her father. There was a large sofa before the fireplace, a writing desk and chair underneath the window for light, and a garden view. The armoire was made of dark walnut that matched the four-poster bed. The colors of the room were in muted tones of pale blue, cream, and silver, and Georgiana was captivated by it.

"I should never want to leave," she said, smiling at the room's beauty.

Walking over to the window, she saw the grounds were immense with a long sweeping lawn that sloped downwards as far as the eye could see and a wooded forest beyond that.

"Would you care for tea, my lady? I can have it brought up directly," Mrs. Trevor asked.

Georgiana turned, surprised at the words. "Tea would be lovely. Thank you, Mrs. Trevor."

Walking the length of her room several times back and forth, she realized it would be a pleasure to be mistress of such an estate. It was such a beautiful home, and everywhere she looked was filled with pretty things. The grounds outside her window were attractive and well-manicured. After tea had arrived and been drunk, she decided to roam the grounds.

After exiting through the French doors, she moved down the lawn, passed the shrubbery, and felt as if she was a thousand miles away from London and all the nonsense going on there. Madeleine was married to a rake who was happy to flirt and proposition her friends, while her father was married to a fortune hunter who wanted his money much more than she wanted Jonathan.

And she was married to Alexander. He had followed her from Boston to Martha's Vineyard to keep her safe. He had entered into a fake engagement to keep her safe. And finally, when Elias's obsession crossed into a demented place and he kidnapped her, Alexander had once more stepped in and married her. He had done it all to keep her safe.

She wandered into the rose garden that had been beloved by Alexander's mother, walked past the brick entrance, and breathed in deeply the serenity of the garden with its lavender bushes, wildflowers, willows, and herbs.

When she returned to the house, Mrs. Trevor sent a maid to her to see if she required anything for the evening. Georgiana felt looked after and cared for, and she sent the maid away, saying she didn't require anything else. She quickly undressed and pulled on a wrap, but before she dressed for dinner, a knock fell upon the door.

She called out, "Come," and Alexander entered the room.

"Are you settled in? Do you have everything you need?" he asked her kindly.

"I do." She nodded, tying the belt about her slim waist. "Mrs. Trevor is most kind. She even sent a young maid to assist me."

"I'm glad. You must let me know if there is anything you want. I'll make certain it's yours," he said, eyeing her quietly.

"The grounds are lovely," she said, moving to the window. "I saw them for a short time earlier, but what I did see was most enchanting."

He came to stand beside her, and they both looked out over the green lawns and shrubbery.

"There's a storm coming," he said, pointing to the sky. Grey clouds were amassing. "You mustn't stray too far. The grounds are immense. It doesn't seem so from here, but there are woodlands and forests beyond the manicured lawns and you might get lost."

"Then you'll come with me," she said simply.

"Would you like me to?" he asked.

"Of course!" She shrugged. "Who better to show me the grounds than the master of it all?"

"Master of it all," he repeated. "That sounds medieval. Very well."

"In the morning?" she asked.

"And wear your warmest dress and cloak. It's going to snow. We won't stay out long."

By the next morning, a light dusting of snow had fallen, and it looked picturesque from the warmth of her room. Georgiana pulled open the heavy doors of her armoire to look through her wardrobe to see which would be the warmest. She found a cranberry-colored woolen dress that would be perfect for the weather.

She rang for the maid, and after she drank a cup of hot tea with a splash of cream, the maid arrived to help her into the dress.

"Are you going out in the weather, my lady?" the maid asked softly. "Surely not. A storm is coming."

Georgiana smiled sweetly at the young woman. "I won't stray, I've been told. I wanted to see beyond the gardens to the woodland area."

"But my lord is going with you?" The girl nodded.

"He is. So, I'll be well looked after."

Alexander was to take her to look about the grounds that morning after breakfast, but she was so excited that she stepped outside alone. There was a chill in the air, and she shivered slightly, but it was also so clear and beautiful. She stepped down the stone steps and walked through the garden that she could see from her window.

In winter, everything looked skeletal and dead as she passed along the shrubs and rose bushes. Moving past them, she saw the beginning of the woodland area, and something jolted in front of her. She was frightened for a moment, and then she smiled. A deer!

She tried not to move as she studied the beauty of the animal before her. Its coat was brown with white spots, and its face was small and delicate, with a black nose and ears sprouting from both sides of the head. She caught her breath as it moved towards her, and then seeing her, it bolted off.

Georgiana moved into the woods. She had never seen a deer up close and wondered if there were others about.

She knew nothing about them. Did they wander about in packs or were they solitary creatures?

As she followed the deer, a light dusting of snow fell from the sky, and she brushed the sprinkling from her shoulders. The temperature was dropping, and she might have been so much colder, but she was excited to see the deer.

As she moved between the trees, two deer were in front of her, both munching on the green grass and paying her no attention at all. She studied them silently and was mesmerized by the serenity of the place. Alone in the woodland area with only the deer for company and the snow lightly falling, she could very well be in a fairyland.

She would exist on berries in the summer and nuts in the winter and find a little cottage to live in. She giggled at her foolishness, and when the deer moved forward unexpectedly, she picked up her hem and followed them quickly. Not looking where she was going, she stepped deep into a rabbit hole and fell to her knees.

She tried to right herself but cried out. She had twisted her ankle badly. The pain in her right ankle was sharp, and when she tried to place her weight on it, it was impossible. She had turned it.

"Damn!" she said, angry at herself.

She looked about the woodland and realized in her quest to chase the deer she had no idea where she was. The woodland looked the same in every direction, and to return to the house, she had no idea which way she should walk. As if she could walk. At the moment, she could only hop, and she would not get very far. She looked about for a large stick to use as a crutch, but there was nothing about.

She would need to find a very large stick to support her body weight and help her return to the house. She shivered for the first time, realizing that after the moment of fascination over the deer had passed, she was now quite cold. Snow had begun to fall again, and instead of being idyllic and picturesque, the situation with her ankle had rendered it dangerous. She could freeze to death.

There was a large tree a ways from her, and she hobbled to it. Sitting at the base of the tree, she cursed herself. What a stupid thing to have done! Why had she set off into the unknown grounds without Alexander? Why?

And Alexander. He would come and find her, but not for some time, and by then she would be half frozen. Her cheeks felt so cold, and her nose was freezing. Her gloves kept her hands warm, and the dress was made of wool, but even that wouldn't be helpful if it got wet from the snow. Then it would weigh her down, and she would get a cold on top of everything else.

She began to get scared. How long could a person be in the snow? Surely, since she was clothed in wool with gloves to protect her hands, she would be fine. But she knew people who had been severely damaged by the snow. A friend of her father's had lost a finger due to being out in the cold for a long period of time, and an elderly person down the street had perished from being caught out in it.

She noticed for the first time that the clouds had shifted and everything was becoming darker. The snow continued to fall, and she shivered again. How long had she been out in the woods? She moved her arms up and down, but everything felt difficult.

Was she the stupidest person ever? She had run off to look at deer and fallen into a rabbit's hole. She was beyond foolish. Her hands were shaking, and she felt drowsy. How could she be so cold and yet so sleepy? That made no sense at all.

When she heard a noise near her, she smiled. The deer had come to watch her die. That was at least comforting.

She wouldn't be alone.

"Jesus Christ!" she heard someone mutter. Since when did deer swear?

"My God! Hold the lantern," another voice said.

Georgiana heard the voice and smiled. "You won't need a lantern. There's enough light where I'm going."

She could hear the slurring of her own voice and frowned at it. She had not had anything to drink. The tea! It was poisoned, she thought wildly. Elias had poisoned her tea. That devious bastard!

She felt a large warm cloak about her shoulders, and someone picked her up. Georgiana looked up and saw that Alexander was holding her in his arms.

"Let's go," he told the footman as he walked through the snow. It crunched loudly under his feet.

"The deer want to watch me die," Georgiana told him.

Alexander gave her a slow smile. "They may, my mad darling, but I do not."

After carrying her back to the great house, Alexander placed her in her room. "Light the fire, Mrs. Trevor, and bring some brandy," he ordered and she exited the room to do his bidding.

Dismissing the servants, he stripped Georgiana of all her clothes and wrapped her tightly in a blanket. She was shivering as he placed her between his legs and held her before the fireplace. When Mrs. Trevor returned, he took the glass of brandy and placed it to her lips.

"Drink, darling," he told her softly.

He was able to get a small bit down her throat before she coughed.

"A brick wrapped in lamb's wool," he directed to Mrs. Trevor. "Quickly!"

When the housekeeper returned with the brick wrapped in wool, he placed it before the fireplace and put Georgiana's feet on it.

"My darling," he said softly.

Thinking swiftly, he removed his jacket and shirt and opened up the blanket, pulling her against him. He could immediately feel his heat transfer to her. Her skin was so cold to the touch it felt inhuman. He held her tightly against him, rocking her like a child.

"Shhh," he whispered. "You're all right. You're safe with me."

Mrs. Trevor backed out of the room, and when he heard the door close, he smoothed her hair back.

"Georgiana." He whispered her name. "Everything is all right. You're safe. You're here with me."

The fire crackled in the room, and the wind whistled outside. Alexander stayed with Georgiana all night, holding her tightly to him. When the fire dwindled, he added several more logs to it and then caught Georgiana up in his arms again.

He had placed several pillows from the bed in a semi-circle on the floor so he could sit and hold her before the fireplace. Georgiana was so pale in the low firelight that he could see the veins underneath her skin.

He loved her fiercely and the thought of losing her was incomprehensible.

"Mrs. Trevor," he asked the woman who was waiting in the hall.

"My Lord?"

"Please send for the doctor and have several more warmed bricks placed in the bed for Georgiana," he directed.

"Right away, my lord."

Alexander went back to his room to change his clothes and wash his face. Looking into the mirror, he knew he looked bad. His face was haggard from little sleep, and there were circles under his eyes. He had not slept much that night, and when he splashed the water several times onto his face, it helped refresh and awaken him.

After dressing in a simple blue wool jacket and breeches, he went downstairs for a cup of coffee and helped himself to some toast and eggs.

Mrs. Trevor came into the room, looking severe dressed all in black. "The doctor is on his way, my lord," she told him.

"Thank you, Mrs. Trevor."

"And I placed several warm bricks into the bed myself for my lady." She nodded.

"Thank you."

"You'll forgive my impertinence, my lord, but perhaps you should try and get some sleep," she noted. "You've been up almost the entire night, so I've heard."

He assumed the footman or butler had come in to stoke the fire and seen him with Georgiana. "I'll be fine, Mrs. Trevor, but thank you for your concern. Did the doctor say when he would arrive?"

"Within the next hour, sir. He's only just in the village."

It was an hour later when Dr. Pelham arrived at the abbey. Dr. Pelham was a middle-aged man who was closer to his father in age. He had been a country doctor his entire life and had helped birth most of the natives in the Derbyshire area.

He was well respected, and his medical knowledge was immense. He could easily have had a practice in London but preferred a quiet country life.

"Lichfield," he said in greeting to Alexander as they shook hands. "Sorry to hear about your father and brother. Good men, both of them."

"Thank you, Dr. Pelham."

"So, tell me about Lady Lichfield. What happened?"

"She was anxious to see the grounds and went out on her own, not realizing how large it is," Alexander explained. "It began to snow, and she was out there for some time."

"Ah." Dr. Pelham nodded. "The cold. Was she shivering a great deal and confused at all?"

Alexander nodded in return. "She was. She was also slurring her words."

"Exposure from the cold," the doctor affirmed. "It can happen and does in degrees. If she's healthy and otherwise fine, the cold she experienced should not have any long-term effects. I'll visit her now."

Alexander didn't join Georgiana and Dr. Pelham. He worried she might be angry at him for not finding her sooner and didn't want to see the blame in her emerald eyes.

It was still only late morning, so he went to find his estate manager to see the work that was going on in rethatching the cottage roofs at the eastern edge of the property. He stepped out of the house and went to the long row of cottages until he came to the largest one.

He welcomed the chance to discuss the estate and grounds and not worry about Georgiana and what she might have suffered in the cold. He felt responsible for her. As they pored over the plans of the cottage roofs, he heard a huffing and puffing outside, and soon Dr. Pelham joined them.

"My God, man! I've been looking everywhere for you!" he said, trying to catch his breath. "What a horrible thing to do! Make an old man spring about this vast estate looking for you!"

Alexander frowned. "Has something happened? Is Georgiana all right?" he asked, his heart racing. "For God's sake, tell me!"

Mrs. Trevor entered the room, carrying a tray with her. She set the tray on the bed before Georgiana and waved at hand at the items. "A pot of tea, eggs, toast with jam, and a spot of bacon. The doctor asked I give you a hearty meal, my lady."

"You're very kind." Georgiana nodded. "I've been very stupid."

"My lady?" Mrs. Trevor frowned.

"I've caused such a problem. I ventured into the estate and woodland and should have known better. Alexander warned me, and I didn't listen," she explained.

"There's no use crying over spilt milk, my lady. What's done is done and no harm." She patted her hand on the bed.

Georgiana smiled weakly. "Still. I should have listened. He told me not to venture out. He told me." Georgiana looked down at the tray and its contents and then back at the housekeeper. "Mrs. Trevor. Was I in the bed all night? I recall being in front of the fire. Being so warm and in a sort of cocoon. Did I dream that?"

"No, my lady. You didn't dream it. When the master found you, he returned straight away to this room. He removed your clothes and some of his and wrapped you in a blanket," she said matter-of-fact, not knowing the married couple had only been together once.

"He wrapped me in a blanket?" Georgiana asked.

"Aye. He did. And he stayed with you all night. He didn't sleep at all." Mrs. Trevor had heard from the footmen. "When the fire died down, he had a log added and hot brick to warm your feet."

"He didn't sleep?" Georgiana felt a catch in her throat.

"He stayed by your side all night. He only placed you in the bed in the morning when he thought you were better," the housekeeper assured her.

"He stayed with me the entire time?" she asked softly.

"You forgive my impertinence, but I've never seen a man more dedicated and in love with his wife," she told her. "He's entirely devoted to you."

"Have you seen my husband? Alexander?"

"I understand he had a meeting with his estate manager."

"I see." Georgiana nodded as the woman left the room.

Georgiana pulled her wrapper tightly about her body, thinking about how foolish she had been. She had put herself in harm's way and not listened to Alexander. If he wasn't angry at her, he should be.

Down in the garden, the greenery was blanketed under the white snow. From high above in her warm room, the garden looked serene and quite lovely. She thought of the night before, and her heart beat quickly as she remembered Alexander holding her tightly to him.

She had been so cold, and he had warmed her using his own body heat. Selflessly he had given her what she needed, just as he seemed to do so often. He always seemed to put her safety first, and she was warmed by the thought of him. Handsome Alexander. Arrogant Alexander. Lord Lichfield. Duty bound to an estate but also to her.

When a knock fell on the door, she turned to it. "Come."

Alexander entered the room, his face warm as he looked at her. "Georgiana! You shouldn't be up!" he told her sharply. "Come and lie back in bed."

"I'm not that fragile," she said but allowed herself to be moved.

"No but you must take care," he insisted.

"Are you angry with me?" she asked, looking up at him.

"Angry? Why should I be?"

"I behaved so stupidly. I was cursing at myself once I knew I was lost yesterday."

He smoothed her hair back from her face. "None of that matters. You're safe now."

"Mrs. Trevor said –" She clutched at his hand.

"Yes?" He held her hand in his.

"She said you stayed with me all night. That you barely had any rest yourself." Her eyes traced the lines of his face.

He shrugged. "I'll sleep tonight. Besides how could I rest knowing you might be in danger?"

"I think I'll be quite happy at the abbey," she said, nodding to him. "Even after yesterday's fiasco."

"You think it might grow on you?" he wondered, looking down at their entwined fingers.

"I do," Georgiana answered. "After all, I can't very well leave the abbey, especially as I've just realized this morning that I'm in love with the master of it all."

Alexander frowned and then he started. "What did you say?" His heart skipped a beat. Had he misheard?

"I love you, Alexander." Her emerald eyes met his. "It's taken me a bit of time to realize it, but I do. And if you can forgive this silly creature for behaving so badly, I want to make a real go of it. I want to be your wife. A true wife."

Alexander kissed her once on the lips and then pulled her tightly against him and kissed her properly, leaving her breathless. "It's just as well, my darling, because I could never let you go now," he said, smiling.

"Oh, yes?" Georgiana grinned. "And why is that?"

"I spoke to Dr. Pelham just now. He didn't want to cause you any undue stress what with last night but you are with child," he said softly.

Georgiana's emerald eyes widened. "With child? I'm with child?"

"Yes, my love."

"But it was only that one time we were together," she said, frowning.

He kissed her temple. "That's all it takes, my love."

She placed her hand along her flat stomach and marveled at it. *A child*!

"So now you see, my love, instead of two of us, we'll be three."

Epilogue

ONE YEAR LATER

LICHFIELD, DERBYSHIRE
The winter snow had come once more.

Georgiana was a doting mother. Their daughter, Amelia, had inherited her mother's lovely face and emerald eyes, and Alexander had never known a year of more bliss and joy.

Georgiana was a loving wife and mother, and though she made her opinion known on many topics, she was also very affectionate with her husband. She gave him sound advice on the running of the estate, and their united goal was to make Lichfield Abbey self-sustaining.

They had brought in more sheep to enable them to have their own wool weaved and dyed, which they also sold to different factories in the north. They created a successful brewhouse that distributed to much of Derbyshire. Georgiana was admired for her intelligence and kindness, and many tenants came to her directly for advice and guidance.

The birth of Amelia had been difficult, but Georgiana was strong and Dr. Pelham had been pleased to deliver another generation of Lichfields. Alexander was more in love with Georgiana than ever, and he could barely keep his hands off her.

Circling her waist as they watched baby Amelia cooing on the rug before them, he nuzzled her neck. "Let's have Mrs. Trevor watch our little darling for an hour so we can go upstairs and nap," he whispered to her.

She giggled and then grew stern. "You're a liar! You never nap. That's just your excuse to get me alone and have your way with me," she scolded him.

"I don't need any excuse, Georgiana," he said, turning her to face him. "I'm absolutely besotted with you. I grow worse with time, not better."

"I don't want you to get better, my dearest," she said, putting her arms around his neck. "I want you as besotted with me as I am with you."

"Mrs. Trevor!" he called out suddenly as Georgiana bit back a smile.

Lying naked in each other's arms a short time later, he kissed the top of her head. "Besides, I'm doing this all for Amelia if you want to know the truth."

Georgiana frowned. "Doing all of this is for Amelia? How is that?"

"We can't have only one child. She'll be lonely."

"Is that so?" Georgiana asked.

"Absolutely. She needs at least three or four siblings." He nodded.

"I'll give you two and no more," she insisted.

"Hmm," he replied, nuzzling her neck.

They remained locked together, holding each other for a short time in the stillness of the room.

"Where are we?" she asked quietly, looking up at the ceiling and then back at him.

"Florence?" he answered.

"No."

"Paris?" he asked again.

"I don't think so."

"Constantinople!" he said, thinking it was the answer she sought.

"We're in Derbyshire."

"Derbyshire," he repeated slowly. "Do you know what?"

"What?" she asked.

"We're exactly where I want to be. I want to be nowhere else on earth than here with you."

"I agree completely," she said, smiling. "This is exactly where I want to be. Here in Derbyshire. With you."

She closed her eyes as he bent down to kiss her slowly and sweetly.

Excerpt

IN THE MIDST OF SHADOWS

1
880
London, England
Prologue

Casimir Kimberly strode resolutely past the throng of people gathered in the alley who were trying to catch a glimpse of the body of the woman lying at the foot of the wooden stairs. His black woolen overcoat reached to his knees, and he could feel the material swirl about his legs as he walked.

Casimir was not a man given to fanciful dress or cologne as some dandies and French men were known to be, but damn, did he love his coat.

He made eye contact with a policeman keeping the crowd under control. The man immediately motioned for Casimir to make his way through the circle of people. Casimir glanced over his shoulder and saw that Ralphie was lagging behind him, as always.

As he came closer to the body lying in an odd position from the fall, a flash of lightning dominated the sky, and he looked up. It was early morning, and most people were still in bed. The gathering crowd must be the dead woman's neighbors or local tradespeople.

He felt around in his coat pocket for his John Millar & Sons tin and took out one drop, popping it into his mouth. As the delicious flavors of black currant and licorice filled his mouth, Casimir began to study the crowd surrounding him. He first surveyed the middle-aged men, then the women.

He knew what he was searching for, and his heart beat faster as the lightning flashed once more through the morning sky.

He sat back on his haunches, surveying the body before him. He had been told a portion of the woman's story when the police had summoned him.

While the charwoman had lived on the second floor, the stairs leading to the flat were out in the alleyway. Sometime during the night, the woman had fallen down the stairs and broken her neck.

Some in the police said it was an accident; others were not so convinced. Casimir had been called in to look over the scene and offer his opinion. Casimir wasn't a detective with Scotland Yard or a private investigator working for the Pinkerton Detective Agency but was blessed—or cursed, depending on whom you asked—with an abnormal understanding of crime, its victims, and most importantly, the offenders.

Casimir suddenly looked up. He sniffed the air distinctly with several sniffs to the right and then to the left and narrowed his eyes.

"Ralphie," he growled once.

"Yes, Guvnor," came the quick reply from the man standing nearby.

"Move that fishmonger down the lane," Casimir said simply. "All I can smell is his two-day-old mackerel."

"Aye, Guvnor."

The fishmonger had moved along, but Casimir's sense of smell was compromised. He swore inwardly. He always liked to get a sense of the crime scene's smell. The blood, the vomit, the rain, the earth.

Each had its own distinct smell, and each told its own story. Casimir looked down at the body and noticed the shabbiness of her nightdress, her small feet, her blotchy skin, and rough hands used to hard work. The woman was probably in her forties, but her weathered face looked closer to sixty. Her forehead was deeply lined, her eyes sunken into her gaunt face.

As he took in her worn hands, he noticed something peculiar.

On the ring finger of her left hand, there was lighter skin where a ring had once been. He knew the woman was married.

Casimir stood up abruptly, causing the onlookers around him to gasp. He shook his head and looked about at the group.

He had been so absorbed in concentrating on the dead woman, he had forgotten about the people surrounding him in the alleyway. He looked back into the group, his eyes searching for what he had seen before to assure himself that he was correct. His eyes narrowed when he saw the exchange, and then he almost grinned.

This was too easy, he told himself.

He strode forward, his long legs covering vast amounts of space before he stood before a stout, well-built man in the crowd. The man had the look of a stonemason, not very tall but built like a solid bull.

He eyed the man quietly, looking over his beefy chest, his bulging forearms, his black hair sprinkled with gray, and the cap he held in his hands respectfully. Casimir narrowed his eyes and watched the man glance quickly to his right and then away again.

Following his gaze, he saw who the man was looking at. A small red-haired woman with an ample bosom and thick ankles. She smiled shyly back at the man before he looked away.

"He did it," Casimir said loudly and firmly, pointing to the stonemason.

Detective Chief Inspector Browne came to stand next to him. "Blast it all, Casimir! You can't know anything yet. You can't!" He said the last part, almost whining.

"Ah! But I do, Monsieur Browne. I know everything. And it's quite simple, actually. It's the oldest story in the book," Casimir said, patting back his curly blond hair.

The detective looked exasperated as the two policemen moved to either side of the stout, muscled man.

Casimir shrugged. "My dear Inspector Browne. You see everything around you and yet, in fact, see nothing at all. It's a travesty."

"Indeed?" Inspector Browne responded. "Well, since I see nothing and you see everything, why don't you explain it to us mere mortals."

Casimir smiled indulgently. "It appears I must. So here we have Madame Charwoman." He pointed dramatically to the woman now being discreetly covered with a blanket again. He spoke the words loudly to the entire group, not just the Inspector.

"She has spent her whole life toiling in other people's homes and businesses cleaning their messes. And we see it has taken its toll," he said and heard someone in the crowd sniff, trying to hold back their tears.

"The years have been cold and unkind. A woman not much older than my own mother yet looks older than my grandmother." He sighed dramatically as the Inspector rolled his eyes. "I imagine she brought several children into the world, but they never lived long," he surmised, and the assembled people said nothing.

"How the devil did you work that out?" Inspector Browne sneered, and Casimir nodded as if addressing a simpleton.

"If the woman had any living children, Inspector, would they not be here mourning her demise?" Casimir replied, and several women watching the scene unfold nodded and agreed with the assessment. "Yet no one has come near the body to touch her except for the police."

"Neither has the husband." The Inspector gestured to the stout, muscled man. "So, what of it?"

Casimir nodded to the Inspector. "Thank you, Browne. You've led me precisely to the point. Here we have a woman who has departed the earth, and yet her husband stands a few feet away, completely removed from the situation at hand.

"Why? I ask you, why?" Casimir flung his hands up into the air, startling the crowd.

The Inspector shook his head. "Obviously, we know why, Casimir. He doesn't care to be around a dead body."

Casimir scoffed. "Of course, that could be the reason."

The Inspector nodded condescendingly.

"But it isn't." Casimir brushed a piece of nonexistent lint from his own jacket.

"Blast it," the Inspector swore under his breath.

Casimir surveyed the people surrounding him and pointed to the redhead. "You. Come here."

The woman looked about her, and several people moved aside to let her through the growing crowd. She came to stand before him, uttering not a word.

"Now, what's this about?" Inspector Browne shook his head, irritated. "What does this woman have to do with anything here?"

"You asked me to come here and survey the situation, Inspector. If you no longer wish me to do so, I can go," Casimir said quietly, turning his head away.

"Damn it all, Casimir. Get on with it!"

"With pleasure." He heard the thunder in the distance and knew the rain would soon be upon them.

"As I said, the charwoman worked hard, did her duty, but ultimately age crept up upon her. Meanwhile, the husband is," he looked over the middle-aged man once more, "working as a stonemason. Barely making a living. His dreams, like his hair, are graying."

"Graying!" he shouted to the crowd, turning in a small circle, his long jacket flaring out around him.

The two policemen looked at each other warily as they stood near the husband of the charwoman.

"Is he really an inspector? He seems more like an actor playing to the crowd," one whispered to the other.

His friend had a slight grin on his face. "I've seen him at work before. He's neither a detective nor an actor. He's a wizard!"

Meanwhile, Inspector Browne shook his head ruefully as he watched Casimir's tall, elegant frame facing the enthralled crowd.

"But one day…." Casimir turned back to the assembled people, his voice filled with intense passion. "One day, he visits a public house and sees a woman serving drinks. He's fascinated by her! Her youth, her vitality—her bosom, most likely." He muttered the last bit, but several people heard him and tittered.

"Casimir—" the Inspector said in a warning voice.

"The stonemason finds his youth again! He believes himself to be in love and she as well. The rub is, he's married. So, he arranges an accident for his wife." Casimir shrugged. "What could be easier? A string pulled across the top of the stairs, and no one is the wiser."

All eyes turned to the stonemason, who appeared shocked. His eyes were wide and frightened.

"Now, the only thing to do is wait a respectable time until he can marry his barmaid," Casimir finished simply.

"So, arrest him," he directed the Inspector.

The group was shocked into silence while the redhead met Casimir's eyes. He could see the fear in them, and he reached down suddenly to grab her left hand in his.

The two policemen clasped the husband by the upper arms, and though he struggled initially, he gave in.

"How did you know?" he yelled to Casimir, standing a few feet away. "My God, how did you know?"

Casimir turned sharply to the Inspector and dropped a golden ring band into his hand.

"The ring." He shrugged.

"The ring?" The husband frowned.

"A woman like your wife with no money, no fine clothes. A gold wedding band would mean everything to her, especially from the man she loves. She would never remove it. Yet you did so the moment she was dead to give it to the woman you thought would be your new wife," Casimir explained.

A shocked intake of breath came from everyone in the crowd, and several words filled the air: "disgusting," "horrid," "monster."

The husband's face fell. "I wanted a new start. Something different," he whispered.

Casimir looked at the redhead and then back at the husband. "What you've earned yourself, my dear Mr. Stonemason, is a quick end at the hangman's hands."

Casimir strode away from the group as the sky opened up and the rain began to fall. His trusty sidekick, Ralphie, trailed behind him, trying to keep up.

Casimir Kimberly, he thought to himself. You did it!

Once more, you solved a murder crime in less time than it takes most men to finish their afternoon cuppa. He was extraordinary, he thought, smiling to himself. Absolutely extraordinary!

Inspector Browne motioned to the policeman to take the husband in custody as well as the barmaid. They would need to be questioned. The two were led away from the scene as neighbors continued to stand in the rain, gossiping.

The rain was falling in steady sheets as Inspector Browne took one last look at the tall retreating figure. The legendary Casimir Kimberly. He was a man made of flesh and blood but still a legend amongst Londoners. He had made it his mission in life to fight injustice and be a champion for the people.

And the people adored him.

In all his many years at Scotland Yard, Browne had never witnessed a man who was able to understand and comprehend a crime scene with such rapid detail. Casimir Kimberly was indeed a legend. And he was also so full of himself that sometimes Browne wanted to smash his face in.

But at least a poor woman's untimely death had been solved, and the husband would hang. The rain lessened, and the sun peeked through the clouds, steadily rising as the crowd dispersed and Browne made his way back to the body of the charwoman.

He looked down at the ring in his hand. Casimir was right. The small gold wedding band was probably all the woman had of any worth in the world. Luckily for her, it had also been the means to point a guilty finger at her husband.

He tucked the ring safely into his pocket. He would make certain sure it was buried with her.

About Nicola

Nicola spent her childhood in Los Angeles. As a young student in elementary school, she had a great fondness for reading and began to write creatively. She graduated from university with a degree in communications and held a variety of positions in journalism, education, government and nonprofit. Nicola has traveled extensively throughout Europe, China and Central America. Nicola's goal is to create rich characters with a strong male lead and a passionate female lead.

https://linktr.ee/authornicolaitalia

Made in the USA
Middletown, DE
04 April 2023